LITTLE BLACK LIES

LITTLE BLACK LIES

Sandra Block

GRAND CENTRAL
PUBLISHING

NEW YORK   BOSTON

Copyright © 2015 by Sandra Block
Reading Group Guide © 2015 by Sandra Block

Grand Central Publishing
Hachette Book Group
1290 Avenue of the Americas
New York, NY 10104

HachetteBookGroup.com

Printed in the United States of America

RRD-C

First Edition: February 2015
10 9 8 7 6 5 4 3 2 1

Grand Central Publishing is a division of Hachette Book Group, Inc.
The Grand Central Publishing name and logo is a trademark of Hachette Book Group, Inc.

The Hachette Speakers Bureau provides a wide range of authors for speaking events. To find out more, go to www.hachettespeakersbureau.com or call (866) 376-6591.

The publisher is not responsible for websites (or their content) that are not owned by the publisher.

Library of Congress Cataloging-in-Publication Data

Block, Sandra.
  Little black lies / Sandra Block. — First edition.
    pages cm
  Summary: "From first-time novelist Sandra Block, a gripping page-turner about a psychiatrist determined to discover the truth about her past" —Provided by publisher.
  ISBN 978-1-4555-8373-7 (paperback) — ISBN 978-1-4789-8330-9 (audio download) — ISBN 978-1-4555-8375-1 (ebook) 1. Women psychiatrists—Fiction. 2. Identity (Psychology)—Fiction. 3. Suspense fiction.
I. Title.
  PS3602.L64285L58 2015
  813'.6—dc23
                              2014020887

For my mom and dad

That a lie which is half a truth is ever the
blackest of lies.

—ALFRED, LORD TENNYSON

Book One: November

Chapter One

She picks an invisible bug off her face.

A pink sore swells up, adding to the constellation of scabs dotting her skin, remnants of previous invisible bugs. Tiffany is a "frequent flyer" as they say, in and out of the psychiatric ward. She's been my patient twice already, both times delusional and coming off crystal meth. She does the usual circuit: emergency room, psych ward, rehab, streets, and repeat. A cycle destined to continue until interrupted by jail, death, or less likely, sobriety. Tiffany sits on her hospital bed staring off into space, the skimpy blue blanket over her knees. She is emaciated, her spine jutting out of the back of her hospital gown. A penny-sized patch of scalp gleams through her bleach-blond, stringy roots, due to her penchant for yanking out clumps of hair (otherwise known as *trichotillomania*, in case Dr. Grant asks me, which he will.)

"I've got to go now, Tiffany. Anything else I can do for you?"

She doesn't answer or even look at me. Either she's psy-

3

chotic or ignoring me or both, but I don't have time to figure out which because we're rounding in five minutes, and I still haven't finished my charts. I run down the hall to the nurses' station, which is in chaos. Jason and Dr. A, the other two psychiatry residents, are elbow to elbow in the tiny room, mint-green charts in precarious towers around them. The nurses jog around us, saying "Excuse me" too loudly, as they sort out meds and record vitals, ready to sign out, punch out, and get the hell out of Dodge as the seven o'clock shift drifts in.

Dr. A grabs an order sheet from the stack. "Did anyone discontinue the IV on Mr. Wisnoski?"

"Mr. who?" one of the nurses calls back.

"Bed nine. Mr. Wisnoski. This should be done expediently."

"Whatever you say," the nurse answers, putting on latex gloves and heading to the room. Dr. A's real name is Dr. Adoonyaddayt, and his first name is just as unpronounceable. So everybody calls him Dr. A. He has a strong Thai accent and obsessively studies an online dictionary to improve his vocabulary. He is, as he told me, "building a *compendium* of knowledge." Dr. A appointed Jason to be his "idiom tutor," to better connect with American patients. He used to be a neurosurgeon in Thailand but is slumming with us in psychiatry now because it's impossible for foreign medical graduates to get into neurosurgery here. Dr. A is easily the smartest of our threesome.

"I thought Wisnoski was mine," Jason says. "He's yours?"

"Mine," Dr. A answers, taking the chart from his hand. Jason is dressed to the nines as usual, with his trademark bow tie (he has more colors than I thought existed, a *compendium* of bow ties in his closet), bangs gelled up and bleached just so. Jason is gay to the point of cliché, which I pointed out to him over beer one night, though he disagreed. "I'm Chinese American. Cliché would be me tutoring you in math."

The new medical student (Tom?) hasn't picked up a chart yet. He watches us running around like beheaded chickens and yawns. I like to play a little game, figuring out which fields the medical students are headed into, which I can usually guess in the first five minutes. This one, surgeon for sure.

"Zoe," Jason calls out to me. "You got the new one?"

"Which one, Tiffany?"

"No," he says. "The transfer. Vallano."

"Oh, the one from Syracuse. Yup, I got her," I answer, grabbing her enormous chart, which tumbles open. "Dr. Grant's special present for me."

Jason guffaws, cracking open his own charts. "He sure does love you."

"Ah yes, such is my lot," I answer, flipping through her chart. It's obvious Dr. Grant doesn't like me, though I can't figure out why. It could be the Yale thing. But then again, maybe not. Could be a lot of things. Could be that I don't like him, and being a psychiatrist extraordinaire, he senses this.

Footsteps thump down the hall as Dr. Grant appears in the doorway. Beads of sweat mix into the curly hair at his temples from walking up ten flights of stairs. In my opinion, anyone who walks up ten flights of stairs on a daily basis needs a psychiatrist. Dr. Grant is wearing gray pants with a thin pinstripe and a checkered blue shirt, a combination that suggests his closet light burned out. He is a small, slight man. I could crush him in a thumbsie war.

"Ready to round?" he asks.

We file out of the cramped nurses' station, and the medical student strides over to shake his hand. "Kevin," he says.

Kevin, Tom, same thing. We stack the charts into the metal rolling cart and then Jason pushes it, clattering down the hallway. We pass by gray-blue walls, sometimes more blue than gray, sometimes more gray than blue, depending on the soot. The floor tiles are an atrocious teal blue (the approval committee was either color-blind or on mushrooms), dented and scraped from years of residents and food carts rattling down the hall.

"All right, first victim," Dr. Grant says, stopping just outside the room. Dr. Grant always calls the patients "victims" when we round. I haven't taken the time to analyze this, but it does seem peculiar. To his credit, he says it quietly at least, so the already paranoid patients don't get any ideas. "Mr. Wisnoski. Who's got this one?"

"This is my patient, sir," answers Dr. A. He calls everyone "sir."

"Okay. Go ahead and present."

"Mr. Wisnoski is a forty-nine-year-old Caucasian gentleman with a long-standing history of depression. He was found unresponsive by his wife after overdosing on Ambien."

"How many pills?"

"Thirty pills, sir. He took one month's dose. He was taken by the EMT to the ER, where he underwent gastric lavage and quickly recovered."

"Meds?" Dr. Grant asks.

"Prozac, forty milligrams qd. He's been on multiple SSRIs before without success but had reportedly been feeling better on Prozac."

"So why did he try to kill himself?" Dr. Grant glances around and zeroes in on me, as usual. "Dr. Goldman?"

I'm still not used to the "doctor" thing, telling nurses "Just call me Zoe." "The problem is," I answer, "Prozac actually was effective."

Kevin is chewing a large piece of pink gum, which smells of strawberry. I can tell Dr. Grant is feeling the stress of ignoring this.

"Tell us what you mean by that, Dr. Goldman."

"Oftentimes a patient is most at risk for suicide when there is some improvement in functionality," I explain. "They finally have the wherewithal to commit suicide."

"That's right," he admits, though it pains him. We all head into the room, but it is empty, the patient's disheveled blue blanket crumpled on the bed. The room reeks of charcoal, which stains the sheets from last night's stomach pump. After some consternation, we discover from a nurse that Mr. Wisnoski is off getting an EEG.

So we move on down the list to the next room. The name is drawn in fat black marker into the doorplate. "Vallano." This is my add-on, the transfer.

"Dr. Goldman?"

"Okay," I say, ready to launch. "Ms. Sofia Vallano is a thirty-six-year-old Caucasian female with a history of narcissism and possibly sociopathy on her Axis II. She has been in

7

Upstate Mental Community Hospital since age fourteen for the murder of her mother."

"Holy shit" escapes from Jason, to a glare from Dr. Grant. Still, you can't blame him; she did kill her mother.

"Any other family members?" Dr. Grant asks.

"One brother, listed as a lost contact, one sister the same. The brother was reportedly injured in the incident."

"Go on," Dr. Grant says.

"After the closure of UMCH, she was transferred here for further treatment and evaluation," I continue.

"And," Dr. Grant announces, "possibly for discharge, pending our recommendations."

"Discharge, really?" I ask.

"Yes, really."

I slide her chart back into the cart. "Based on what findings? Has her diagnosis changed?"

"Well now, Dr. Goldman, that's our job to find out. She's been a ward of the state for over twenty years now. If she's truly a sociopath, I grant you, we may not be able to release her to society. If she's narcissistic, however, maybe we can." He skims through her old discharge summary. "From what I can see, UMCH has been kicking the can down the road on this one for a while now."

"She never went to prison?" the medical student asks, still chewing gum.

"Not fit to stand trial. Okay, let's see how she's doing." Dr. Grant knocks on the door in a quick series.

And there is Sofia Vallano, perched on the bed, reading a magazine. I'm not sure what I expected. Some baleful creature with blood dripping from her eyeteeth maybe. But this is not what I see. Sofia Vallano is a stunning mix of colors: shiny black hair, royal blue eyes, and opera red lips. Something like Elizabeth Taylor in her middle years, curvaceous and unapologetically sexual. They say the devil comes well dressed.

"Hello," she says with a smile. A knowing smile, as if she's laughing at a joke we aren't in on. She does not put down the magazine.

"Hello," says Dr. Grant.

"I'm Dr. Goldman," I say, extending my hand. My skin is damp in hers. "I'll be the main resident taking care of you, along with Dr. Grant, who's in charge. Just saying hello for now, but I'll be back to see you later."

"Okay," she answers and looks back down at her magazine. Obviously she's been through the likes of us before. A cloying scent rises off the magazine perfume ad on her lap. Redolent and musky.

We say our good-byes and all head back to see Mr. Wisnoski, who still isn't back from EEG.

"Who's next?" Dr. Grant asks. "Dr. Chang? Do you have anyone?"

"Yes, I have Mrs. Greene," Jason answers.

"Would you like to present?"

"Fifty-six-year-old African American female with a history of bipolar II. She came in today after a manic episode, now apparently consistent with bipolar I."

"And how was that determined?"

"Last night, she climbed onstage at *Les Misérables* to sing during one of the solos."

Sandra Block

"Which one?" I ask, immediately regretting the question, which is not terribly relevant to the diagnosis and also tells me my Adderall hasn't kicked in yet.

"'I Dreamed a Dream,' I think," he answers.

"Ah, the Susan Boyle one," says Dr. A in appreciation. "I find that song most gratifying."

Dr. Grant surveys us all with incredulity. "Doctors, could you at least *pretend* to be professional here?" Dr. A drops his gaze shamefully, and Jason twirls his bangs. Kevin chews on. "Meds?" Dr. Grant asks.

"She was on Trileptal," Jason says. "Three hundred BID but stopped it due to nausea three weeks ago. The history is all from her sister because the patient is not giving a reliable history. Her speech is extremely pressured."

"Ah yes," Dr. A says. "In bouts of mania, actually,"—he pronounces this *act-tually*, with a hard *t*—"the speech is quite rapid, and one cannot get the word in edgily."

"He means 'edgewise,'" Jason explains.

"Ah, edgewise, so it is." Dr. A pulls the little black notebook out of his lab-coat pocket, where he jots down all his ill-begotten idioms.

Dr. Grant crosses his arms. One summer when I was in high school, my mom enrolled me in ADHD camp (sold to me as a drama camp) to boost the self-esteem of her ever-slouching, moody giant of a daughter. We played this game called Name That Emotion, where one group would act out an emotion and the other group would call out what it was. If I had to name that emotion for Dr. Grant assessing his crop of psychiatry residents, it would be disgust. We head to the next victim, our Broadway hopeful, but alas, she is getting a CAT scan, so we head back to see Mr. Wisnoski, who is *still* in EEG.

Dr. Grant looks supremely frustrated. "Anyone else to see?"

"I have Tiffany," I say.

"Oh, Tiffany, I know her. She can wait." He chews on the inside of his lip, thinking. "All right. I guess we'll finish rounds this afternoon. Just make sure you see all your patients and write your notes in the meantime."

So we split up to see our respective patients. The nurses' station has slowed to a hum now. I settle down to Sofia's chart, which is massive, not to mention the three bursting manila envelopes from UMCH, but at least I can feel my focus turning on. As I open the chart, the perfume card from the magazine falls out, the heady smell of perfume rising up from the page like an olfactory hallucination.

Chapter Two

The nightmare is always the same. Bloodstains on my hands, red as finger paint.

I am hiding, but I don't know why. I don't know where I am, or who I'm hiding from.

A whirring noise buzzes in time with my hands; my fingers are pulsing in pain. Moonlight streams through the window, spattering the tile floor, interlaced with shadows of tree branches. I rub my cheek against my teddy bear. Soft, blue teddy bear, bristles stiff with drying blood. Teddy's name is Po-Po. His black-bead eye glints in the moonlight. His other eye went missing weeks ago, rolled some-where, under a kitchen rug or in between the couch cushions maybe. No matter, I love my one-eyed teddy. I am hiding Po-Po, too.

The room is warm, blazing warm, and I smell smoke all around, like sweet tobacco. Like the smell of my dad's rolled cigarettes.

The shadows of the tree branches move on the floor, like witch's fingers.

"Zoe?" a voice calls out, sweet as pie, patient. "Zoe?" It is a *singsong voice. I tuck myself in tighter, barely breathing. If I fold myself up, they will not find me. My heart bangs in my ears. I watch the slit of light beneath the door for movement. My teddy trembles in my wet, bleeding hands.*

"Zoe? Honey, come here. We just want to help you. Come on, honey."

The voice is calm, soothing. Mommy? Is she calling me? Relief surges through my body like water on a fire.

"Mommy!" I scream with every fiber in my body. I forget that I am hiding, forget that someone may find me. "Mommy! Mommy!" It is a shriek, a prayer.

And then the door opens, and my heart stops.

⌒

"Zoe!" Scotty is shaking me by the arm. My heart leaps out of my chest and I sit up like a shot, my pajama top slimy with sweat.

"What the fuck?" he asks. Charitable, considering he is my brother. And my screaming just tore him from the arms of his latest paramour, now wide awake and wondering why he's living with some crazy woman bellowing in the next room. "What was that all about?"

"The fire," I say, confused, catching my breath.

"The fire?" He looks confused, too, maybe because he just woke up, or maybe because the fire was over twenty years ago. "I didn't know you were still having those nightmares," he says, his voice gravelly with sleep.

"I didn't either." I haven't had a nightmare about the fire since high school.

My brother stands up from my bed, all limbs, hair tousled. Half of his face looks monstrous in the shadows, like the Phantom of the Opera. He stretches up his arms with a yawn, his eyes turning toward his bedroom. "You okay?"

"Yeah, I'm fine." I'm not sure this is true, but after all, he does have someone waiting in his bed. And I am old enough to go back to sleep without my mommy.

"Thanks," I call to his retreating figure. Soft voices float into the hallway as he returns to his bedroom, "What's-wrong-with-her?" noises. I lay back down in bed, my pattering heart slowing. Headlights flash on my wall as a car rumbles down the street.

Three in the morning.

A brown spider twirls on a web in the corner of the ceiling. Thinking back to my medical school lecture on poisonous spiders, I vaguely recall it's the brown ones you have to watch out for, that would kill you dead in seconds. Or maybe it was the brown ones that were harmless, and the red ones that were deadly. This does seem like an important distinction, though not necessarily at 3:03 a.m. I shut my eyes and try to sleep, but I've played this game before, and sleep has no intention of coming, not anytime soon. Sleep is perverse in that way, abandoning you just when you need it most.

Unless I have some Xanax left.

This hope drags me to the bathroom, the bright light stinging my eyes. I untwist the cap and peer in to see my little white pill shining up at me like a beacon from its orange plastic bottle. Thank God. I'm not addicted to the stuff, but it's easy to see how that could happen. I have, in fact, seen it happen.

I pop the pill into my mouth and climb back in bed. My brain slows to a thrum, listening to the Xanax. Arms jelly, legs jelly, brain jelly, melting into the bed. But before I fade off, the finest gossamer of a thought sticks in my brain like a burr.

The fire. After twenty years, why am I dreaming about the fire?

Chapter Three

T ell me about the dream," Sam says.

I am lying on the stiff, chocolate-brown leather couch in his office, playing with an iron puzzle. Rings and figure eights that supposedly unlink into a necklace, with the apparent purpose of driving crazy patients even crazier.

"It's about a fire," I say.

"Okay," he says, in a measured voice. Sam always has a measured voice, part of the psychiatric bedside-manner thing I need to work on. He taps his knuckles on his glossy wooden desk. Everything in his office is glossy. It reminds me of the inside of a yacht: shiny, dark-cherry wooden furniture, deep navy-blue walls, anchor bookends, and a brass barometer on his desk. He has an oversized compass, too, with a desert-tan face and red and blue hands that always point true north. Which is odd, because the room faces east. I pointed this out once, and he gave me a polite smile that said, *Maybe your Adderall needs adjusting.* "Tell me more," he says.

"About the dream? It's a nightmare, really. A memory."

"A memory of what?"

I shake some blood back into my feet, which are dangling over the couch. This couch is not meant for tall people. Then again, most people probably don't actually lie on the couch. "Does anyone else actually lie on the couch?" I ask, since the thought strikes.

"Zoe, how about we try to focus on the dream?"

I sit up, clanking the iron puzzle back on the table. Focus, right.

"You say the dream is a memory. A memory of what?"

"A memory of the fire. The fire that killed my birth mother."

Sam stares at me. "Go on."

"It was just the two of us in the house when it happened. I was four years old. I survived, obviously, but she didn't."

"Wow," he says, though it's a measured "wow."

"My mom, my adoptive mom, told me about it when I was little, because I don't remember it very well. Only what I can piece together from the nightmare."

"Mmm-hmm," Sam says. "Mmm-hmm" is big in psychiatry. Another thing I have to work on: getting just the right tone for my "Mmm-hmm." "And what do you remember?" he asks.

I think back to the house. My parents showed it to me when we visited their old neighborhood once, a boring sub-urban house with skimpy dental trim around the front door. Somehow I had envisioned a different house, wet with ashes, smoke still rising. But of course, this was years later, and a new house now stood in its place. Phoenix will rise again.

17

"I remember the smell of smoke," I say. "And my hands, I remember my hands being cut." I show him the fine white lines that zigzag my palms. Show-and-tell. "Something fell off the house when it was burning, sliced them up."

"How about your mom? Can you remember her at all?" he asks.

I shake my head. "Not really. I wish I could. I have a photo of us from when I was a baby. That's all I really have of her. Everything else was destroyed in the fire." I pick up the heavy metal puzzle again from the table and clink it around. "My mom knew her, though. My adoptive mom. She was her best friend."

"Really?"

"Yeah. She agreed to raise me if anything should ever happen. And then the fire happened."

Sam leans back in his own chocolate-brown leather chair with a creak and crosses his arms. I can tell he is viewing me in a new light. I've met with him only a few times since I came back home, so it's been mainly a getting-to-know-you affair, mixed with some Adderall tweaking to keep my thoughts from flying too far. We haven't had the "My mother died in a fire" chat yet; I like to go two or three dates before springing that on a new psychiatrist.

"But the real issue," I say, "is why am I dreaming about the fire again?"

"What do you mean by that?"

"I used to have the nightmare every single night when I was a kid."

He considers this. "Likely a form of post-traumatic stress disorder."

"Yes, PTSD was my official diagnosis for a while," I say. When my poor new mom didn't sleep for years, comforting me as I screamed out night after night for my other mommy. We tried a spate of medications for the nightmares: cloni-dine, clonazepam, melatonin, phenobarbital. Nothing worked. Then one night, freshman year of high school, the nightmares just stopped. Like magic.

"Do you have any ideas about it?" Sam asks. "Why you had the nightmare again?"

"I don't know." I unlink a knot in the dull metal chain, the leather crunching as I lean forward on the couch. It is a spectacularly uncomfortable couch. "Probably because I'm back in Buffalo."

"Now that you're home for residency, you mean?"

"Right, because I didn't have the nightmare at all when I was at Yale. I didn't even think about it, actually."

Sam nods, playing with his beard. His beard, eyes, and hair are all the same exact shade of coffee brown. He matches the room. Sam is better-looking than most psychiatrists I've met. I'm always surprised to find him attractive. Not that I would date my psychiatrist, but you know.

"Let's give it some time," he says. "If you keep having the nightmares, we can talk about possible therapies. Like dream rehearsal, did you ever try that one?"

"I don't think so."

"Okay. We can always come back to that if we need to." He looks down at his notes. "How is your mother doing?"

"She has her good and bad days." I tinker with the metal puzzle. "It's weird. We'll have this almost normal conversation, and then she doesn't even remember she's in Buffalo."

"Not unusual. Social graces can stay intact for quite a while."

"I guess." I put the puzzle down. "Sometimes I wonder if we did the right thing though. Moving her there."

"It's natural to feel guilty, Zoe. But you want her to be safe."

"Yeah, but it was Scotty's idea, really. I never thought she was *that* bad."

Sam gives me a questioning look. "Didn't you say she almost burned the house down?"

"Well, yes, that one time," I admit, "when she forgot she was cooking." And then there was the time the police found her wandering down Elmwood in the middle of the night. Which is when we finally decided to move her. "I just hate seeing her in there."

He nods. "It's hard."

I nod, too, because it is. Sam speaks the obvious sometimes, but he means well.

"And Jean Luc?"

"No change there," I answer. "Holding pattern. Still taking a break." "Taking a break" being a euphemism for "breaking up," kind of.

"How's the Adderall working for you?"

"Pretty good," I answer. "Not perfect, though."

"Any palpitations?"

"No."

"Appetite?"

"Fine." Unfortunately, stimulants never did curb my appetite. "My focus isn't great. I just wish it could do a bit more."

Sam checks his computer, leaning his face into the screen. "You're on a fairly high dose already. Are you using any other measures to control your symptoms? Nonpharmacological methods?"

"A bit," I hedge.

"Such as?"

"Running, some. Though I haven't been doing it much lately. In college, I used to row. That helped a lot, even more than running."

"There's a rowing club in Buffalo," he offers.

"I know," I answer. "Maybe in the spring."

He smiles. "Get back to running, Zoe. You need to find a way to keep things in check for yourself when the meds aren't working for you."

"Yeah. I know."

Sam glances unobtrusively at the large pewter clock above my head. Looking at your watch in psychiatry is a big no-no, so most psychiatrists go for the big-clock-above-the-couch technique. He opens the drawer with a squeak and pulls out a script pad. This is where we say good-bye.

"Adderall?" he asks, scribbling.

"Yup." So I keep my mouth shut most of the time.

"Lexapro?"

"Yup." So I don't jump off the Peace Bridge.

"And Xanax."

"Yup." So I can sleep. "Can I have a few more pills this time? Just in case I have the nightmare again?"

There is a pause. Patient asking for more controlled sub-
stances, huge red flag. He raises his eyebrows just a milli-
meter. If my psychiatrist reads me, I read him right back.
"Okay," he says.

His okay speaks volumes as he tears off a script.

"Want to take a ride, Mom?" I ask.

Her room, replete with family pictures covering every flat
surface, a spindly, yellowing plant Scotty never remembers
to water, and a roommate who keeps calling out "Nancy" is
starting to feel claustrophobic.

"Okay," she agrees with some relief. I roll her wheelchair
out of the carpeted doorway onto the shiny, pink-tile floor
and feel as if we are making an escape. We wheel around
for a while, killing time, making the usual rounds and the
usual hellos, folks my mother will not remember tomorrow
and vice versa.

We pass by the rose-pink walls, topped with a creamy bor-
der with wild burgundy roses. The nursing home has taken the
rose-pink theme to a new level. If Sam's office looks like a ship,
this place looks like a huge Victorian tearoom: dark mauve
carpets, mauve Formica, mauve toile window treatments with
happy mauve peasants playing flutes and toiling in fields.

"How's the weather up there?" one of the patients croaks
out with a smile. I give my best, beatific smile, as if I've never
heard that one before.

"She's like a giraffe, isn't she?" my mom says, as though she, too, has just discovered my height and finds it as laughable as I do.

"Thanks a lot, Mom," I say, when we run into the orderly, and I mean literally.

"Mrs. Goldman!" she says in a peppy voice, avoiding our wheelchair. This woman is perpetually cheery, and given her work and her pay, this attitude borders on delusional. "I've got something for you," she says, cooing.

"What do you have?" my mother asks, distrustful. She has never been distrustful, my mother. This is new in her dementia. But I understand it. When you can't trust your mind, what can you trust?

"Your meds, silly!" The woman pulls out a tray with my mother's room number on it and pours the full bounty into a small, white, ruffled paper cup. Ten pills. For my mother, who bragged she was never sick a day in her life. My mother takes the cup in her hands and looks up at me, unsure. *Should I take them?* I have become my mother's mother, but I'm used to this. "Go ahead."

She glances up at me, as if she just remembered something. "Zoe, did you take your pills today?"

"Yes," I answer, laughing at this little nugget from the recesses of her temporal lobe. A question she has asked me a million times over my schooling. I went through a trough of meds for my ADHD, though sometimes I think they didn't help because I was just a natural pain in the ass. The orderly laughs, too, and moves on to her next lucky customer. We roll past the Impressionist prints with muted mauve frames, and past the nurses' station with holiday decorations and re-minders of the date.

Today is Thursday.
The date is the 5th.
The month is November.

Smiley turkeys are posted up on one side of the wall and, on the other, happy pilgrims and Indians are joined hand in hand, all future squabbles (smallpox-infested blankets, mas-sacres, etc.) glossed over. Halloween was quite a sight last month: witches, goblins, and ghosts, and spooky orange spider-web cotton laced across the nurses' station. Scary enough if you weren't already hallucinating.

"How's your father doing?" Mom asks.

"Dad died a while ago, Mom. Remember?"

"Oh right, right, I knew that." Sometimes she remembers this, sometimes she doesn't. Lately, more often than not, she doesn't.

"Car accident," I add, fending off her next question.

My father died when I was a freshman in high school and my brother, Scotty, was in fifth grade. It confirmed my nagging suspicion that Forrest Gump was right. Life *is* like a box of chocolates. But someone already ate all of the caramels.

"That's right," she says. "Now I remember." She is silent for a while, fumbling with her hands while I wheel her around. The smell of soiled sheets wafts out from one of the rooms, mixing with the smell of apple-pie air freshener by the nurses' station, an unpleasant juxtaposition. I'm used to hospital smells, but I've never liked them. We roll back to her room, where her roommate is carrying on to herself about an injustice that happened thirty years ago. Or yesterday, hard to know.

"Let's go outside?" I ask, and my mom nods. I wrap a fluffy lilac afghan around her shoulders. It is a blanket my mom knitted herself, "BD" as Scotty likes to say, "Before Dementia." Or as my mom used to say, "In my current state," to differentiate this from her former state of intelligence, independence. She doesn't say this anymore. Now she doesn't know what state she's in. Or even which city, according to the Mini-Mental-Status-Exam. Her afghan is pilled now, with some stains, but she loves that blanket, and I'm afraid a round in the washing machine might just do in the thing.

It is bright out, a rarity in Buffalo this time of year. Leaves are just past changing, bright, garish reds turning brown. We roll down the narrow pavement path with dried orange leaves skittering past us in the wind. I wrap the blanket tighter around her shoulders.

"So how's your work?" my mother asks, by way of conversation, and because she does not remember what I do.

"I'm a doctor, Mom."

"I know that!" she says, offended. "You're a plastic surgeon."

"Close, psychiatrist."

"That's what I meant."

I shrug; this is possible. "Pretty good." We park her chair

by the flowering crab tree, water beading on the red berries like jewels. "Actually, to be honest, things aren't so terrific right now."

"Why?" she asks.

"You want the list?" I laugh. "Or just the top three?"

She laughs with me. "Let's go for the top three."

"Okay. One"—I lift my finger to count off—"my attending is a jerk who hates me for some reason. Two, I miss Jean Luc. And three, I'm living with my brother."

"Jean Luc?" she asks. "Who's that?"

"You remember," I say. "The chemist, from Yale."

She looks blank.

"The Frenchman?" I remind her.

"Oh," she says with delight. "The Frenchman!" I told my mom about Jean Luc when she was still on this side of lucidity enough to be her old, wisecracking self. She usually teases me about him ten times per visit. Mom takes my hand. Despite the cold, her hand is warm. A young hand, I realize, not arthritic or knotty. Smooth, too young for this newly old mind. "Things will get better," she says.

I squeeze her hand in response, then she lets it go. My mom, despite her lapsing mind, knows how to empathize. It comes naturally to her, more than it does to me with my patients. She empathizes with the nursing-home residents, too. I catch her counseling them, advising them about some problem or another, though neither usually remembers the conversation the next day. Maybe it's her social work training from all those years ago kicking in.

"My coworkers are nice," I add, to make her feel better.

"Now that's something," she encourages, smiling. My mom always did look on the bright side of things.

I move to sit down next to her on the cold iron bench, sick of towering over her chair. The wind kicks up the leaves again and starts the wind chime tinkling in fits, spinning on the branch of the little tree. I recognize that wind chime as a creation from Craft Wednesday a few weeks ago. My mom was quite proud of hers.

"Scotty told me you and the Frenchman were getting married in Paris."

"Nope. He's pulling your leg."

Now she laughs, her low, rumbling, Lauren Bacall laugh. I have seen men fall in love with this laugh. "My son is funny, isn't he?"

"Hilarious." I hug my sweater against the breeze. The wind chime twirls and twirls, tinkling out its song in mad spasms. "So I had my nightmare again."

She turns her head to me. "What nightmare?"

"The fire."

"Oh," she says, pulling her blanket in closer. "I thought you were over that."

"Yeah, so did I."

Mom stares ahead at the tree, the wind chime still going.

"Sam thinks it's because I'm back in Buffalo."

"Who's Sam?"

"Sam, my psychiatrist."

"I thought Dr. Lowry was your psychiatrist."

"Yeah, when I was, like, ten. I've been through a few now, remember, Mom?"

She nods. "I guess."

"I've been seeing Sam since I've been back home. I like him."

She rubs her arms. "I'm getting cold, honey. Ready to go back in?"

"Sure," I say, fighting a yawn. I have to get home to study anyway. So we wind our way back into the Victorian palace, past the disinfectant smells, the nurses laughing at their station, back to Mom's small, rose-pink-carpeted room, with her roommate mercifully gone.

"Home," I say, depositing her in her favorite corner rocker. I smooth the blanket around her and gather up my things.

"See you later, Mom. I love you."

"I love you, too, Tanya," she answers, her eyes closing.

I stare at her a moment as she descends right into sleep, her breath evening into a soft snore. Tanya? I jiggle my car keys, debating, but don't have the heart to wake her. And the whole drive home the name burrows itself in my head: Tanya. Who the hell is Tanya?

"No, I don't know any Tanya," Scotty says, clearing up dishes from the next table. "It's probably just someone from her past. She's not exactly all there, Zoe, in case you haven't noticed."

"Yeah, I guess not," I answer, handing him another plate, but he's already charging off to the register to take an order. I pick up my coffee cup, and the bronze foam leaf twirls around in a circle. The baristas do make an artistic cup of java here. The first sip is heavenly, though I smear the leaf and end up with a milk mustache. Raindrops squiggle down the window, racing each other. The weather has gone from blue skies to gray, foggy drizzle in a couple of hours. The smell of nutmeg rises from the mug, and I take another warm, foamy sip.

I could sit here all day, staring out the window in my favorite settee by the hearth, procrastination being one of my favorite pastimes. It takes all my will, but I peel my eyes off the raindrops scurrying down the window and focus on the book in my hands, smoothing down the first page of the first chapter.

Personality Disorders
Antisocial personality: Long-term pattern of exploiting the rights of others. The behavior can be criminal. Patients may be charming and magnetic as well as gifted at flattering others.

I've never been called charming, magnetic, or gifted at flattering others. So I think I'm okay as far as antisocial goes.

"You good? Or can I get you anything?" Eddie asks.

"I'm great, thanks."

This is the longest string of words Eddie has ever said to me. To call Eddie "shy" is being kind. He is not far from "Cluster C Avoidant" in the personality disorder chapter. Reportedly Eddie has a crush on me. I take this with a mountainous grain of salt, however, coming from my brother. Eddie is a type of handsome: pale, lanky, with a ponytail and leaf tattoos vining up his arms. Being six feet, five inches, he is taller than I am, so he likely gets asked, "What's the weather like up there?" ten times a day as well, though I am not sure how much else we have in common. Eddie likes philosophy and Russian poetry; again, per Scotty. I haven't thought much about Russian poetry or philosophy, other than as a risk factor for suicide.

High-pitched laughter rings out over at the bar, mixed with the noise of beans grinding. Ditzy laughter, from girls hunched over their phones, rapidly texting. Scotty is head barista today, flirting with as many women as possible. Scotty has a way with the ladies, as they say. I'm not sure why. He's on the taller side, but not as tall as I am. And he's skinny, boyish-looking. But if I had to venture a guess for his success with women, it would be his eyebrows. Expressive, with a hint of James Dean.

The Coffee Spot is a place that prides itself on not being Starbucks, which isn't a grand achievement, but it does have a certain charm. If Sam's office is a yacht, and the nursing home a Victorian tearoom, then the Coffee Spot is a funky bachelor pad. The walls are mocha brown, as are the stained wooden floors, but everything else is without color scheme or theme, except maybe "cool." The furniture is all secondhand and beat-up but comfortable: mismatched chairs and sofas, including my favorite eggplant settee by the fireplace. Local avant-garde artwork covers the walls. The bathrooms don't say Women or Men but are labeled by bronzed torsos, that kind of place. This was Scotty's college job, which soon became his actual job when he flunked out of the University at Buffalo. He claims this was due to the stress of dealing with Mom. I claim this was due to smoking too much dope. So we have a difference of opinion.

An antisocial person may be superficially attractive and charming but has little regard for others. Patients often have a history of oppositional defiance disorder (ODD) in childhood. They show a pattern of lying, stealing, and having problems with authority, and as a result, may end up incarcerated. Many in the prison population would fit this diagnosis.

Funny trivia fact: Tattoos used to be included as a sign of an antisocial personality. Now they're just a sign of trying to fit in. If tattoos were still part of the diagnosis criterion, everyone at the Coffee Spot would be on their way to jail, including Scotty, who has several tattoos strategically circling various muscles. My mom tried to warn him off ink by telling him he couldn't be buried in a Jewish cemetery with any marks on his body. "Give me a break, Mom," he said. "Every fucking person in Jerusalem has a tattoo." This was after his summer trip to Israel, which had the unintended effect of making him more rebellious and less religious, if this was possible. "Language, Scotty!" my mom yelled, which is something she said a hundred times a day.

Laughter wafts over the bar again. This time it's an older woman giggling with Scotty. When I say older, I mean older for Scotty. That makes her about thirty.

"Pumpkin spice latte," Eddie calls out, and the woman shimmies up to grab it. Pumpkin spice latte? How anyone could choke down that swill is beyond me. The woman is in a cheap, blue business suit. She has red hair and freckles, completely not Scotty's type. Scotty goes for girls with implants and skinny arms, spray-on tans and white teeth. Barbie girls. Those are the girls who usually end up in Scotty's room, a red handkerchief tied jauntily around the handle to let me know to knock first. He goes for girls who shop at Abercrombie, not Dress Barn. But then again, he appears to be flirting back all the same. Getting her number even, I'll be damned.

"Could I get you anything else, Zoe?" Eddie asks. He sounds petrified. I don't think he's ever called me by name before.

"Still good, Eddie. Thanks." I hold up my cup in evidence, still half-full. Or half-empty, you know, depending.

He nods and looks as if he is about to say something, then veers off to another table as fast as his lanky legs will take him. Poor guy. If he had an eighth of Scotty's moves, he'd be shacked up right now, bright red handkerchief tied around a doorknob, reading Russian poetry to some dewy-eyed damsel. Probably not me. I haven't been dewy-eyed for a while.

Dum-dum-dum-dah.

Beethoven's Fifth. This is the text tone for Jean Luc. My heart always thumps when I hear that tune, pathetic as that may be. Scotty programmed the text tone as a lark. Scotty does not like Jean Luc, whom he routinely refers to as "Frog-Boy." My brother has never actually met Jean Luc, so I'm not sure what the issue is. Maybe it's a Freudian thing.

Vous êtes mon petit chou, the text reads. Literally, "You are my little cabbage." Jean Luc knows I find this endearment hysterical.

How's my little broccoli? I write back.

Skype?

Sure. I move my coffee over to boot up my laptop. In a minute, Jean Luc's face fills up the screen. I never tire of looking at Jean Luc. I am not proud of this superficiality, but it's a fact. He is beautiful, Ralph Lauren–model beautiful: brooding eyes, ropy muscles from years of soccer, and dirty-blond, unkempt bangs that always fall into his eyes. When I first met Jean Luc, winter break of my last year of medical school, I spent the entire day trying to classify him. He is a curious mix of awkward, clueless, and handsome. You could mistake him for snobby, but he's actually shy. Aloof, when he's just solving chemistry problems in his head. And then there is his beauty, which is unavoidable, though he doesn't seem to notice. But women notice. They zone in on him in a bar, attracted to the Darwinian fittest, the peacock with the most outstanding feathers.

Yet he picked me—the tall one—much to the shock and unalloyed dismay of the other female contestants. This fact surprises me to this day because I am not beautiful. It's not that I'm bad-looking, just forgettable. It's like once you get past the six-foot thing, it's hard to remember anything else. If I robbed a liquor store at gunpoint, the victim would tell the criminal sketch artist, "She was over six feet tall," then be at a loss. No one remembers my eye color (hazel, whatever hazel means, sometimes brown, sometimes green) or hair color (brown, but just brown, not chestnut brown, for instance) and freckles (which I'm told are cute, but not in an *I want to bed you* kind of way). But Jean Luc disagreed with my assessment. He said I was too stupid to see how lovely I am, which was the first time I have ever been called either stupid or lovely.

"How's life in DC?" I ask.

"Going well," he answers. "The government job is promising." Jean Luc had his doubts about going into government work instead of academia, but the tenure prospects weren't encouraging last year.

A girl runs behind Jean Luc on the screen, wrapped in a towel like she's fresh out of the shower. Her blond hair is slicked back and dripping. "Sorry!" she calls in a singsong voice.

"Did I interrupt something?" I ask him.

"That's Melanie." He pronounces it in the French way, *Meh-lah-NEE*, with the accent on the last syllable. "Robbie's girlfriend," he explains. Robbie is his flatmate, someone he met from the classifieds for the apartment. Robbie is quintessential DC: power ties, lunch meetings at pricey restaurants where he might be seen, twice-a-day workouts. He is everything Jean Luc is not. Jean Luc widens his eyes and mouths. "She never leaves."

This gets a chuckle from me, a relieved chuckle. We talk awhile. I tell him about everything: my newest patient—the lovely Sofia Vallano, the annoying Dr. Grant, my mother's fading mind, Scotty's latest dalliances, the return of the nightmare. Everything, in short, except how much I miss him. Because I don't know how to tell him that. It is logical, he explained, that we should date other people when we are miles apart. And Jean Luc is logical. He thrives in the reliable world of chemistry, a world of absolutes. One night, as we sat in damp grass and gaped at the fireworks springing up against the sky, he pointed in the air and said, "You see, fireworks are chemistry. You mix them together, and they explode. It is predictable. It is..." He searched for the word in English. "Accountable. People are not always accountable, but chemistry"—he smiled, as if he were talking about a lover—"chemistry is always accountable."

A cat jumps up on the table in a gray flash. Jean Luc pets her absentmindedly, even though he's allergic to cats, then she flies off the screen again.

"You have a cat?"

"It's Robbie's," he answers. "Kitty."

"The cat's name is Kitty?"

"Yes." He shrugs. "Melanie named her."

"Hmm." So Melanie is either a complete dullard or woefully ironic.

Jean Luc glances at his watch, a silver and blue one that I gave him for his birthday. "Zoe, I have to go. We are going for dinner soon."

"Okay," I say, noticing the fading blond in his hair, the summer sun long gone now. "Where are you going?"

"Sushi," he answers with a grimace. "This is all they eat around here. So expensive for little fish pieces that are not even cooked."

I lean back in the settee, laughing. Half the time, Jean Luc doesn't even realize he's being funny. "Have fun."

"*Je t'aime*," he says.

"*Je t'aime*," I answer. We are taking a break but still saying *je t'aime*. I close Skype, and my gaze wanders back to the window, where some of the raindrops are now freezing in beads. I smooth the book page again.

Patients with antisocial personality disorder are not necessarily sociopaths. Many are nonviolent unless provoked.

The woman with the pumpkin latte is leaving, huddling up against the cold rain. Sleet thuds against the window, threatening actual snow. The flames flicker against the grate on the hearth. I lean my head back against the soft leather and take another lingering sip of coffee before looking down at my book again. Internally I sigh, if this is possible.

Hours to go before I sleep.

Chapter Four

The psych ward is buzzing as usual. The heater in the resident room clangs away as cold leaks from the window. Patches of last night's snow checker the ground.

How is my little kumquat? I text and drop the phone in my stiff lab-coat pocket, behind my *Psychiatry Pearls* book, before I have a chance to fret over whether I will get a response or not.

"Who are you texting?" Jason asks, sneaking up behind me.

"No one."

"It's your boyfriend, right?"

I don't answer, and he starts jabbing my arm. "Give it up, girl. Pictures."

"He's not even my boyfriend anymore," I say, showing him a photo on my phone.

"Holy shit." Jason grabs my phone to take a closer look. "He's fucking hot. He looks like Beckham." He pauses to consider. "I'd have sex with him."

"Oh, thanks, Jason. He'll be so pleased."

Jason was on call last night and looks a bit bleary-eyed, the gelled, bleached tuft of his bangs starting to droop and the trademark bow tie long gone. He sits down heavily in his chair and leans back, the two chair legs precariously digging into a stain on the rust-brown carpet. The carpet is dotted with such stains, in various shapes and shades, like islands on a map. The resident room is a metaphor for our department: broke and run-down. Psychiatry is a poor man's medical field. The neurosurgery resident room, on the other hand, looks like the Taj Mahal.

Dr. A enters the room and takes a seat next to Jason. "Anything for me?" he asks.

"Yeah," Jason answers. "You ready?"

"Ready as I'll ever be," Dr. A says, remarkably not screwing up any part of the phrase.

"Who's yours again?" Jason scans his page.

"Wisnoski, Hillbrand, and Edwards."

"All right," he shifts papers. "Wisnoski, Wisnoski, Wisnoski," he says, pointing to the name. "Still on twenty-four-hour one-on-one. But they're watching him today, may d/c it for the weekend if he's no longer verbalizing clear suicidal ideation. He pretty much still is, though."

Dr. A nods.

"EEG normal. We upped his Lexapro to fifty milligrams qd and added Abilify at ten. No privileges right now, no phone if he asks, which he will."

"What's the plan if there is not significant improvement from the medication changes?" Dr. A asks.

38

"Possibly ECT," says Jason. He is talking about electro-convulsive shock therapy, one of the last resorts for depression. But this is Mr. Wisnoski's third suicide attempt in the last five years.

"Ah, that is why they got the EEG," he says.

"That's the fact, Jack."

Dr. A looks puzzled and pulls out his idiom notebook. "Who is this Jack?"

"Forget it, man. Just yes, you're right, that's why they got the EEG." Jason scans farther down the sheet. "Fuck, I need some coffee. Hillbrand is finished with detox and is awaiting transfer to rehab."

"He's off suicide watch?"

"Yeah, turns out he drank window cleaner to get drunk, not to kill himself."

"Lack of insight," I offer.

"Yeah, I'd say," answers Jason. "And Edwards is stable, awaiting discharge."

Dr. A pats him on the back and grabs his charts to start seeing his patients.

Jason turns to me. "Who you got?"

"Just two right now. Miles Featherington and Vallano. Tiffany Carlson got discharged."

"Okay. Featherington has group therapy in the morning. Going up on Risperdal and Depakote for OCD. Limited to ten-minute showers, and watch that no one gives him a toothbrush or he gives himself a thorough rectal cleaning." I wince. "Oh, and he gets to look at his stamp collection every Wednesday if he doesn't refuse meds."

"How about Vallano?"

"No fireworks yet," Jason says. "She's the model patient, I guess. She has a nail file for her manicures that has to be locked up nightly to prevent someone else grabbing it, and she also has charcoals that have to be locked up."

"Charcoals?"

"It seems she's quite the accomplished artist," he says.

"A woman of many talents," I say, grabbing the charts. "What's her privilege level, by the way?"

"Level three," he says. "As long as she cooperates in group, which she has been." Level three is the highest. It means she's allowed magazines or books from the library, makeup and nail polish, one phone call per week (which she never takes), and group outings. Though she's still not allowed off the floor without an aide. I check over the orders from last night before going on to see my charge.

Sofia Vallano is lying on her bed, propped up on her elbows, her hands cradling her chin. She is flipping through another magazine that has a waifish woman telling you "what men really want" on the cover, the sort that casually describe fellatio in an elevator. I would think finding out "what men really want" doesn't come in very handy in a mental institution, but who can tell. She is bouncing her feet together in an absentminded rhythm. She looks as if she could be at overnight camp, were it not for the fact that she is over thirty, on a psychiatric ward, and a probable psychopath. She is just missing the Dubble-Bubble chewing gum and posters of *Teen Beat* heartthrobs taped to the walls.

A couple of small, framed charcoal drawings sit on her

bare desk, along with the hospital-issued pink-plastic pitcher of ice water. The pictures are quite impressive, actually. One is a landscape of branches in a night sky, with a moon shining through. The other is a self-portrait, not surprising for a narcissist.

"Did you draw these?" I ask, picking up a frame, starting in safe territory.

"Yup," she says, eyes still on the magazine. A teenager ignoring her mom, except that she killed her mom. And she's no longer a teenager.

"They're good."

"Yup," she repeats, nonchalant. The silence builds as she flips through her magazine, refusing to interact with me beyond monosyllables.

I sit down in the chair next to her bed. "So how are you finding the new place?"

Sofia crosses her legs, still lying on her belly. "It's a variation of the old place."

I nod, flipping open her chart, and scoot my chair closer to her bed. I wait a long thirty seconds to see if she'll break the silence, but she doesn't. "Do you want to talk about why you're here?"

Sofia's upper lip flinches a millisecond, but she keeps her face buried in her magazine. "Haven't you heard?" she asks.

"Well," I say, leaning back in the chair, faking a laid-back posture to match hers. Mirroring: another big one in the psychiatry bag of tricks. "I have read through your chart, of course."

"It's all in there then. You know more than I do."

"Maybe. But, even still, I'd like to hear it in your own words. Do you feel ready to talk about it?"

Sofia pauses to consider, looking at the ceiling. "Not really."

I sigh inwardly. So far this is going really well. She flips through the magazine pages, though I can tell she is not reading the words. The branches of an old maple tree sway in the fogged-up window, a few faded orange leaves clinging stubbornly.

"We're talking about releasing you, you know," I say, to test whether she does know this.

Her shoulders tense, then release. She clears her throat but does not look up. "I heard," she says. But I can tell she is lying. A piece of black hair escapes into her eyes, and she pushes it back behind her ear. "And who makes that decision?"

"We all do. Dr. Grant has the final say, of course, but it's a team approach."

"Of course," she answers, not hiding her smirk.

I tap my foot on a loose tile. "Sofia, do you know why I'm asking you about the release?"

"No," she says, the glossy magazine page catching the sun's glare as she flips it.

"Do you want to know?" I ask.

"Sure," she says. "Enlighten me."

Wow, "enlighten." Big word. Did you learn that in college? Oh no, I'm sorry, I guess not, that's right: You were confined to a mental hospital. But of course I say none of this. Adderall forces all my best zingers to stay in my mouth.

42

"I won't know if you're ready for discharge until we can talk about the reason you're here."

She keeps flipping pages and licks her lips, which look chapped. "Guess I'll be here for a while then."

I shrug but don't stoop to answer. Grabbing her chart, I stand up to leave, wondering at her purposelessly self-destructive attitude: I won't talk to you, even if it means I'm stuck here forever. "I'll be in tomorrow, Sofia."

"Okay, Zoe," she says.

"That's Dr. Goldman, actually," I say, feeling for the first time like Dr. Goldman. As I leave the room, my phone sings out: *Dum-dum-dum-dah*. Jean Luc. My heart does a polka. If I were Pavlov's dog, I would salivate.

What is a kumquat? The text reads.

Fruit. Look it up. I type.

U r calling me a fruit?

U call me cabbage.

:) Je t'aime.

Je t'aime, I answer and get ready to see my next patient, who I hope to hell doesn't have a toothbrush.

Chapter Five

W arm blood on my hands, my nightgown damp with sweat, buzzing in my ears. All day long, jagged pieces of the nightmare creep into my thoughts.

"I'll try anything," I say.

Sam folds his hands together. "Unfortunately, as you may know, there isn't much research on treating nightmares."

"Yes, I know." I tap my heel against the scratchy blue carpet. "What about dream rehearsal? You mentioned that before."

He nods. "That is probably where I'd start."

"Okay, let's do it then." Patience has never been my strong suit. I had the nightmare again last night. So it wasn't a one-off. They could be back for good. And I want this fixed, now.

Sam leans back and uncrosses his legs, his corduroys whisking together. He is wearing brown again, blending into the room as usual. Even his glasses (readers—he only wears them sometimes) are tortoiseshell. I'm surprised they don't have little anchors on them.

"We have to start by delving into the dream. I need you to tell me every detail, from the very beginning," he says.

I take a deep breath. My nightmare, not my favorite topic of conversation. "Okay. Well, it always starts with my hands."

"All right."

"They're bleeding. Like I told you, from something that fell off the house, but I don't remember that part."

"Okay. What happens next?"

"It's me as a little girl, and I'm confused. Or maybe it's me as an adult being confused, I'm not sure."

Sam squints his eyes. "I don't think I'm following you."

"Yeah, I'm not sure I follow myself."

He puts down his yellow pad. "So you're a little girl in the dream."

"Yes, and I'm hiding, but I don't know who I'm hiding from. I don't even know where I am. But what I'm saying is, I think the little girl knows; I just don't remember."

"Okay, I see now." Sam pauses, staring at the wall. "Is it possible you were confused, maybe a little oxygen-deprived, when you were hiding from the fire?"

I feel myself smiling. This is what I love about therapy, both giving and getting these moments of insight. "Yes." I never considered the possibility of oxygen deprivation before. *Of course* I was confused. The thought is exhilarating.

"So you're hiding," he confirms.

"Yes, and I hear a whirring noise."

"What's that from?"

"I don't know," I say. "And actually, it drives me a little crazy. I'm always trying to place that sound, even in the dream."

"Okay, so there's a whirring noise."

"And I'm afraid."

"Naturally."

"And I've got my blue teddy bear, Po-Po, who is missing an eye."

Sam smiles at the image.

"And someone's calling my name, but I'm afraid to come out."

"Okay. Do you know who that someone is?"

"Not really," I say, but this is only half-true.

"Go on."

"Then the person opens the door." My heart speeds as I recount this. "And that's all."

Sam nods, digesting this. I catch him glancing at the pewter clock, then down again. "I'm going to give you some homework for next week. I want you to write down the dream, every instant, every little thing you remember. Can you do that?"

"Sure."

"Sometimes just the act of writing down the words diminishes their power over you."

"Okay, that makes sense."

"Then I want you to extend the dream."

"Extend it? What do you mean?"

"I think part of the problem here is the confusion. The

unknown. That may be what's truly scaring you. The lack of a real ending."

"But how do I extend it? I don't know what happens when the door opens."

"Right," he says, "and I think that's the crux of the problem."

I shift, and the uncomfortable leather couch creaks with me. "So you're saying give it another ending?"

Sam sits up in the chair with a smile. "That's *exactly* what I'm saying. An ending that you dictate. That you control. An ending that's not a question mark."

"Like?"

"That's up to you to decide. What's a more optimistic, and perhaps realistic, ending to the dream?"

I pause, thinking. "I don't know. A fireman coming?"

"Sounds like a good one." Sam crosses his legs, the corduroy rubbing again. "You need to bring resolution to the nightmare. I think that could really help."

"So how does this work? I just hope the fireman shows up in the dream at the right moment?"

"Not exactly," Sam says. "You need to practice it. That's where the rehearsal part comes in. You run through the dream before you go to bed. Every single moment, especially the end, when the door opens and the fireman enters. You insert your new ending and rehearse that part before you go to sleep."

I am picturing a fireman, dressed in bright yellow, bursting through the doorway, ax in hand. Face grubby with soot and sweat, helmet tipping down over his forehead. Saving the day. The thought gladdens me. Much better than the alternative—the unknown, or even worse, the suspected. The idea so terrible that I can't let it sneak into my brain for a second without falling into a well of self-loathing and guilt. The idea that I *do* know who was calling me, but I didn't answer her.

And maybe, if I had answered her, she would still be alive.

Chapter Six

"Tell me about my birth mother," I say.

We are sitting in her room, Mom in her rocker and me on the corner of the bed, on her crumpled Amish quilt. The evergreen air freshener I bought last week is pumping its heart out to cover the competing smells. We have arranged it so she now has the luxury of a cramped private room, so we don't have to hear her roommate rambling on about "Nancy" anymore. Mom looks up from her magazine, which I notice with some distaste is the same magazine Sofia was reading. "What about her?" she asks.

"Just about her." I stash my *Narcissism* book on her night-stand, next to a Gideon Bible. "Beth Winters," I say, reminding her.

"Yes, Beth Winters, I know. But why are you so interested in her all of a sudden?"

Which is a fair question. Probably because I'm dreaming about the fire again. "I don't know."

"Hmph," she says, glancing back down at the magazine.

"I have this patient," I tell her, "who's a sociopath. She killed her mother when she was, like, fourteen."

She looks up abruptly. "That's terrible," she says, smoothing the magazine cover with her palm. "We had a few patients like that when I was in social work. So sad, these troubled, troubled kids." Her eyes take on a faraway glaze. "I remember one case in particular. This young boy who killed his whole…" She shivers. "Never mind. Just sad, so sad." Then she lets out a chipper, unexpected laugh. "I can't remember what I had for breakfast, but I can still remember those kids."

I wait for her to say more, but she doesn't. She just stares at the wall. I clear my throat, trying to sound casual. "So it got me thinking about my own mother, how she died. I just want to find out more about her."

She nods, putting the magazine on the nightstand with only a hint of a sigh, as if she is sick of telling this story but will do it just one more time because I insist.

"Beth Winters," I say again.

"Yes, that was her name," she answers.

"And she was your best friend," I say, jogging her memory.

"Beth was my best friend. You know the story, Zoe. She asked me, if anything ever happened to her, would I raise you, and I said yes." She takes off her reading glasses, cleaning the lenses with her blanket. "Of course, when someone asks you this you never really think about it. You just say yes. No one ever thinks something will actually happen. If you really thought about it, you might say no."

"True," I say, considering this. There is a pause, my mom mindlessly rubbing her glasses. "And then?"

"And then she died in the fire, not six months after asking me." She puts her glasses back on, though they are still dirty. Her rocker knocks against the rose-pink wall, smudging it with wood stain. "You know, I didn't think I would ever have children. We tried so hard, your father and I, for years we tried. Nearly divorced over it."

If I were a cartoon, my mouth would be hanging open. She has never told me this about her and Dad before. She fumbles with the pilled lilac blanket on her lap. Then she starts to clean her glasses with the blanket again. I'm not sure if she forgot she just cleaned them or if she noticed they were still dirty. Then she drops them, silver rims glinting in the sunlight. I pick them up and hand them back to her.

"Then Beth died. And suddenly, I had a baby of my own." She smiles at me. "A four-year-old baby."

I smooth out a wrinkle in the quilt, pulling the plum diamond straight. "But I never understood something. Why didn't her family just take me in?"

She squints as if trying to remember the answer. "I think it was written in her will, so no one could contest it." She throws me a defensive look, as though I might want to contest it.

"And my biological father?" I ask. "No one knew his whereabouts?"

She pauses. "Larry something, I think."

She had told me before it was a one-night stand. "Did you ever try to find him?"

"I don't remember, honey. Maybe. Probably."

"What about her parents?"

"What is this, twenty questions?" she asks with a nervous smile.

"No, I'm just trying to fill in some things."

"Her parents were gone," she says, then pauses, thinking.

"You told me they died of cancer when she was young," I offer.

"Yes, that's right," she says, relieved to get the answer. "Very sad."

"No other family?"

She looks at the ceiling; the rocker thwacks the wall again. "A sister I think. She was into drugs, I want to say."

"Heroin, you told me."

"That's it then."

I'm not sure why I'm asking her these questions when I'm the one providing all the answers. She lifts her glasses off her face and starts cleaning the lenses again. This time they are definitely clean, though, sparkling even.

"It was hard. Of course, your father and I were over the moon with you. But on the other hand"—she drops her glasses again, and I pick them up, as if we are in some bad vaudeville routine—"I lost my best friend. We were like sisters." She pauses, takes a deep breath. "But I had you. And six months later, I was pregnant with Scotty. After all that time thinking I couldn't have kids, I stopped worrying about it, and boom." She laughs her deep, throaty laugh. "In a weird way, I always felt like that fire was meant to be, as awful as that sounds."

I nod, and she reaches over to take my hand. Her nails have been freshly painted, a French manicure. This is one of the many offered activities in the nursing home, and something she never would have bothered with BD. My hands are ruddy and dry, in need of some lotion. We sit in comfortable silence for a few minutes. In her dementia, there are these odd, unexpected rewards, moments we are closer than we ever have been, or ever would have been.

"I wish I could remember my birth mom," I say. "But I don't. Except for the picture." My mom knows the picture I'm talking about. The only one I have of my "real" mom, a dog-eared photo of a woman with dark hair and brown eyes. Big, lovely, doe eyes with liquid brown eyeliner and permed frizzy black hair, as if she could have been on her way to a seventies disco. She is looking right at the camera in triumph and holding a fuzzy-headed, puffy-eyed baby: me. And on the back of the photo, in faded blue cursive, was my mom's writing: "Beth and Zoe—5 days old."

"She was the real thing, your mom," she says. Her hands are fidgeting. I hand her back her magazine.

"By the way," I ask, "who's Tanya?"

The magazine trembles in her hands. "Who?"

"You called me Tanya when I was leaving last time. I wondered who you were talking about."

"I don't think I know a—"

A knock on the door interrupts us. "Med time!" the orderly calls out in her bright voice, poking her head in the room. Her name, I remember now, is Cherry. Cheery Cherry, I thought when I heard it, so now I don't forget it. Though

53

Cherry is not a name you might forget easily anyway. My mom never remembers, but that's my mom. She throws back her pills, a pro by now, and Cheery Cherry gives her a thumbs-up of approval and pushes off to the next room.

"So you don't know who Tanya is then?"

"No, honey." She sinks down farther in her rocker, her face tired and drawn. "I'm not so good with names anymore."

I pat her arm, standing up from the bed. "That's okay. It doesn't matter." I straighten the magazine, and the spindly plant that is fighting for its life. "I'm going to let you go."

She nods. "Good night," she says, though the sun is out.

"Good night," I answer, remembering how the therapist told us to "meet her where she is at." It took everything in me not to point out the dangling preposition, but then again, that's why I'm on Adderall.

Mom's eyes are closing. Maybe the meds are making her tired. Her Aricept just got increased. I'll have to remember to ask the neurologist about that when he comes back next week. The neurologist who can't explain why my mom suddenly needs a walker, and can't give her a diagnosis.

"Could be frontotemporal dementia, Lewy Body. Could be Alzheimer's." He rubbed his hands together rapidly, as though there were a fire, not making eye contact. His blazer looked as if he'd slept in it. "Problem is, we never really know until autopsy."

Problem is, the diagnosis is not really helpful at that point! I wanted to scream. Just about as helpful as the neurologist coming to check her eye movements, rotate her arms around, and ask her to remember three things (bread, church, twenty dollars, always the same three things that she never remembers), spending a total of five minutes in the room (possibly eight if I happen to be around) before writing a script for another pill that "may or may not help very much," and then moving on, shall we say, to the next victim.

"Tits on a bull," my brother said as the neurologist squirreled out of the room last time. My brother tightened his arms around his chest, fingers splaying his lightning-bolted biceps out of his sky-blue T-shirt. "Tits on a bull."

And on this point, I must say, we most definitely agree.

Chapter Seven

I can't believe this," I say, skimming through Sofia Vallano's chart to catch up on anything from overnight.

Jason bites into an apple. "What?"

"You should not talk with the food in your mouth," Dr. A scolds him.

"I really can't believe this," I repeat.

"Again, what?" Jason asks, opening his mouth and sticking his apple-covered tongue out at Dr. A, who shakes his head in disgust. I have been working with these guys so much lately that sometimes I feel as if I have three brothers. A regular dysfunctional family, us.

"He hasn't been listening to a word I've said," I answer.

"I still don't know what in tarnation you're on about," Jason says, in a Southern drawl he just made up.

Dr. A whips out his notebook. "And what would be a 'tarnation'?"

Jason ignores him.

"I'm talking about my patient Sofia. Remember, the lady killer? Dr. Grant interviewed her yesterday. His note is completely wrong. It sounds like he was talking to a different patient."

"Oh, that," Jason says, bored, turning back to his patient chart and chomping into the apple again. "Grant hasn't listened to a word I've said since July. Don't feel so special."

"Yeah, but the woman is insane, and he's talking about releasing her."

"Dr. Goldman," Jason says, "this *is* a psychiatric facility. If you wanted to work with sane people, you should have gone into internal medicine."

"Act-tually," Dr. A says, "I do not think this would be a safe bet." "Safe bet" is probably one he has been practicing. I have noticed he has started peppering phrases with idioms. "There are plenty of crazy people in internal medicine."

"Yeah, you're right. Radiology then. Lots of sane people in radiology," Jason says. "And I'd be making a shitload more money when I got out. Remind me why I didn't go in to radiology again? Oh yeah, dark rooms, not good, kept falling asleep."

I read out loud to them: "'Patient voices regret over her past actions. States she would like to visit Children's Hospital or become a Big Sister to help other children. Her dream is to become an elementary school teacher or social worker to help troubled kids, as she feels she was not helped.' Is that not unbelievable? She's acting like Mother Teresa, and he's falling for it, hook, line, and sinker."

"It's a fishing metaphor," Jason says as an aside to Dr. A, who is already writing.

"It's bizarre. It's like she's gaslighting me," I say.

Jason holds up his hand. "Old movie reference, don't write it down." Dr. A pauses with his pen above his notebook. Jason pitches the apple core into the wastebasket five feet away with a flourish and misses, earning some miffed stares from the nurses in the station.

"I'm not cleaning that shit up," says one of said nurses.

Jason ambles over and scoops it up, shooting again and missing again. "Yeah, I was in the drama club," he explains, picking it up and dropping it in directly above the can.

"I was, too!" says Dr. A, a bright smile bursting onto his chubby face. "Which plays did you perform? Although we did mainly Thai theater."

"Would you people listen to me?" I say.

"Yeah, yeah, yeah," Jason says. "We heard the big news. Your patient is crazy. Not your issue, girl. It's going to be Dr. Grant's problem if something happens."

"Like, you mean if she *kills* someone?" I shake my head. "That is completely fucked-up."

"Hmmph," Jason says. "What's not?"

"Ah, this is true," agrees Dr. A, as if we have just uncovered one of the world's great truths. "What is not?"

⌐

Sofia is facing the window, sketching with her charcoals, when I walk in. Stepping closer, I see she is drawing a branch from the maple tree in the window, all the knots and whorls, the naked twigs. She stops when she hears my footsteps, holds the charcoal still for a few seconds, then starts up again.

"Looks good," I offer.

"Hmm," she responds. Even she has learned the "Hmm."

I sit down, pulling open her chart on my lap. "Any more thoughts about what I said?"

"About what?" she asks.

"About talking about your mom."

"Not really," she says, her arm swaying in strokes. The room smells flowery, sweet. Like jasmine.

"Are you wearing perfume?" I ask.

She scratches out more detail in the bark. "It's my body lotion. You like it?"

"Yeah," I say. "It's nice."

Sofia turns around from her drawing and smiles at me. It is an all-knowing, mocking smile. Then she turns her head again and goes back to her drawing. Her smile unsettles me, but then again, I might have imagined it.

"Everything okay in group therapy?"

"Yeah," she says, noncommittal.

"How about the food?" I ask, half in jest.

"The food sucks. That's nothing new."

"Do you have visitors bring you anything from the gift shop?"

Here she lets out a withering laugh. "What visitors?"

I have no answer for this. You kill your mom, and you don't get a lot of visitors. I decide to circle back to my original question. "You know, Sofia," I say, jotting down my note on the lined hospital paper, which looks much the same as yesterday's note, "we're going to have to talk about it eventually. If you ever want the chance to tell your side of things."

"Hmm," she says again, to the window, still drawing.

I pause, toying with a paper clip from the chart. "I noticed, from looking at the notes, that you seem to open up more with other members of the team."

She looks up from her sketch. "You mean Dr. Grant?"

"Yes."

"Oh," she says, scratching into the paper, "I just tell him what he wants to hear."

The paper clip squeezes lines into my index finger. "What do you mean?"

She shrugs, dotting the page with her charcoal. "It's not like I just started playing this game, Dr. Goldman. I've been doing this for twenty years now. He's just like everyone else I've ever met in this kind of place. He loves to talk. Talk, talk, talk, talk, words, words, words, words. So I'm just giving him what he wants."

I pause. "You mean you're lying to him?"

"I didn't say that," she amends. "No one said the word 'lying.' It's not like what I'm telling him is untrue." She is grinding the charcoal on the page now, and dark knots spring up on the bark. "I *would* like to become a teacher or be a Big Sister for some underprivileged kids. It's never going to happen, I know that. But talking about it doesn't hurt anyone."

Now she's talking in circles. "But you just said you were only saying what you thought Dr. Grant wanted to hear."

Sofia gazes at me with pity in her eyes. "It's complex, Dr. Goldman. Maybe I'm saying what we both want to hear."

"Okay," I say, realizing we are not any closer to the truth.

I close the chart and stand up. Therapy dispensed, on to the next victim. "See you tomorrow then."

"Yup, see you tomorrow."

I walk out, the scent of jasmine lotion trailing into the hallway.

My phone buzzes in my pocket, and my heart leaps like a gazelle. It has been over a week since Jean Luc's last text, not that I'm counting. The number is unlisted, which means he's probably at work at the new government job.

"Hello," I say in my sexiest, "Happy birthday, Mr. President" voice.

"Dr. Goldman?"

"Yes," I answer, confused, realizing this is not my little kumquat.

"Dr. Grant here. You just have the two patients, right?"

"Yes," I say, my heart slowing to the pace of a geriatric gazelle.

"There's someone in the ER, needs to be seen for a consult. Delirium versus new onset schizophrenia."

I am taking this all down. "Okay?"

"Elderly female, bed eight. Just do the consult, and we can all see her later after we round on the floor patients."

"Okay, is she—" I ask, but he has already disconnected with his typical social grace. Looping my stethoscope over my neck, I head off to the ER.

The place is packed as usual. Patient beds overflow in lines up and down the hall. Snatches of conversations float around the room.

"Can we get an NG in room eight?"

"So I'm like, 'Don't tell me he did that because I am not about to hear that...'"

"Nurse, nurse, please! I'm in agony over here!"

I sidle up to bed eight, ignoring stares as I walk by. You would think the man vomiting blood in room ten would be more interesting than a six-foot-something female in a lab coat, but apparently this is not the case.

"How's the weather up there?" a nurse asks me with a cutesy smile as I enter and she exits the room. I smile until my teeth hurt.

As I leaf through the chart of kind old Mrs. Rosenberg, aka Bed Eight, an ER resident strides into the room and looks me up and down. "Hey," he says by way of greeting. "You the psych resident?"

"That'd be me."

"Mike," he says, and I shake his hand.

"Zoe."

Mike is cute. He's tall with an athletic build verging on gym rat from working out against the bloat of night work and all the crappy snacks at the nurses' station.

"So what's going on with this one?" I ask.

The patient is looking at me warily. "I'm not going to answer any questions, so don't even ask," she says. Her voice is querulous and shaky. "My husband put you up to this, didn't he?"

I stare at her, startled by the charge.

"Don't lie to me, I know he did," she continues, getting angrier.

"It's okay, Mrs. Rosenberg," I say in as soothing a voice as possible. I can have a soothing voice when I try; I've been practicing. I don't touch her hand because I can tell that would set her off.

Mike puts his hands on his hips, revealing impressive biceps from under his scrubs. This may have been the purpose of putting his hands on his hips. "Her husband went to the cafeteria," he says. "But over the last few weeks, he says she's been acting odd. Accusing him of poisoning her, saying he's having affairs." He shrugs. "He's eighty, so that would be pretty impressive."

Mrs. Rosenberg's eyes veer back and forth, as if she's watching a tennis match. She turns to Mike. "She's in on it," she says, pointing to me. "I know she's one of his hussies."

Mike laughs and raises his eyebrows at me. "Now, now, Mrs. Rosenberg."

"'Now, now' nothing," she crows. "I know what I know."

The room curtain clinks open. "Hello?" an elderly voice calls out. "Can I come in?"

It is Mr. Rosenberg. He looks kindly enough, in his navy V-neck and khakis, carrying coffee for his wife. He doesn't look as if he's poisoning anyone, much less having an affair with me.

"And her labs are?" I ask.

"One hundred percent normal. Little hypertension, nothing else. She just got back from CT, so we're waiting on an official read, but I didn't see anything. No big stroke or bleed anyway."

So this could actually be elderly onset paranoid schizophrenia and not a completely bullshit ER consult after all.

"Wanna take a peek at the CT?" Mike asks.

We duck through the checkered peach curtain to a Stone Age computer in the center of the room and scroll through the images. No bleed, no stroke. Mike is standing close to me, close enough for me to smell his aftershave. Pine something.

He clears his throat. "Hey, I know you're kind of involved with Mr. Rosenberg and all, but if that doesn't work out for you, would you ever want to grab some coffee or something?"

I stare at him for an uncomfortable four seconds, ascertaining that he is in fact serious. "Mike, you seem like a nice guy—"

Here he winces melodramatically and says, "But…"

"But…I'm kind of seeing someone already." As I say this, I wonder if this is true. My pseudoboyfriend, who is five hundred miles away, whose last text was over a week ago, in tersely written French I had to look up. I'm starting to wonder if "broken up" means broken up. "Someone not married to my patient," I add.

He laughs and crosses his arms, biceps poking out through his sleeves again. "Oh well, the best ones always are. I had to try," he says. "Maybe I could get your number, just in case."

I grab the patient's chart, ready to head back to her room and be pummeled by a woman scorned. Hell hath no fury. "If you really want me," I say, flirting I suppose, but not quite ready to give up my digits, "just ask for a psych consult."

Chapter Eight

Moonlight is spattered on the tile floor.

A whirring noise buzzes next to me, vibrating in my head. I am curled up, so they can't see me.

"Zoe?" a voice calls out. "Where are you?"

I don't answer, curl myself tighter. The smell of smoke tickles my nose, and I hold my breath. My heart beats in my ears.

"Zoe? Come on out, honey!"

Footsteps track outside the door and I watch them, still holding my breath. My lungs are blowing up, aching. I cling to Po-Po. My hands are smeared with blood, seeping under the cuffs of my nightgown. I wonder if I'll get in trouble for staining it, the way I did when I spilled hot chocolate on my new pants and Dad got angry.

Shadows of tree branches sway on the floor, like snakes.

I can't hold my breath anymore, my heart is thumping out of my chest, and I gasp.

The footsteps stop as the door opens.

A muscular man in a yellow rubber coat stands in the door-

way, blocking the light. He has a huge ax over his shoulder as if he might be chopping trees. "Zoe?" he asks.

"Yes?" I say, hesitant.

His face is stoic, serious, but then he smiles. At first it is a kind smile, but it changes into an eerie, spooky smile, and he pulls back the ax in slow motion, and the sharp silver edge shimmers as it flies right toward me.

"Mommy! Mommy! Mommy!" I scream out, falling to the floor as he winds up for another swing.

⤚

"Hey!" Scotty shakes my shoulder. I leap away from him as if he is on fire, smacking my elbow against the wall. Shocks race down my arm.

"Zoe, what the fuck?" He stares at me across the bed. "Seriously. What's going on? Isn't your psycho doctor helping you out with this shit?" That's his pet name for Sam, and all of my previous psychiatrists: "psycho doctors." And now I'm becoming one.

I shrug, my mouth too dry to speak, and I'm too shaky to trust my voice anyway. He stares at me another long second, and his eyebrows soften into a look akin to tenderness. I feel a flood of love for him and understand in a flash what all these women are seeing in my annoying little brother, more than just a cheap James Dean imitation.

"I'm fine," I say, throat sore from screaming. "Go back to sleep."

He doesn't get up from the bed. "Are you sure?"

"I'm sure. Really. Go to sleep."

Scotty stands up, stretching, looks at me a last time, and turns around to pad off to his bedroom. Whereas, I pad off to the bathroom, where my new stock of Xanax is patiently waiting to still my nerves. I do not yet have to ration my supply this month. Then I am in my bed, lying on my back and waiting for the Xanax to kick in, like a bride waiting for her spouse. Without realizing it, I am plunging into another dream.

A panicky dream of looking for something, but I don't even know what I'm looking for. I'm asking everyone if they know where it is. I ask Jason, Dr. A, my mom, Scotty. It's as if they are all in some kind of "Zoe's subconscious" cocktail party, and I'm weaving my way through them. They are talking, trying to tell me where I put this thing, but I cannot hear them. I just see mouths moving, which sends me into a deeper panic. They are all milling around, ignoring me and talking silently to one another. Finally, I reach Jean Luc. I ask him if he knows what I am looking for, and he opens up his beautiful mouth (I find it beautiful, even in the dream) and says, "*Que sera, sera.*"

"But that's not even French," I point out, but he doesn't hear me.

Chapter Nine

Another day in paradise.

I'm running late because I couldn't find a parking spot in the resident lot, so I had to drive over to the overflow parking on the opposite side of the hospital. I slip into the seat between Jason and Dr. A, scalding my hand with coffee and simultaneously staining my new khaki pencil skirt (which lightened my credit card by fifty bucks last week), and last but not least, earning the unambiguous glare of Dr. Grant for being late.

This morning's Grand Rounds lecture is "The Theory of Memory," given by Dr. Wong from the neuropsychiatry department. Neuropsychiatrists are geekier than either psychiatrists or neurologists, which is no easy feat. In the Olympic sport of Geekdom, neuropsychiatrists would win the gold medal hands down, psychiatry silver, and neurology a close bronze. Dr. Wong is no exception. He wears khakis and a short-sleeve yellow button-down shirt every single day, win-

Little Black Lies

ter or summer, along with large, white sneakers you might see elderly folks wearing for laps through the mall, though Dr. Wong is in his forties. He surely invited his share of Kick Me signs in his time.

"Ahhhhm, there are many theories of memory, starting back in 1896 with Sir William Osler," Dr. Wong drones. His voice is more powerful than Xanax. I may doze off despite the third-degree burn on my hand.

"He gave this lecture last year in medical school," Jason whispers to me. "Brutal."

Dr. A, meanwhile, is sitting on the edge of his seat, eyes wide open, as if it's the last inning of the World Series.

"Ahhhhm, then, in the early 1900s was the empiricist theory of the association by contiguity."

"Brutal" is being kind. I am fighting the urge to check my e-mail with every fiber in my soul, knowing if I do, Dr. Grant might leap out of his chair to throttle me.

"John Locke and John Stuart Mill, ahhhhm, are prime examples of philosophers of empiricism." His voice carries on in its monotonous tone for another ten minutes. Jason has started a tally sheet on his "ahhhms" and even Dr. A's eyes are a touch glazed now. Dr. Grant is checking his e-mail on the sly.

I slump back in the chair and allow my brain to wander, an activity that's a true pleasure for me, as I've been working on coping skills since birth to keep my brain 100 percent focused. Every once in a while, a dog likes to be off his leash.

My mind instantly fastens on to last night's dream. Of course, the kindly volunteer fireman turns out to be homicidal. I am probably the only person who could use dream rehearsal to make a nightmare worse. At this point, I have to face the fact that the nightmare is not a fluke, but a recurring problem. And if inserting a fireman won't work (in fact, I dread ever seeing his face again), I have to try something else. The best way to quiet this beast, to steal it out of my subconscious and kill it dead in the light of day, is to solve it. I open my iPad, pull up a note, and start writing.

Dissection:

1. age in nightmare: four years old
   Meaning: my age when fire occurred
2. hands bleeding
   Meaning: sliced by metal from the house
3. the smell of smoke
   Meaning: obvious, from fire
4. moonlight
   Meaning: also obvious, fire at night
5. one-eyed blue teddy bear, Po-Po
   Meaning: useless detail
6. a whirring sound
   Meaning: no idea what this is
7. hiding
   Meaning: unknown, why am I hiding from the fire? oxygen deprivation?
8. someone calling my name
   Meaning:

I pause but do not fill this one in. This is the question that taunts me at three in the morning when I'm out of Xanax and the clock is glowing a malicious blue. Meaning: Did my mother die because she was trying to get me and I wouldn't come out?

"Ahhhm, another more recent movement in memory has been the repressed memory phenomenon."

Now my ears perk up. Repressed memory.

I know a bit about this subject. In medical school, I did a research paper on women with suppressed childhood memories from some type of trauma, mainly incest and rape. One woman I interviewed recovered a memory of her father killing her best friend. The child was three years old at the time, and she remembered his burying her friend six feet deep in the sandbox and warning her never to tell anyone, or she would end up there, too. Twenty years later, her own three-year-old started crying and throwing a tantrum in a sandbox at the local park, and the memory came hurtling back. The authorities thought she was crazy until they dug up the sandbox at her parents' old address and found a young girl's skeleton.

"One of the major methods to uncover these so-called lost memories, ahhhm, has been hypnosis."

Hypnosis.

A lightbulb clicks on. Hypnosis, of course. The way to remember what your brain doesn't want you to remember. That could be the answer to my nightmares! If the mind can bury a memory so deeply in its own sandbox—a child's skeleton, a mother dying in a fire—maybe I just need a shovel to dig it up.

"Ahhhhm, though, due to many false memories obtained by this therapy, this theory has largely been debunked," Dr. Wong continues.

But I am no longer listening; my brain is off to the races with endless potential. I have read about hypnosis before but never went so far as to pursue it. Then again, I wasn't having the nightmares. I wasn't waking up with the feel of blood on my hands, shellacked by the guilt of hiding from the woman who was trying to save me. Hypnosis: how to wrest a memory from your truculent, uncooperative subconscious.

Forget dream rehearsal, I don't need a fireman to save me.

Chapter Ten

I forgot my Adderall this morning and my brain is on spin cycle, with my foot tapping just as fast.

I am waiting, which is generally what you do in a waiting room. And while waiting is just this side of annoying for most people, it is torture for us ADHD-ers, especially those off their meds. Sam's waiting room reminds me of a nicely appointed bus station, dark gray walls and seats, with strangers sitting side by side, avoiding eye contact. The room is hot, inducing stupor in minutes, so you're just hitting REM sleep when the secretary comes to get you. Glossy, black-framed prints of silver and gold abstract figures hang on the wall, each one about three millimeters crooked. The stereo plays country music in the background, an odd choice for a psychiatry office. I mean, why choose the one genre that could depress even the sunniest disposition?

The man across from me coughs, and everybody looks at him as if on high alert, then just as quickly looks back down at books, magazines, various personal electronic devices. I can tell why he's here by the way he keeps smoothing out his magazine so the pages are exactly symmetrical: OCD. The three-millimeter-off pictures must be driving him to distraction. I have to stop myself from playing Guess That Diagnosis every time the bell rings with a new patient walking in, letting some fresh air into the Hansel-and-Gretel oven of a waiting room. The surly teenager to my right wearing a black T-shirt saying "I love my authority problem": definite oppositional defiant disorder. And his poor, beaten-down mother sitting beside him: bad mom haircut, bad mom jeans, worn-out face.

That kid right there is the reason I will never have children. The whole thing is such a crapshoot. You roll the dice and hope for the best, but you could give birth to the punk to my right, or to Sofia Vallano, for that matter.

I spent my entire month of pediatrics in medical school wanting to stick a fork in my eye. They say doctors who go into psychiatry need their heads examined. I say ditto for pediatrics. Dress in cartoon scrubs and Mickey ties, hand out stickers, and take care of runny noses all day? Kill me. One trip to a restaurant on "kids eat free" night should convince you, with those animals fighting over crayons and which balloon is theirs. Kids are one big, gratuitous, expensive time suck. Jean Luc laughed outright when I explained my reasoning on this one, but he didn't disagree. He is a chemist, after all, and I am empirically correct.

"Hello, little lady," the secretary says, heading my way. This is our private joke. I am nobody's definition of a "little lady." I stand up and everybody looks up, then immediately back down. This is one place where no one stares at me.

When I enter his office, Sam stands in greeting and then sits as I arrange my coat, scarf, purse, phone, and iPad next to me. I have too much crap. "It's hot as hell in there, you know."

"I know, I'm sorry. There's some problem with the heater." He pauses a second, reading me. "So how are you today?"

This is a loaded question at a psychiatrist's office. No one expects you to say "Fine."

"I want to do hypnosis," I say. Nothing like jumping right in. I find small talk especially annoying when off Adderall.

Sam raises his eyebrows, looking at me doubtfully. "Hypnosis?"

"Yup."

He scratches his beard. There is a fingerprint on his tortoiseshell lenses. "You know that's controversial, right?"

"Right. But I still want to try it." I notice my foot tapping and stop it.

"Do you mind if I ask what brings this up, Zoe?"

I shift on the stiff couch. "Grand Rounds."

"Okay. How's that?"

"The topic yesterday was memory. And they talked about the memory recovery process. So hypnosis came up as part of that."

"I see," he says. "Did they talk about the problems with hypnosis?"

"Yes," I admit.

"False memory syndrome, for instance?"

"Yes," I repeat. "They did. Actually, I learned about it in medical school, too. I did some research on recovered memories."

"So you know that it's really grown out of favor recently. And there's a good reason for that. Many women went through this process and ended up 'remembering' things that weren't even true. Sexual abuse, for instance, that never actually occurred."

"I have heard about that."

"You can imagine this was quite disruptive in their lives."

"Yes, yes, yes," I say. "I know all this. I know it's controversial. I know it doesn't always work. I'm well aware of all of the potential pitfalls. But I still want to try it."

Sam twiddles his thumbs. "Why? What are you hoping to achieve?"

I tug up my black leather boots. My legs don't know what to do with themselves. "I had the nightmare again."

He nods. "Okay. Did you try the dream rehearsal like we talked about?"

"Yeah," I say. "I tried it. No go. Bust. Complete and utter failure."

"Tell me more."

"It didn't work," I say, throwing up my hands. "The fireman was a maniac."

"Okay," he says. I could swear he is fighting off a smile.

"Seriously, he had an ax. He swung it at me. Twice."

"That's..." He bites his lip. He is definitely trying not to laugh. "That is unfortunate."

"Yeah. I would say. But it doesn't matter. Because I think I figured it out."

"The nightmare?"

"Yes, kind of. The reason I'm having the nightmare at least. Why it's resurfaced."

"And what did you figure out?"

My foot thwaps against the carpet, catching on some threads. "It *does* have to do with my mom."

"How is that?"

"So my mom is demented, right?"

"Right," he agrees.

"And I feel like I'm losing her."

"Okay, I can see that."

"That's why I'm having the nightmare. I'm losing one mother so, somewhere, deep in my subconscious maybe, I want to find out about my other mother, my birth mother."

"I don't see how that follows entirely."

"Don't you? All my life I've wondered about her. My mom would tell me this and that, little things. But I've always felt like a piece was missing. But I guess I also felt guilty that, if I told my mom, she would feel bad, like she wasn't a good enough mother for me. But now I have my chance. I can't hurt my mother by finding out—she won't even know."

Sam stares out the window, nodding. Burnt-yellow leaves are scattered around the base of the tree like litter.

"I think I'm ready to find out about her now. And maybe the nightmare is like a clue. Or a message."

"The nightmare is a memory, Zoe."

"Yes, yes, I know." I scoot forward on the couch to quiet my legs. "But it's more than that. It's also my last memory of her. My real mother." I feel a spike of guilt for my real, real mother—the one who raised me—sitting on a rocker with a dilapidated blanket and a dilapidated brain. But mixed with the guilt, a surge of freedom. "I want you to hypnotize me back to that night."

Sam puts his hands up like brakes. "Hypnosis can be very disruptive, as I said. You're dismantling protective mechanisms." He looks right in my eyes. "Zoe, sometimes there are good reasons we forget things."

"I know," I say. And I do know. Freud was right about a lot, and my subconscious is probably a hell of a lot smarter than my flitting, ADHD-riddled conscious ever will be. But I still want to try it.

"How about we give dream rehearsal one more try?" Sam asks. "Before we abandon it completely."

The fireman's ax jumps into my mind. "I don't think that's such a good idea."

"We could practice it together," Sam offers.

"Let me ask you," I say, ignoring the suggestion. "Have you ever done hypnosis before?"

Sam clutches the front of his dark, glossy desk, the captain of his ship. "I have carried out hypnosis before," he says, as if he is admitting he used to inject heroin.

"And how did it go?" I ask, trying not to betray the excitement bubbling in me.

"I've had cases where it went very well, and others where it was not at all successful. More than not successful, harmful." So he's injected more than once. He grips the desk, staring out the window. In a word, deciding.

"I'm not asking for a miracle," I say. "If it works, and I remember more about that night, even a glimmer of my mom, I'll consider it a success. If it doesn't, and I'm hounded by that nightmare every night of my life, at least I can say we tried."

Sam keeps staring, weighing my words. I see him reflected in a mirror on the wall, a large, dark wooden circle that looks vaguely like a ship's wheel. "I've tried dream rehearsal. It didn't work. And you yourself said there are no good therapies out there," I continue.

He nods absentmindedly, then looks down at his notes. "So how is your mom doing?" he asks, changing the subject none too subtly.

"Not great," I say. "She called me 'Tanya' a couple weeks ago."

"Oh? Tell me more."

"There's not much to tell." I lean back on the most uncomfortable couch ever made. "She's losing it is all, like Scotty says. But it's sad, because sometimes she's so with it."

"Who's Tanya?" he asks.

"Probably some old friend of hers. I don't really know any Tanyas. But it's familiar somehow."

"It's tough," Sam says, shaking his head. Then he pushes his chair back, which is the sign. The pewter clock has announced my departure. "I need to think about this, Zoe, and you need to think about it. Take some time."

I nod vigorously.

"Think about the fact that if you uncover painful memories of the fire, of your birth mother, you may go back to a very scary, very raw place. A place where you may not be able to function very well, especially during residency."

I nod again, more vigorously. I must look like a monkey.

"If you still want to do it next week, I will consider it."

"Okay," I say, pretending I will contemplate every angle. But I already know my answer, and hope swells in my chest as he pulls out his pad.

"You seem a little jittery today. Any problems with the Adderall?"

"Only problem being I forgot it this morning," I say.

"Ah," he answers with a smile. "That explains a lot."

I wonder what the hell that means but manage to hold my tongue, even without Adderall.

"Remember the nonpharmacological things we discussed to help the ADHD," Sam says.

"Yeah, I know," I mumble. "I really have to get back to running."

"Yes, you do," he says as he scribbles off my litany of medications.

"That is completely fucked-up," Scotty says as we enter the nursing home. Scolding elderly glances, murmurs, and tut-tuts are thrown our way. "Hypnosis?"

"It is not at all fucked-up, actually," I answer in a whisper to avoid murmurs and tut-tuts. "It's something I really need to do right now. For the nightmare."

He laughs, a scoff more than a laugh. "What does it have to do with the nightmare?" he asks, pulling off his hat and shaking out his hair. "I thought you were into that dream re-hearsal shit."

"Yeah, it didn't go so well." I unbutton my coat, which I just notice is missing the middle black plastic button. "And I'm trying to remember some things about my mother."

"Why don't you just ask Mom? They were best friends."

"Believe me, Scotty, I *have* been asking her... my whole life. She's never told me much. And now, I'm not even sure she could if she wanted to."

We are standing just inside the lobby. The automatic outside door keeps grinding open and closed, blasting us with cold, rainy air.

"What do you want to know?" he asks.

"I don't know. Anything. Did she like gardening, for instance, or roller coasters?" I have no idea where I came up with that one.

"Yeah, right. Very important things like gardening and roller coasters. What about your real *father*, Zoe? Don't you want to find out about him? How about your real third cousin once removed? Maybe he liked roller coasters."

"Listen, Scotty. My father didn't raise me for four years. He was basically a sperm donor." This last part comes out a bit louder than intended, and a mother steers her young daughter away from us as they walk by. I move farther into the lobby toward the vast expanse of mauve, determined both to end the conversation and to get out of the freezing doorway.

Scotty follows me, wiping his wet, grassy sneakers on the black rubber mat. "You are seriously fucked-up, you know

81

that? I always thought you were a little fucked-up, but you are majorly, royally fucked-up."

"'Majorly, royally,' huh? What are you, twelve?"

We have finally cleared the doorway when Mom comes heading our way, swooping in to break up her squabbling children as always. Cheery Cherry is pushing her wheelchair.

"Hi," Mom says, beaming at us. Every time she looks at me this way, I feel guilty for not visiting more often.

"Hi yourself," I say, hugging her, and Scotty moves in for a hug, too. One big happy family.

"You okay, honey-doll?" asks Cheery Cherry, releasing Mom with some trepidation to her obviously less-qualified children.

"Yes, thank you," my mom answers, turning to us. "Let's sit here today," she says, pointing to the dark cherry table in the lobby. The idea of us all in her square of a room, with Scotty and me about to throttle each other, does seem ill advised. I sit down by the table in a formal chair, with upholstered swirling blue and mauve, and Scotty takes a similarly floral seat next to Mom. Outside, a robin picks at a patch of grass, swiveling its head around to look out for any competition. I'm wondering when he flies down south. Do robins fly down south? I really need to take my Adderall.

"So how's the coffee business?" Mom asks Scotty, perhaps to verify that he is indeed still in the coffee business.

"Good," he answers. "Got a few more Web-site clients, too," he adds, to verify that he is not a complete fuck-up. Scotty has a stack of business cards at the cash register for his Web-site design business: Spyder Web Designs. You might think actual, responsible entrepreneurs would not want to put their entire Web presence in the hands of a flaky barista, but apparently I am wrong. The cards disappear quickly, and I must admit he puts together an eye-catching Web site on the cheap. My brother is probably the next Zuckerberg.

"So," Scotty says, apropos of nothing, "guess what? Zoe wants to find out about her *real* mother."

I glare at him. *Glare* is not a strong enough word.

"What do you mean?" she asks.

"Oh, she has this brilliant idea that she's going to be *hypnotized* by her psycho doctor."

My mom looks at me blankly. "I don't think I understand."

"Listen," I say in my calmest voice, "this nightmare is very disturbing to me. And I think hypnosis might help me understand it a little better."

Mom chews on one of her French-manicured fingernails. Most of the polish has worn off. My mother was never one to chew her nails BD. "Do you really think this is wise, Zoe?" she asks. "Don't you think sometimes it's better to leave well enough alone?"

"Maybe." The robin darts to another bit of grass. "I don't know."

"She wants to know if her real mom liked gardening or roller coasters," Scotty adds.

A blast of cold air comes in behind us as the next visitors tromp in, unwrapping scarves and shaking off boots on the black rubber mat. The automatic door grinds shut again. "What do you want to know about Beth? I can tell you, honey. She *loved* roller coasters. In fact, she once dragged me on Montezuma's Revenge seven times in a row. I threw up in a garbage can, but she was still running to get into line again."

I laugh at this image, as does Scotty, though this doesn't sound like a very sensitive friend. "Was Dad there?" I ask, having a hard time visualizing him anywhere near a roller coaster.

"Oh no, of course not," she says. "And about gardening." Mom pauses. "I don't remember her gardening much, but she was very young."

Old enough to have kids, but too young to garden? Somehow this doesn't jibe with the disco-haired, doe-eyed picture of Beth Winters I had in my head. I have always pictured a small side garden with pink hollyhocks, deep purple salvia, and shades of red zinnias in the fall. I visualize this pathetic little garden charred by the fire, sopped from the heroic firefighters' efforts from the night before, still smoking days later. But I don't know if this is a true memory or not.

"I remember a garden, Mom, from after the fire. At least I think I do."

"What fire?" she asks.

I shoot Scotty a glance.

"The fire," he says. "You know. When Zoe's mom died."

She smiles at him solicitously and chews on her fingernails again.

"The fire, Mom," he continues. "Don't you remember the fire?"

"Oh, wait a second," she says brightly, "the fire, of course!"

She gives an unsure smile. "My memory's not what it used to be. What about the fire?"

"Nothing," I say morosely. So now I know Beth Winters loved roller coasters and gardening, not so much.

"Honestly, honey, I don't remember that much about it anymore. I do remember the fire. Vaguely. Every day, I lose something else." She looks down at her nails. "I can hardly even remember Beth's face anymore."

The bird is chirping now, his gray head wet and matted from the rain. He is yanking something from the ground with glee. A worm!

Mom puts her hands in her bathrobe pockets. "Oh," she says with excitement, as if she just remembered, "you guys want to see something?" She pulls out a ratty Popsicle stick (or tongue depressor in my line of work) with bright feathers glued on it in a million directions. Fuzzy neon-pink, electric-blue, and lilac-purple feathers.

I examine it in my hands, and she waits for a pronouncement, like a child handing over a piece of artwork in first grade. After identifying its wattle, I realize this is a turkey. A glam turkey, sort of stuck in the nineties, but a turkey nonetheless. A Thanksgiving craft.

"That's great, Mom," I say, and Scotty murmurs his agreement. Mom smiles ear-to-ear and then reaches over and takes it back. We sit there awhile, watching the birds, a gaggle of them now, leaping from patch to patch of soggy grass while Mom smooths the turkey feathers in her hands as if she is holding on to a newborn.

⟵

The smell of buffalo dung hangs heavy in the air.

The rain has cleared into a cool, blue November evening, the light watercolor blue that comes before night falls in earnest, streaked with pink. I have decided to take Sam's advice and go for a run, taking my favorite route in Delaware Park. The park edges the zoo so, if you look over the fence, you can see the buffalo, or at least smell them. Buffalo in Buffalo, we know the art of self-parody.

My pink sneakers slap the pavement, and immediately I feel my brain relaxing, as if it's a muscle that's been tense. I run into the wind, the cold numbing my cheeks, my phone strapped to my arm like a gun holster in case a *Dum-dum-dum-dah* should ring out and I might, God forbid, miss it. This is the exact reason I swore I'd never fall in love, so as not to be one of those women waiting by the phone, or strapping it to my arm in this case.

I never understood the illness of romantic love. I had seen friends devolve into this delusional, schizophrenic, love-stricken state, one after another, and I just didn't get it. I didn't get holing yourself in your room and texting for hours. I didn't get the crushed depression that followed when so-and-so stopped calling/texting and was seen tonguing someone else at someone else's soiree. The whole thing seemed ridiculous.

It's not that I didn't *want* to fall in love, I had just given up on the whole concept. I didn't think it would happen to me. If love was going to hit anywhere, I figured it would be medical school with its intense relationships forged by hours together, reeking of formaldehyde, cheek to cheek over a corpse, sleeping two hours in the same call room before blared awake by pagers. (Friendships that in fact evaporate like smoke when all the medical students fly off to their new residencies, turning into internists, orthopedic surgeons, neurologists, or maybe even psychiatrists.)

It was December of my last year of medical school when I found out I was not immune to such madness. I met Jean Luc and saw that love wasn't a choice but a foregone conclusion.

Perhaps it was the romance of the setting I couldn't withstand. We were staying at my friend Eva's ski lodge in Vermont for winter break with Karen (ophthalmologist), Allison (pediatrician), Eva (plastic surgery, probably owns a yacht by now), and her distant cousin Jean Luc, a postdoc in chemistry. Karen was engaged, Allison a lesbian, and Eva not interested in dating her cousin, so that meant my odds were decent, and I fell hard for him.

We were the best skiers in our group and shrugged off the others with politic haste, mapping out baroque ski plans, weaving through Mistletoe and Whoopsie-Daisy, Jean Luc with his ruddy cheeks, snow melting in his eyelashes. The first night we all went in the hot tub, and Jean Luc and I stayed in talking long after the others had gone back inside the lodge. The snow drifted in lazy flakes, steam misting my vision, and I sat with my head back, dark green pines all around, snow tumbling down at me as if in a 3-D movie. And right then, I got it: the delusional, psychotic, blissed-out state of love.

That night I lay beside him in bed, wide awake, wired to the gills, watching his chest rise and fall and the rust-colored stubble on his chin. The foolish rush of dopamine, the tingling of every Pacinian corpuscle in my dermatome. And the next morning we were walking together, and I was admiring his bootprints in the snow, rows of squares like a waffle iron. And I felt an odd sort of terror, because I was admiring his footprints. Who does that? And I realized, yes, this is love, and I am not immune.

A man in dark blue spandex runs by me and smiles. His dog, a huge, furry black thing, is plowing on next to him like a small gorilla on a leash. The puddles glow pink in the sky's reflection, and I wipe the sweat off my forehead with my rough sleeve. My phone pings a text, and for an instant my heart jumps, but then I realize it's not his text tone. I swing my arm around to look at the screen.

Coffee sometime? Found ur number, not giving up!

It takes a moment for this to register.

P.S. in case u forgot. This is Mike, a.k.a. obnoxious ER resident.

I smile. It is a good feeling, being wanted. But my heart isn't doing a dance.

Chapter Eleven

Sofia's pencil scratches against the paper like a rat burrowing in the trash.

She faces the window, her hand a blur of motion, and I notice a tattoo on her arm. I have spotted it before but never really looked at it closely. The tattoo is an intricate Gothic design, in grays, like her charcoals. A black skeleton knight on a silver-white steed, holding up a flag with the symbol of a shield, with a flower and the Roman numeral VIII. I have seen the image before, though I can't place it.

It is a dark, sinister tattoo.

"Like it?" she asks, extending her arm.

I lift my eyebrows in answer. *Like* is a strong word. "When did you get it?" I ask, trying to work that one out. She's been institutionalized since fourteen, and I doubt anyone would have inked her before that.

"I was eighteen." She looks up from her drawing for a moment, gazing off dreamily. "Me and some girls from UMCH earned a trip to the ice cream parlor for good behavior. With a chaperone, of course," she adds. "So we convinced the chaperone to get lost for a couple of hours and went looking for some real fun."

I am picturing the Pink Ladies in *Grease* out for a night on the town and wondering how exactly the convincing of the chaperone took place.

"And we found it, right next to the ice cream parlor. The tattoo parlor. Cool Licks Ice Cream and Bad to the Bone Tattoos." Her fingers cradle the charcoal, hand streaking across the page again. "So me and my girls got ice cream *and* tattoos."

"What kind of ice cream?"

Sofia's eyes dart off the page and look at me like blue marbles. "No one's ever asked me that one before," she says with a half smile. She twirls the charcoal in her fingers like a mini-baton. "Rocky Road. It was delicious. Haven't had it since." She looks down at her arm, rubbing the tattoo as if she just got a flu shot. "I got in some severe fucking trouble for that one," she drawls with a laugh.

"Yeah, I bet," I answer, forcing a laugh myself. Ah, those halcyon days, getting grim reaper tattoos with my pals from the insane asylum. "Where'd you get the money?" I ask, just thinking of it. "For a tattoo. Those things aren't cheap."

She shrugs. "I have my ways."

Of this I have no doubt. She doesn't expound any further, so we sit, staring at each other in silence that grows uncomfortable. Sofia puts her picture down on her bed. "The thing about what happened," she says as if we were just talking about it, "is that I really don't remember it."

I put the chart down next to me, mirroring, I guess. "What do you mean?" A surge of excitement runs through me. Is she finally going to talk about it?

"When you asked me why I killed my mother."

"Yes."

"The truth is, I don't remember any of it."

A voice booms out over the intercom: "Jenny in room one? Jenny, IV change needed in room one."

Sofia looks up at the intercom above the bed. "Does that all day," she says. "Drives me crazy."

The word *crazy* hangs in the air.

"You're saying you don't remember anything?" I repeat.

"Very little," she says. "Just patches of things, here and there."

"Like what?"

"It's hard to explain. It's like pieces of memories."

"Hmm," I say, for lack of something better to say. I did read this in her old records. This has been her party line all along from UMHC: "Patient claims she does not recall event. Fugue state suspected." And I can't rule out her denial completely. It is possible, the fugue state, under dissociative disorders in the DSM V: "A state lasting hours, days, or longer with amnesia for the events during that time frame, usually provoked by severe stress." It's not impossible, but it's exceedingly rare, usually emerging as a bullshit insanity defense.

"Was there any stressor you know of around that time? Any physical abuse, for instance?" I pause. "Sexual abuse?"

Her upper lip twitches. "No, there really wasn't. They went through all this at the old place," Sofia says with some annoyance. "And I told them the same thing: I don't remember. I wish I could, but I don't." She taps her charcoal on the arm of her chair. I can see smudges on the wood from where she tapped it before.

I glance up at the clock, an industrial behemoth with a cage around the face, and realize I have three more patients to see before rounds. "Okay then. I guess I'll see you tomorrow."

"I'll be here," she answers and turns back to her drawing.

Chapter Twelve

I've made my decision," I announce. "I want to do it."

Sam does not look surprised. "Let's just go over this one more time. You understand that it may not even work."

"Yes. I'm aware of that."

"And that if I do get you into a state of hypnosis, the memories may not be valid."

I nod. "I'm aware of that, too."

"But you still definitely, absolutely want to do it."

"Definitely, absolutely."

"Okay," Sam says, resigned. "I'm willing to give it a try. But let's go over some ground rules." He lifts his glasses off his face and rubs the bridge of his nose.

"Fine."

"First things first. What we're going to do today is to see whether you're susceptible to hypnosis. Not everyone is. If we find you are susceptible, then we will go further into it."

"Susceptible? I don't get it."

Sam cleans his glasses with the sleeve of his navy blazer and puts them back on. The brass buttons from his sleeve shine in the sun. "Some people aren't able to get into a re-laxed enough state to go into hypnosis. That's what we have to find out."

"Oh, okay," I say, trying not to give away my disappointment. Given my oft-skeptical and utterly unrelaxed nature, I have a snowball's chance in hell of being "susceptible." I'm the one always saying, "That would never happen in real life" during a movie. Suspending my disbelief, another weakness of mine. But I can only try.

"Another important thing is that this is an extremely vulnerable state for a person. So you need to keep my voice with you at all times, even when we're going in deep. I will be there as your support and your guide. I'm not willing to let you do this alone. If you don't follow my prompts, we'll have to abort therapy."

"Abort therapy" sounds like a space mission. "So you're like my shaman," I say.

"Sure," Sam says, looking a little worried about what he got himself into. "So, remember, throughout the sessions, I'll be keeping close tabs on you. Wherever you are in the process, you need to keep checking in with me."

"Yes, I get it."

"And another thing: If things get difficult, we may need to come up with a safe word. Something you or I can say if you need to get out of a situation, and I can pull you back immediately."

"A safe word."

"Yes. The truth is, I don't usually start out with a safe word because then people tend to use it as a crutch. I first try to work through what may be uncomfortable without resorting to a safe word. But we can always create one if we need to."

I nod again, though I think he's laying it on pretty thick here. It's not as if he's about to perform brain surgery.

"Again," he repeats. He puts his hands up to his mouth, like he's praying. "You are totally sure."

"Without a doubt."

Sam pauses a beat, then stands. "Okay then, let's give it a try." He heads over to his bookcase and pulls a worn, gray, thick text. He flips through, settles on a page with a corner turned over, returns to his desk, and sits back down. "Do you have a quarter?"

"A quarter?" I reach down and scrounge around in my purse. "What for?"

"You'll see." He is rifling through his top drawer to find one, too. "I may have one if you don't."

"No, I got it," I say, retrieving one from the bottom of my purse. The quarter is cool in my hand.

"All right. Go ahead and lie down."

"Okay." I move my coat to the floor and lie down on the couch. My knees tremble for just an instant, and I work on relaxing.

"How are you doing?"

"Couldn't be better," I answer, squeezing my quarter, which is warming up.

"This first part, as I said, is to see if you are susceptible to hypnosis or not. Listen closely. I am going to ask you to drop the quarter during the session. Try not to drop it."

"*Not* to drop it?"

"That's right. If you are able to disobey this command and keep holding on to the quarter, we'll know this is not going to work for you. You will not be suggestible enough to get into the necessary state. If you do drop the quarter, however, as I tell you, then we know it will work."

"Okay." I doubt to hell I'm going to drop that quarter.

"I want you to listen to my voice," Sam says. "Listen to my words and follow everything I am saying." His speech is low and melodious, honey in my ears. "We are taking a journey together."

I am trying to focus on his voice, but it is not easy. Hyperactivity and hypnosis do not appear to be good bedfellows.

"I am your guide on this journey, and you will follow everything I tell you to do." His voice is strong and deep, resonating. Not the voice I have been talking to every session. "I am going to count to fifty, and you will take a deep breath with every count. I will start now. One…two…three… four…"

My shoulders relax, though I hadn't realized they were tense. He is counting, I am breathing. My neck is wobbly, my hands tingling. Hyperventilation? Hypoxia? My brain interjects but is quieted. Stop, focus, don't try to figure it out, just listen. "Thirty-one…thirty-two…thirty-three…" The tingling travels down my legs, settling in my knees, rubbery. The sensation is like Xanax. I am still holding on to my quarter. "Fifty…."

My brain disengages.

"You are in a forest, a huge forest, bigger than you have ever seen." Walls of dark green rise up around me. Birds scream in different pitches.

"You are walking to the river. There is a boat there for you. It has your name on it." Pine needles crunch under my feet, and I am at the opening of the river. Blue water sings around me. The boat is small with a fresh coat of red paint. "Zoe" is written in black script on the corner. I step in and it rocks a second, then steadies. I sit on the warm wooden bench inside and pick up an oar, which is smoothly sanded, made for my hand. I start rowing. Has he told me to row? I'm not sure, but I am aware of myself lying on the couch and at the same time perched in the boat. The oar dips into the dark blue water, drags, and lifts. Drops jet off the bottom of the oar, in perfect parabolas, then slip back into the water. Dip and lift. Dip and lift, again, and again, and again. The sun shimmers on the water.

Where am I going?

Calm suffuses my body into the rhythm of rowing. It is different from the feeling I had rowing at Yale, when every nerve ending was on fire, pulsing in time with the coxswain's screams, and every thigh muscle begged me to stop but I refused. Jean Luc flashed by on the sidelines, a cheering pink blob, but I did not break my rhythm, sweat leaking into my eyes. I could hear my breathing like someone else's, scratchy, huffy, and I kept rowing. Because the fast thoughts in my head finally shut up and slowed down. And it was the best way I had ever found to do this, better than running, even better than Adderall.

Sandra Block

But this is completely different.

We are not fighting, my body and me, my brain and me. We are in perfect alignment. My water, my boat, my arm, my oar, my brain. Calm, at one, we are all in this together.

"Zoe?" I hear Sam's voice, deep, sonorous.

"Yes." I feel my lips move, my voice sounds as if it is underwater.

"Do you feel the quarter?"

"Yes."

"It is heavy. It is getting heavier and heavier in your hand. It is weighing down your hand. It is weighing down the boat."

"No," I say, gripping the quarter.

"Yes, Zoe. It is heavy. You can't hold it anymore. Drop the quarter now, Zoe. Drop the quarter."

"No," I mumble, and I try with all my might to hold on to it, feeling the ridges digging into my skin, but it is too heavy.

And the quarter rolls out of my hand.

Chapter Thirteen

That night, I'm in an uncommonly good mood.

I glance around to see all the other regulars in their usual spots, all creatures of habit, like me. Hot coffee in a pleasantly hefty mug, with just the right amount of cream (Eddie is skilled at that), and the design of a bronzed leaf staring up at me in all its foamy goodness that I am about to decimate with my tongue. My favorite leather settee with just the right grooves to fit my body. Feet up on the hearth of the fireplace, heat wafting out, enveloping me in a cloud of warmth. Black-velvet night sky pressing against the window, with pinhole stars gleaming through.

I have a rosy outlook tonight, like Scrooge maybe, after he came back to the present, handing out sixpence and turkeys and such. Things seem to be, at least for the moment, going my way. Sofia opened up with me, even if just an inch; hypnosis was a smashing success.

In a word: I am happy.

Dum-dum-dum-dah. The DSM V book skitters out of my hand, and my heart does a tap dance. Finally, radio silence has been broken!

Skype? I read in the text.

Sure. I pull my laptop out as fast as my hands will let me and boot up, connecting to him. Jean Luc is blurry for a few seconds, then crystallizes onto the screen. He looks good, as usual, maybe a little on the pale side.

"Sorry I haven't texted you. Things are crazy around here." His accent sounds stronger than I remember.

"That's okay," I assure him. "We're all busy." As if I haven't been pining away for the sound of Beethoven's Fifth every day.

Jean Luc takes a deep breath, ducks his head into his hands, then lifts it again with a pained smile. My stomach starts sinking.

"Zoe, there is not a good way to say this, so I'm just going to say it. I've fallen in love with someone."

My heart stops dancing.

"I want us to stay the very best of friends, if we can. But if we can't, I do understand." His speech sounds rehearsed, but there is a tremor in his voice. I watch the words come out of his mouth as if he is talking with the volume off. "Zoe, are you all right?"

"Fine, fine," I answer, sounding far off. "Anyone I know?" I ask this half in jest. Who would I know in DC?

He looks down at his butcher-block kitchen table. "Melanie."

"Melanie?" A sour laugh escapes me. Of course, the beau-

tiful siren, the honey-voiced, blond-hair-slicked-back Melanie. I picture the whole nasty affair like a movie going
fast-forward. The irresistible Melanie, the tried-to-be-true
best friend, the cuckolded fool, all the usual characters in the
same old, tawdry soap opera from time eternal. My broken
heart is not just unoriginal, it's cliché.

Jean Luc leans toward the camera, his gray eyes looming.
"We didn't mean for this. Robbie was away for the weekend,
we had dinner together, and one thing led to the other thing,
as you say."

"Right," I say, nodding. One thing led to the other thing,
isn't that always how it happens?

"Zoe?" I hear again, and I realize I have been nodding at
the screen for the last minute. My head is about to fall off
from all the nodding. "I am very sorry about this," he says.

"Yeah, I have to go," I say.

"Zoe, please, do you—"

But I don't let him finish. I close the laptop, folding him
in half and stuck in DC forever, then have the odd feeling I
have trapped him in the computer. Puzzling over this, I look
up to see Scotty standing in front of me.

"What's wrong?" he asks.

"Nothing. Why?"

"You look like you're about to hurl."

"Gee, thanks."

"No, seriously, you're pale as a ghost."

"I'm fine," I insist.

He shrugs and walks away. Scotty's right, I feel like vomiting in my coffee. Jean Luc fell in love with his roommate's

girlfriend? The supposedly annoying Meh-lah-nee who named her boyfriend's cat Kitty? Analyzing this ridiculous notion for a half second, I know I should feel as though I have dodged a bullet. But I don't. I feel as though the bullet is lodged inches away from my spinal cord.

I blow into my coffee, holding on tightly to the mug like a lifeboat. Water stings my eyes, and my nose starts to run. It is at least a small mercy I am not crying over Skype. Because, as in all other things, I am not a pretty crier. Out of the corner of my eye I see Eddie pointing to me, trying to look inconspicuous. Scotty strides over and sits down, folding his long limbs into the velour chair next to me.

"All right, what's going on?"

I stare out the window, hiccuping like an idiot. The night, oddly enough, is still gorgeous. Snowflakes float through the sky like feathers, an early November snow.

"Is it that asshole, Frog-Boy?"

"Jean Luc," I choke out to defend him. After all, he has a name.

Scotty stares at me, the James Dean look softening his face. "You know what? Fuck him," he says. "Eddie is a hundred times better than that French piece of shit."

"I know. I'm sure he is."

I sit there a minute, wiping my eyes while he pretends not to notice. Boys are never good at watching girls cry.

Finally, Scotty heaves a sigh. "Love sucks," he says, which is as good a consolation as any, and I give him a weak smile in thanks. Scotty pats my knee uncomfortably and gets up to go back to work. Eddie (who is undoubtedly a hundred times better than Jean Luc) wanders by, apparently to tidy up and straighten chairs, but all the while peering over at me to be sure I haven't launched myself out the window yet (which, as it's on the ground floor, would result in only minor injuries, a skinned knee perhaps).

I finish my lukewarm coffee and head home. The apartment is dark and empty, cold. Our place is an old Buffalo house, Arts and Crafts with original leaded windows, full of old-world charm. *Old* also means drafty, however, and tonight I am chilled to the bone. I flick on some lights, turn on the gas fireplace, and fall into our beat-up, red corduroy couch. Sam needs a couch like this, instead of that monstrous, dark brown thing. We got it cheap from an estate sale when Scotty had volunteered to shop for some new furniture for the Coffee Spot. I pull my phone from my purse but suddenly realize that the only person I really want to talk to is my mom. But I can't bear the thought of her asking me, "Who is Jean Luc again?"

So I put down the phone and just sit on the couch, warmed by the fireplace. The grandfather clock (from the same estate sale and heavy as hell to get into the apartment) gongs out ten o'clock. Yawning, I decide that's a respectable time to admit defeat for the day and drag myself upstairs to my bedroom. I sit down heavily on my bed, the burgundy comforter ballooning around me. Looking around my room, I see Jean Luc's gold-framed picture on the middle shelf of my bookcase. A cork is right next to it, standing up at attention, a stupid souvenir I kept from a date at Yale. An overly expensive Italian meal complete with corny violin serenade and a red rose. I walk over, pull the cork off the shelf, and sniff it. The red wine scent used to thrill me, sending a bolt of desire through my bones. Now it just makes me sick. I toss it in the garbage, along with his framed picture, with a crash.

Within minutes, I am pulling on my favorite comfy, blue-cotton pajamas, peeling my drying contacts out of my eyes, and swallowing three magic white pills. I know full well that this is a bad idea. I am supposed to take only one at a time, and I will run out early, but I take them anyway. Then I climb into bed, the cool sheets welcoming me, and slowly, slowly, my brain stops humming.

Book Two: December

Chapter Fourteen

I want you to look for a house up ahead," Sam's voice intones. "Do you see it?"

I am gliding in the bright-red boat, sun shimmering on the river. I shield my eyes, gazing into the ceramic-blue, cloudless sky. Suddenly I see a house up ahead on the grass riverbank, as if it were conjured up from thin air. "Yes," I answer in a disembodied voice.

"Describe it to me."

"Dark brown wood, dirty windows," I tell him. It is a foreboding, decrepit house. Spartan and bare, like something you might find falling apart in the middle of the woods.

"I want you to go in the house," he says.

So I do. I am magically off the boat and transported onto the front steps. The stairs creak, and the porch is stained a muddy, black-brown color. A tall maroon vase hovers next to the door, like a spittoon, with a cobweb lacing it to the front door. The place looks like a haunted house on a movie set.

Even in the midst of hypnosis, it strikes me that my imaginary house does not suggest a sanguine state of mind.

"Go into the house," he repeats.

I don't want to, but Sam's voice is strong, and I pull open the heavy door to a gleaming white room. The floor is marble white. I step in gingerly, feeling like a little kid who is trespassing. The walls are freshly painted white. When I turn around, I see my own black footprints following me. I am tracking in soot.

"Do you recognize anything?" he asks.

"No," I answer. Except maybe some heavy-handed symbolism I'll have to decode in a later therapy session. I look ahead to stairs, which are covered in a run-down, puke-green carpet, threads pouched up from years of catching book bags, high heels, puppy claws. Years of wear and tear. My feet are taking me up the stairs. I don't want to go, but I can't stop them.

"What is happening?" Sam asks.

"Stairs," I answer. As I ascend, I realize something strange is happening. Time is spinning forward at a rapid pace, as in a reality TV show where the camera pans in on a house from daybreak to sunset in a few seconds, pictorially flipping through the hours with the clouds racing by. With each step it turns darker outside, until I'm at the top and it is pitch-black outside the window. Silent. I have been here before.

"What are you seeing?" he asks. "Don't forget. You have to stay with me, Zoe."

"The laundry room," I say, surprised at my answer. The laundry room? I walk into the gray darkness. I can hear whirring, and I put my hand on the dryer. Warm. The room is warm. "That's the whirring!" I yell out, surprised and thrilled.

"What is?"

"The dryer. That's the sound I always hear in my dream!" I could never identify that rhythmic motor. Now I hear it clearly, the soft rumbling. I look down at the floor and see shadows of branches, swaying. Outside the moon is out, white-bright.

I hear footsteps, whispers. I reach out and shut the door, by millimeters, careful not to make any noise. The door clicks, and the footsteps stop. My heart freezes. Whispers, and then footsteps again. I am panting in fear.

"What's going on, Zoe?" Sam says. "Stay with me here. Don't do this alone."

"They're coming."

"Who?"

"I don't know," I say, my voice shaking. My mother? My father? I hear the rumble of the dryer. Outside the door, music is playing. Loud classical music. Crashing cymbals, scratching cellos. "I hear music," I say.

"What else?" he asks.

I sit down, rag-doll exhausted, on the cold, white floor. The moon is a marble in the sky. I put my hand against the moan of the dryer, which is comforting. The orchestral music blares and fades from down the hall. I hear a bedroom door opening, then slamming shut. The sweet smell of smoke is wafting into the room.

"I smell something now," I say.

"What is it? Can you tell?"

"Smoke, I think," I say. The smell is a deep cedar. Tobacco? Maybe the fire started with a pipe.

"Do you see any smoke?"

"No, not yet," I answer, looking under the door. I envision a plume of smoke wafting outside the door. I picture this but I do not actually see it, because I will not open the door. I touch the doorknob, which is warm, but not hot.

"Do you see your mother?"

"No," I say, my voice desperate. "She's supposed to be here."

"It's okay," Sam answers, his voice calm and soothing. "I want you to focus on one feature of your mother that you remember. One feature, and see if she appears before you. Then she'll be there for you, Zoe, and she can help you. We can both help you. I know you're scared, but you're not alone."

Of course I choose her eyes, her big, deep, brown doe eyes. I am staring into them, summoning them forth. Brown eyes, shining, sad. But she does not come. Footsteps. I slump down against the dryer again.

"She's not coming," I whisper. I am stroking Po-Po, my pale-blue, lovely bear. But he is larger than I remember. He fills my arms.

Scenes of a carnival flitter into my mind. I'm out of the house for an instant. Happy organ music fills the air, kids yelling and screeching. Rows of blue and pink cotton candy jog by us, and then I see a huge, sharp dart dive into a balloon with a loud "snap!" and freckly teenage arms handing me a big blue bear, which I can't believe is mine. I reach up to hug my mom. My mom! I can smell her sweet, sweaty scent on her T-shirt. I can feel her, the warmth of her arms, though I cannot see her.

"Do you see her now?" Sam asks.

The carnival disappears, and the whirring moans in my ears again. "I don't know. She was here, but she's gone now. She's gone. I don't know where she went." I feel myself growing panicky again.

"Can you call her?" he asks. "Try to call her, Zoe."

"I can't," I whisper. "I'm hiding."

"Who are you hiding from?"

"I don't know," I answer. "It's hot." I feel myself crying. Sweat glistens on me in the heat, and then I feel the burning in my hands. Blood springs up from zigzag lines across my palms, dripping on Po-Po. I am horrified to get Po-Po dirty. I might get in trouble. My hands are throbbing with my heartbeat. Searing red pain. Nauseating pain.

"Mommy!" I scream at the top of my lungs. "Mommy, Mommy, Mommy, Mommy, Mommy!" If I can scream loud enough, she'll come. She'll find me, and she won't die. As Sam pulls me out of the trance, I watch the red slice marks seal up into fine white scars on my palms like magic.

But I am still calling out for my mommy.

Chapter Fifteen

Sofia is filing her nails when I make my announcement.

"You're going to have a visitor this week."

"Oh yeah?" she says, putting on a bored front. But I can tell her interest is piqued. "And who would that be?"

"Your brother," I answer, watching for the effect. I am not disappointed. Her nail file starts trembling like a leaf between her fingers. She puts it down, and it rattles against the table. Her face has gone chalky white.

"Are you okay?" I ask.

She doesn't answer for a minute, and I almost think she didn't hear me.

"Sofia?" I ask.

"I'm fine," she says in a whisper, staring at the dingy tile floor.

"Sofia," I say gently, "you don't look fine."

Again, she doesn't speak for some time. The caged clock ticks above us. "I'm afraid," she admits, her voice just audible. "I'm afraid to see him."

"That's natural. It's been a long time."

She shakes her head. "He hates me."

"I don't know about that. There is probably some anger there." I mean, after all, you did kill his mother.

"For what I did to him."

I nod, playing with my blue pen, squeezing my pinky in the cap. "For killing your mother, you mean?"

"No, I hurt him."

I pause here, vaguely recalling a mention of her brother being injured in the initial reports. But I don't remember this very well. He was listed as "lost contact" until Dr. Grant found him without much trouble at all. UMHC obviously didn't try very hard. "Do you want to talk about it?"

Sofia looks out the window, where a line of snow powders the gray maple branch. "I hurt him."

"Okay."

"I hurt his eye," she says in a monotone, like a robot.

"You hurt his eye," I repeat.

She turns away from the window and back to me again, but looks past me. "He was bleeding."

"Okay," I say again, trying to draw her out some more.

"Oh God," she moans, an actual moan, as if it hurts to say the words. She grabs her head as if she is about to rip it off and stands up, pacing the room. "I can't do this."

"What? Can't do what?"

She keeps pacing, not answering. "I can't do this, I can't do this, I can't do this."

"Sofia." I stand up from my chair, startled by her sudden change in behavior. "Tell me what's going on here."

She keeps mumbling, pacing. For the first time since she was admitted, she looks as if she actually belongs in a mental institution. I thumb through her chart to look at her medication list and am surprised to see none. I don't think I have one patient on my list without medications. I write down an order for Ativan, two milligrams, and sign it.

Sofia stops pacing, standing stock-still in the middle of the room. "He was gone. He was doing okay. I wasn't hurting him," she says as if she is begging. "Why would he come back? My sister never bothered to. Why did *he* have to?"

"I don't know, Sofia. I think Dr. Grant contacted him about releasing you. Your brother wanted to talk to us. To talk to you. I think that's understandable."

She shakes her head furiously, then sits back down, hands tight on the arms of her chair. "What if I don't want to see him?" she asks, raising her head. She looks like the queen of the mental hospital.

"I'm not sure you have a choice on that one, Sofia."

"But I was doing so well," she argues, dropping her regal stance, her voice plangent, almost whiny.

"Yes, but we also have to consider how he is doing." I walk over to her, putting my hand on her arm, my fingers interlaced with her tattoo. "It's going to be all right, Sofia."

"Nothing is all right." She pulls in her arms, away from my touch.

"Listen." I step back a foot to give her some space. "You hurt him. You hurt his eye. That's okay. We'll work through it. This is something we can work through together."

114

Sofia doesn't answer. She squeezes her own arms so tightly that she is leaving red fingerprints.

"Are you afraid he doesn't want you to be released? Is that it?"

"It has nothing to do with that."

"Then what is it? Tell me, Sofia. Maybe I can help you."

"I'm afraid…" She is rocking back and forth.

"Yes. What are you afraid of? Tell me."

She looks up at me, her eyes pure desperation. "I'm afraid he's going to make me remember."

⤺

Through the window, Tiffany looks thinner than when I saw her last, if that's possible, with more scars mapped out on her face.

We are in the psychiatric ER, also known as the PER, also known as the Fishbowl. From the main office inside where the doctors sit, patient intake rooms radiate out like spokes on a wheel. Patients are constantly peering out of their rooms and looking at command central to see what's going on. Thus the Fishbowl, and we are the fish. It is a well-armed Fishbowl, however, with double-plated glass and reinforced, solid-wood doors, should all hell break loose, which is not a rare occurrence in the PER.

The guard picks one of ten keys hanging from a long chain on his belt, clinks it through the keyhole, and lets me into room seven. When I sit next to her, I can see her teeth are decaying. Her breath is horrid.

"Can you tell me what's going on?" I ask.

She doesn't answer. She looks morose, not high, so we must have caught her coming down this time.

"How are you doing?"

At this her eyes fill up with tears, tracking lines down her dirty, ruddy, pocked face. "I'm such a fuckup." Fine hair coats her chin. We see this in anorexics, too. Lanugo from starvation. Her jaw muscles expand and contract as she clenches her teeth.

"Tiffany," I say, patting her knee, "maybe this is your chance."

She turns to me, the briefest glimmer of hope in her eyes.

"I mean it. Let's stabilize you, get you to rehab. Then stay there, Tiffany. Get clean. It gets better than this, I promise."

"I've tried," she says, the glimmer dimming. "It never works."

"This time it'll work. Give it another try." I feel like a cheerleader. But I hardly know what else to offer at this point. To this patient, who might have been a cheerleader herself not so long ago, with her own hopes and dreams, but who instead is dying before my eyes.

"What do you want to be when you grow up?" I ask her.

Tiffany lets out a hoarse, bitter laugh, tears staining her face again. It's hard to tell if she is laughing or crying. Both, I guess. "That's all over now," she says, shaking her head.

"Maybe not," I insist. She is only twenty-nine, though she looks fifty. "Do you remember? Did you ever have a dream of what you wanted to be?"

"An airline stewardess," she says, laughing again. She

sounds a million years old. "Ever since I was a kid. I loved their blue uniforms, their lipstick. Everything."

"Listen," I urge her, "that can still be you, Tiffany. With your hair done up, wearing a crisp blue uniform, making announcements, helping out passengers." It didn't sound all that exciting from my description, however. "Traveling around the world," I add, and her eyes light up again.

"Yeah, maybe," she says, and I can see the battle on her face: hope versus drugs. It's rigged, though. Every neuro-transmitter in your brain screams for the drugs, and it's hard to ignore your brain. Your brain fashions excuses, talks you down, and basically betrays your whole body to get its fix. And the more you take crystal meth, the more your brain disintegrates into itself. Her brain is just as pocked with holes as her face at this point.

"Think about it, Tiffany," I say, leaving her to her thoughts, which I know, coming off meth, are unfathomably dark and low. I do a quick check and see no shoes, no shoelaces. I write "Suicide precautions" on the order sheet to be certain. All the crystal meth and cocaine patients go directly into suicide precautions because sometimes their brains convince them, one, that they are terrible, worthless people, and two, that it's not worth living without drugs. Her new, puffy, hospital-issued white socks glow against the grimy floor. They will be stained gray soon, like all the other patients'.

The door lock clinks again, and a tall body strides in. Mike. The ER resident and former suitor. Suitor via one text

117

and one phone call, both of which I ignored, basically due to his lack of being Jean Luc.

"Hi," he says, surprised. I stand up from my chair in greeting. We regard each other not with displeasure. In fact, a smile is sneaking onto my face.

Tiffany looks up at him, then at the wall again, as if it's not worth the effort to register this newcomer in scrubs, just another one of "them."

"So what's up, Tiger Lily?" I ask him, wondering why I am quoting Woody Allen. I realize it is something my mom used to say. He shrugs, still smiling, not getting the reference. "So what brings you to this neck of the woods?" I ask, still sounding like my mother.

"You know, this and that," he says, jiggling a mammoth chart in his hand.

"They sent you up from the ER?"

"Someone needs stitches out. One Mrs. Carl," he says, glancing at the chart for the name.

"Oh, this is Tiffany Carlson, not Carl. Carl's in... I'm not sure. She might have been transferred to a room already. Here, come with me, we can check it out." I turn to my patient. "Do you mind if I leave for a minute? I'll be right back."

She doesn't respond.

We head out to room three, where Mrs. Carl is. But Dr. A is already there, removing stitches, even though she's Jason's patient. Long, angry purple lines run up and down her wrists. Vertical, so she meant business. Scars she will have forever. I trace the scars on my own hands.

"Healed quite well," Dr. A says proudly, as though he

stitched them himself. "Fairly superficial, which is helpful." He reaches into his ever-ready black bag for another pair of smaller scissors.

"So," says Mike, "it appears I'm not needed."

"Oh yes," Dr. A says. "I've got this all covered up and around."

Mike raises an eyebrow.

"He just means covered," I say.

Dr. A is humming quietly. "This one's not quite ready to come out," he says.

"No?" says Mrs. Carl, who, for someone who just attempted suicide, seems in good spirits. Her hair has been recently permed, her body a bit doughy. She is a neighborhood mom. Someone who would have baked you cookies.

"Not quite," repeats Dr. A. "In fact," he says, scrounging around for yet another instrument, "it could use one more knot." His hands spin acrobatically as he ties off a few more knots.

We give him a wave to signal we're leaving and head back to command central to drop off the chart. The guard unlocks the door for us. "Your boy's got some skills," Mike says.

"Dr. A? Yeah, he used to be a surgeon back in Thailand. Some super-duper neurovascular guy supposedly. Couldn't get into the program here."

"That's too bad," Mike says.

And then we stand there. He has no further reason to stay in the PER and I have no further reason to keep him. Except that I like the look of the patch of chest hair fanning out in the V-neck of his scrubs.

"About that coffee," I say.

"Yeah, about that coffee."

"I'm thinking I need a redo on that one."

He whips out his phone and starts typing. "I'm texting you my number. Call me." Mike snaps the patient chart shut and points a finger at me. "Don't make me beg, Dr. Goldman. Because I will if I have to, and it's not going to be a pretty sight."

And my heart didn't leap, but it maybe skipped a little.

Chapter Sixteen

Jack Vallano is a handsome man, despite his eye patch. Or maybe because of his eye patch. "Ain't got no eye," he says, pointing at it. "Maybe you noticed." He might have caught me staring, though it is difficult to look at him without staring.

"Never could get an eye that fit right. So I went for the pirate look," he says, smiling now, bright-white teeth, Hollywood teeth, though he is a not a Hollywood guy. His smile reminds me of someone, and I realize with a stomach quiver that it is his sister. Jack is a burly man, not fat, though, every inch bone and muscle. He has on a dark brown leather jacket that again, could look fashionable but isn't meant to. It looks weathered because it is weathered, ditto the jeans and T-shirt. His face is weathered, too, though he's only thirty, ruddy with pale freckles laced across his skin.

We sit in the conference room, Jack, me, and Dr. Grant, discussing the perfectly terrifying prospect of meeting with his sister. The woman who killed his mother and left him scarred and half-blind, or as Jack himself put it, "Yeah, she fucked me up pretty good," and whom he has not seen since that very night. But he seems less antsy than I am, given that I ran out of Adderall last night. I tense my toes to stop them from tapping.

We are sitting in our family therapy room, which does not inspire confidence or even a sense of well-being, though it is meant to. Inspirational photos line the wall in cheap, thin metal frames—Achieve, Anything Is Possible, Together We Can Change the World—with the appropriately matched picture of people climbing mountains, or kayaking rapids, or what have you. Old, coffee-stained, dusty mugs sit in the corner on a small wooden table. Toys with layers of bacterial grime, from when Johnny wiped his nose and Susie was still getting over enterovirus, are all thrown into a plastic play oven with a perpetually open door after the fastener succumbed to its last yank. The sides of the room are lined with plastic chairs in various shades of bright blue and orange, like an airport from the seventies. This is a room that could have been decorated by one of our more functional schizophrenic patients.

Jack Vallano loops his heavy leather jacket over the chair.

"So," says Dr. Grant, breaking into the silence. Today he is wearing a tie with diamonds, a checkered shirt, and the same gray pin-striped pants. He reminds me of a child dressed up for Clash Day. "It is a pleasure to meet you."

"Likewise," Jack returns.

"Let me ask you, if I may, before we start: What are you hoping to achieve in meeting with your sister?"

Jack has his elbows planted on the table, his chin in his hands. He rubs his face as if to wake himself up, maybe from this nightmare or just the long car ride. His scar turns magenta and twists, then settles back into a jagged peach line.

"I got your letter," he says.

"Yes," says Dr. Grant.

"Talking about possibly releasing my sister. 'She may not warrant further treatment' and this and that," he adds, as if he is reading from the letter.

Dr. Grant nods. "And what do you think about that?"

Jack pulls out a pack of Marlboros and tilts the pack our way in offering.

"Um," says Dr. Grant with a glimmer of panic, "there's actually no..."

"Oh, right," Jack answers, apologetic, stuffing the pack back in his jacket, the packet crinkling. "So what do I think of that?" he repeats. "I think she's full of shit. That's why I came up here."

I take an instant liking to Jack Vallano.

"And why do you say that?" asks Dr. Grant.

Jack leans back in his wooden chair, which squeaks as if straining with his bulk. "Simple. She's the devil."

"Okay," Dr. Grant answers. "Let's put a pin in that, if you don't mind, and change our focus here a little bit. Can you tell me about yourself, if you feel comfortable doing that?"

"Sure," he says. "What do you want to know?"

"How about we start with the incident?"

"The incident, right. Let's see. I was eight years old when

my family was murdered, and my sister stabbed me in the eye. So that was a pretty good setup."

"Mmm-hmm."

"Went to a string of foster homes. Didn't go very well. I had 'trust issues,' I read on one of my social worker reports. Stands to reason, I figure."

"Uh-huh," I say, working myself into the conversation.

"Homeless at sixteen. Heroin addict at seventeen. Guess I was a late bloomer on that one. Living on the streets, getting by however." He looks at his feet. I can guess what "however" means. "And then Jesus found me, or vice versa maybe. Been blessed ever since."

This was not the turn I expected. Nowhere is "Jesus freak" written on Jack Vallano. He crosses his legs and leans back in the squeaky chair again. If he had a cigarette, he would be smoking it.

"If I may," Dr. Grant says, smoothing his hand against the dull wooden surface, "what do you do now, for your living?"

"Postal service in Chicago," he answers.

"Okay, great. How did you end up there?"

"Found a job through my sponsor from NA."

"Narcotics Anonymous?" I ask, and Jack nods.

"My sponsor knew I wouldn't make it at home with all my same old triggers, so he gave me a bus ticket to Chicago and two hundred bucks. Got to Chicago and spent the toughest hour of my life right outside the bus station, deciding whether to shoot up the two hundred or get an apartment. Jesus won. Got the apartment. Been there ever since. Still go to a meeting every single day."

"So you took some time off to come down?" I ask.

"Ain't had a sick day in years," he says. "Plenty of time saved up."

There is a pause in the conversation. I tap my foot, hear myself doing it, then stop. In the silence, Jack swings his face to me with a jolt, not taking his eyes off me for a long moment.

"Is everything okay?" I ask finally, to break the silence.

Jack swallows and readjusts his eye patch. "Yeah, fine. It's nothing." He reaches for his cigarettes again but his hand remembers and stops midway. "This place has got me pretty fucked-up," he says, shaking his head with a strained smile.

"Okay," Dr. Grant says, redirecting the conversation. "So let me ask you...and first let me say, I understand your apprehension at the talk of releasing your sister." "Apprehension" being a mild understatement. "But," he continues, "if you found a new life through Jesus, what makes you so certain your sister can't change, too? I mean, as you say, it's been twenty years."

Jack nods and crosses his large arms across his chest. "That's what I'm going to find out."

"How's that?" Dr. Grant asks.

"If she's changed, like you say, I'll be the first to congratulate her. No, even better. I'll be the first to give her a hug. Hey, I wasn't no saint myself. One more year and I would've ended up dead or in jail, no doubt. I would've stolen the shirt off your back for drugs, killed you as soon as looked at you." He raps his knuckle lightly on the table. "People change. I know I did. So that's what I come to find out: Did she change, or is she the devil?"

Dr. Grant nods then rubs his smooth, pink chin as if he has a goatee. "How will you decide that, do you think?"

Jack nods, furrowing his eyebrows. "I'll look her in the eye and talk to her. That's all I can do. Find out if there's any room for Jesus in her." He squints his good eye for a second. "I'm not one to talk about Jesus every other sentence. Not my way. Everyone's got their own business and don't nobody care most of the time." Here he looks straight at me, his blue eye bright, Sofia Vallano blue. "But you all can't afford to make a mistake on this one. And I don't take this lightly."

"No, of course, not," says Dr. Grant. "I can assure you none of us take it lightly."

There is a pause then, and I move my chair an inch toward him. "What is your biggest concern here, Mr. Vallano," I ask, "if we were to release her? Do you think she might try to come after you again?"

"No," he answers, thinking about it. "She wouldn't dare touch me now. But it's more the principle of the thing."

"The principle?"

"Yeah," he answers. "The principle. If you got the devil locked up, you don't let him out for nothing."

～

Sofia is tapping her nails on the table. Tap...tap tap. Tap... tap tap, like some kind of tinny Morse code. She looks around at the inspirational photos with feigned interest, covering what is likely abject terror at facing her brother again. Jack grabbed a bite to eat while I collected Sofia Vallano, and we are now waiting in the same family therapy room for his return.

We sit across from each other in silence, having run out of small talk about the weather and hospital food a long time ago. Sofia holds on to her pink plastic nail file, glances at her nails, and starts filing, though she already has a perfect, pearly half-moon atop each one. If anything, she is ruining her French manicure with each violent scrape, bits of white dust flying off. But then she has more than enough time to fix this once she returns to her room. Filing her nails seems inappropriate for such a momentous occasion. But this is her chosen coping mechanism, and it seems cruel to deny her that much.

Dr. Grant's slapping footsteps announce his arrival as he walks in with Jack Vallano. They look as if they were joking about something, and Jack Vallano appears as calm as Sofia appears petrified. She glances up at him, then back to the table, as if the look burned her.

The men sit down and settle in, and everybody stares at one another in silence. If the room weren't carpeted, you could have heard a pin drop.

"So we meet again," Jack says.

Sofia raises her eyebrows. "So it appears." Her eyes are fixed on the table, avoiding his face.

"You afraid to look me in the eye for some reason?" he asks, his voice booming but restrained. I get the feeling you would not want to be anywhere near Jack Vallano when he was actually raising his voice.

Sofia looks up at him, accepting his dare, and they stare at each other.

"There, that wasn't so bad, was it?" he asks.

I can tell he has been waiting for this moment, maybe for his entire life. Even if he never even realized it before.

She holds his gaze. "I'm not sure what we're accomplishing here," she states, a stab at the cool, confident Sofia Vallano.

"I'm not sure that's up to you to decide," Jack answers, practically baring his teeth.

"Yes," Dr. Grant breaks in, "I know there are a lot of…emotions floating around the room right now. So let's all take a deep breath and try to be as calm as possible." He glances at both siblings, giving them a chance to take a deep breath, though nobody does.

"Sofia," Dr. Grant continues, "you ask what we are trying to accomplish, which is a fair question. And I would put it to you this way: Before we make the decision about your release"—he turns to her—"and I know you've been anxious for us to consider that issue"—he turns back then to Jack—"we wanted to allow your brother to visit. Let him have his say in the matter. And maybe get some closure, too." He pauses, looking over to her brother. "Isn't that right, Mr. Vallano?"

"Yeah, that's right," he answers without taking his eye off his sister.

"Okay," Sofia says, the sullen teenager again. She picks

up her nail file clumsily, the finest tremor in her fingers. She studies her overly filed nails and starts the rhythmic scraping again. "So what do you want to know?"

There is a pause while Jack watches his sister, his chest rising and falling, and red splotches flaming his cheeks. The scratching of her nail file fills the silence, and he watches for a minute that feels like ten. "Let's start with something simple," he says. "Why did you kill my mother?"

This is met with stony silence. The filing sound crescendos and decrescendos with each nail. "I couldn't possibly answer that."

Jack nods, backing up his chair a few inches from the table, his chest expanding as he leans back. "And why would that be, exactly?"

"Because I don't remember," Sofia says.

"Oh," he laughs, an angry bark of a laugh. "You don't remember. That's rich. She doesn't remember! What, are you saying you blacked out or something?"

"Not completely," she answers.

"Just the part where you killed Mom?"

She blows the dust off a nail. "I am told I was in a fugue state."

He laughs again. "Oh. So that's it then." He shakes his head, registering his disbelief. "I've read all about that, Sofia, your so-called fugue state." He turns to me, taking me by surprise. "You believe in all that crap, Dr. Goldman?"

I swallow, feeling my face go hot. Dr. Grant is looking at me, too. "It is uncommon," I say, "but it can happen in severe emotional states."

Jack shrugs and half smiles at me to clarify that I am not the true target of his ire. "Okay," he says. "Let's just say, for the sake of argument, that you were in fact in a fugue state, and you don't remember anything that happened."

Sofia nods, staring at her nails.

"Let's just say," he repeats, "for a millisecond that I believe that load of crap. Okay, so then what caused this fugue state? Dr. Goldman says it can happen in severe emotional situations. So what was that for you, Sofia? What was this severe emotional problem that made you descend into this fugue state?"

She doesn't answer.

"Come on, let us in on the secret. I'm dying to know. Did"—he looks around the room—"did you get a B in math class? Was that it? I can see how that might be deeply emotionally disturbing."

Sofia looks up at him for just an instant, the scraping sound dropping into a vast silence. "You wouldn't understand," she says. Her eyes tear up, glistening, then she stares at her hands again and starts filing in earnest. The tears do not spill over, sinking back into her eyes.

"No," Jack says, voice quieter now, but just as angry, "I probably wouldn't. I wouldn't understand a thing you had to say to me. And you can save those crocodile tears, Sofia. They don't change a goddamn thing."

Her tears seems real to me, but he may be right. Sofia stops filing and places the file on the table gingerly, as if it is a friend. "Listen, I know you're angry at me."

Jack snorts. "How insightful."

130

"You should be," she says. "But, Jack, I honestly don't remember very much about that night. I'm not trying to lie to
you. I don't know if it was a fugue state. I don't know what it
was. But I just don't remember."

He doesn't respond.

"But I can tell you what I *do* remember about that night.
If it might help with closure."

"Closure," he repeats. "Whatever, Sofia. Go ahead."

She leans forward onto the wooden table, her gaze on the
carpet by her brother's feet. "I was into bad stuff that year,"
she says, her voice soft. "Bad friends, drugs, you know." She
glances over at me.

"Mmm-hmm," I offer.

"I was smoking a lot of pot. Pretty much every night. Life
sucked. Dad left. Mom was useless, didn't do anything except
lay on the couch drinking vodka. You remember that, Jack? I
was practically raising you for a while, when she wasn't really
there."

He rolls his eyes but does not contradict her.

"You probably don't remember," she allows. "But the
point is, I was heavy into drugs. Going for anything that
could kill the pain."

Here he nods, as if he understands.

"The night it happened, I was smoking pot, as usual, with
some friends. But later my friend told me the weed was mixed
with PCP."

"Angel dust?" I ask.

"Yeah, angel dust," she says. "And I remember, I was
higher than a fucking kite. Higher than I've ever been in my

entire life. But it wasn't a good high, you know? Not like heroin," she says, as if everyone knows how heroin feels. But Jack nods—he does know.

"And this part I remember like it was yesterday: That stuff just lit me up. Lit me up in a really bad way. Like every hurt I ever had, every piece of anger I ever carried, was multiplied by a hundred. By a thousand. I was so angry. It's like every cell in my body was filled to the brim with hate."

Sofia toys with the pink plastic file again, but then leaves it spinning on the table. "I remember that feeling, that out-of-my-mind, angry feeling, but then everything else fades. Like watching a bad horror movie or something. I remember scenes. I remember watching over scenes like I was out of my body."

The room is absolutely silent, everyone watching Sofia.

"There was blood," she says with a shiver. "I remember all the blood. And I remember stabbing you, Jack. I know you might not believe me, but I felt like I had no control over my body. Like I was a puppet, and someone was pulling my strings. I couldn't help it. I couldn't stop myself. I just watched my body keep doing it." She picks up the file again but does not start filing, tapping the pink plastic end on the table instead. "But I don't remember killing Mom. I don't re-member that at all."

We all wait for her to continue, but she has no more to say.

Jack redirects his chair with a creak, facing Sofia. He folds his hands together in a posture of prayer. "I don't know what happened to you, Sofia. I don't know what happened that night. I mean, hell, I was only eight years old." He adjusts his eye patch, which was creeping up the scar. "But I do know what I was left with. And Sofia, you know what that is?"

She doesn't answer him, but I think it was a rhetorical question.

"Absolutely nothing. Less than nothing. And you did that, Sofia. You. Not some fugue state, not PCP, not some kind of force pulling you like a puppet." His voice is calm, gentle even, completely different from the angry, sarcastic person he was minutes ago. "You took everything I had, Sofia. Everything. My whole family. My mom, my sister. You took my life. And I just wish"—he exhales, and his lip trembles—"I just wish I understood why."

Sofia doesn't answer right away, then without warning, drops her face in her hands and starts crying. "I don't know why. I really, really wish I did. But I don't remember."

Jack stares down at the table, not at her, this sobbing mess of a sister. He stays silent while she cries, and I fight the urge to reach over and comfort her. For the first time since I met my patient, I feel just a tincture of empathy for her.

Before I head home, I run over to Sofia's room for a quick debriefing after her brother's visit. She is lying on her bed, flimsy blue blanket bunched up at her feet. She stares out the window, the sky gun-smoke gray, with snow clouds piling up.

"Hi," I say, grabbing the metal chair across from her.

She lifts her head. "Hello."

"Just came in to see how you're doing before I leave for the day."

She nods. "Is he still here?"

"Who, Jack?"

"Yeah."

"I'm not sure, but he is planning on leaving today. We said we'd keep him posted with any new developments."

She gives me a half smile, folding her arms. "I don't develop all that much."

I smile back.

"It wasn't as bad as I thought it was going to be," she says, surprised. "It was actually kind of a relief."

I nod. "Yeah, I can see how that might be. Sometimes the unknown is scarier than what's in front of your face."

"Do you think he's still mad at me?" she asks.

Sofia asks this as if they just got in a tiff over a stolen pack of bubble gum and not her stabbing him in the eye and killing his mother. Sometimes I'm unsure if she's being intentionally obtuse or if her psyche is that severely underdeveloped.

I pull a light purple bottle of lotion off her desk and turn it around in my hands. The smell of jasmine emanates from it. "Why, are you worried about it?"

"A little."

"That he didn't believe you?"

Sofia rolls her eyes. "I don't expect him to believe me."

"Why not?"

"Don't you know?" she says facetiously. "I'm the big bad boogeyman. He'd never believe anything I had to say." The sky is spitting bits of sleet now, minipellets thudding against the window. She taps her fingers together, and the shadows dance on the wall like finger puppets.

I nod and stand to leave but then think of something. "Why didn't you tell me about the PCP before?"

Sofia looks down at her hands, still tapping them, as if it is a finger game. "I don't know. It was in my chart," she says on the defensive side.

"Really? I don't remember seeing it there."

"Yeah." She sits up. Her face is pale, as if the meeting exhausted her. "I remember when I first got to Upstate, they used to urine-test me all the time."

I did remember a section on THC use, her last test being negative over a year ago now. But PCP? Angel dust? I don't remember a word on that one. But then again, she was a transfer. I'm sure in twenty years of charting, some things didn't make it to our hospital.

"It's not an issue. I'm just surprised it didn't come into your defense. PCP-induced psychosis is a well-known phenomenon." I've seen it land people in jail, but not in psychiatric institutions, at least not for this long.

Sofia shrugs. "I was so young back then, you know. That whole time was a blur for me. I honestly don't remember what was or wasn't said. Maybe they did try to use it to defend me. I'm not sure they even believed me when I told them about it. You'd probably have to look in my chart."

"Sure," I say, and we make our good-byes until Monday.

I head over to the nurses' station, my mind batting around the PCP question. It seems like a rather large oversight not to mention. If it were me (not saying I would ever kill my mother), but still if I were in her shoes, that would be the first thing out of my mouth: "I didn't mean it. It wasn't me, really. I was on PCP!"

As I stand at the counter with my chart, the nurse slaps down a pack of cards and drops her pink stethoscope next to it.

"Where'd you get these?" I ask. The top cards fan out and I pick one up.

"Oh, they're from a patient," she says dismissively. "I had to confiscate them. People were fighting over them in the rec room. Causing quite a ruckus."

I take a closer look at the card, which is unsettling and familiar. A black skeleton on top of a white horse. "What are they?"

"Tarot cards," she says. "And that right there in your hand is the Death card." She shrugs. "If you believe in that bull-shit, which I don't."

And it dawns on me then where I've seen it before. The Death card: It's Sofia Vallano's tattoo.

Chapter Seventeen

H*ickory* is my safe word.

We are now utilizing a safe word after the last hypnosis fiasco, when I bellowed out for my mommy and cleared half the waiting room of people who were just this side of emotionally stable to begin with. So the plan is, if I start to lose it, Sam will say "hickory" and I will snap out of it, and he will not have to reschedule thirteen follow-ups with people spooked by the goings-on in the exam room.

"Are you sure you still want to do this?" Sam asks, assuredly hoping against all hope I'll say no. And I am not at all sure, given my last experience, but I'm game for one more go.

"Yes."

"All right," Sam says. He puts his glasses on his desk with a clink and drops his voice to a low, hypnotic monotone.

I settle into the rough, uncomfortable leather couch as much as possible. The heater hums in the background.

"Close your eyes and listen to my voice. I am going to count to fifty."

I follow his voice through the numbers, the pine forest, the bright-red boat, the jewel-blue sea, and end up back in the white-white foyer of my ugly, haunted brown house. I don't know how long this takes. It feels like hours but may take minutes. I am ascending the worn, puke-green carpeted stairs again, as if a spirit is launching me up them, with no will of my own. I am heading for the laundry room, though I do not want to go in there. I can feel with every fiber of my being that I do not want to go in there, but my legs are pushing me. And again, it is pitch-black night outside, seconds after it was a sunny afternoon with a blue, cloudless sky.

I am watching the girl huddled by the dryer. I can see her trembling, clinging to a big blue bear with one eye. The smell is acrid. Sweat, fear, urine. She has peed herself. I want to reach out to her, but I cannot. I sense this is against the rules somehow, that any contact might kill her.

"What's happening, Zoe?" The voice floats into the laundry room. "Don't forget, stay with me this time."

"I am watching her," I answer.

Moonlight lays the crisscross shadow of the windowpane across her nightgown. A blue, frilly nightgown, the same color as Po-Po. A nightgown for a child who is loved. And maybe this is all I need to know about my mother—that she loved me. I feel my throat get heavy with sadness.

"Talk to me, Zoe. Don't do this alone."

"I need to help her." The girl is crying, and I try to reach out, rules be damned, but I cannot. I'm frozen, as in a dream where you are running, your legs heavy as lead, pushing through water, as the attacker gains. I am trying to reach her when I smell sweet, tangy smoke and feel my hands, which burn as if they are on fire. Lipstick-red blood turning magenta, drying and clotting on my sleeve. My heart is smacking against my ribs, my breath coming in asthmatic puffs. I see footsteps in the light streaming from under the door. I gather further into myself, folding myself up into a ball.

"Zoe?" the voice calls, sweet as honey.

It's my mom, but I won't answer her. Why won't I answer her?

The door flies open, and I am peeking up through my slimy, bloody fingers at a giant figure. My eyes hurt from the sudden light of the hallway bursting into the room. The face leans down close to mine, and I am clenching my teeth to stop them from chattering. The features of the face align themselves.

It is my mom, BD. "*I* am your real mother, honey," she says. "Don't worry about finding anyone else. I love you, honey."

But then her face transforms, morphing into another.

"Don't listen to her, Zoe," she says. It is Beth Winters, fresh from her photo, frizzy black hair, seal-brown, eye-lined eyes. "*I'm* your real mother. I was trying to call you. But you wouldn't come. Why wouldn't you come, Zoe?"

"I'm sorry," I call out. "I'm sorry."

"Zoe," Sam's voice says, as if coming from a speaker in the laundry room. "Talk to me. What's going on?"

My birth mother's face melts away, forming yet another face. It is familiar, a sardonic grin.

"No, *I'm* your mother, Dr. Goldman." It is Sofia Vallano, handing me a card, which I take. A stiff black-and-white card, with my bloody thumbprints on the edges. It is the knight and the horse. The Death card. "This one's for you," she says with her *Mona Lisa* smile.

And I hear the word *hickory*, but I can't stop screaming.

Chapter Eighteen

Mike lifts his coffee cup to his lips and leans back in the blue velour chair, crossing his long legs. He's wearing dark jeans and a gray sweater. Date clothes. I barely recognize him out of his scrubs. "So you're actually doing hypnosis?" he asks.

"Yup," I answer but don't offer any more.

"That's all—'Yup'? Come on," he says. "You've got to tell me more than that."

I peer down at my coffee, the foamy candy-cane design disintegrating and turning fuzzy. Scotty tells me Eddie is working on a dreidel next. "You want the long version or the abbreviated version?" I ask.

He shrugs. "I've always gone for the CliffsNotes."

So I tell him the basics, including yesterday's nightmare-esque hypnosis session. His eyes widen as the story goes on, with the "This girl has a lot of baggage" look, which is why I try to avoid offering backstory on any date for as long as possible. But somehow today, sitting here with Mike, I just don't care.

"I know a little bit about my biological mother, but not much," I say. "My dad, I guess, was not in the picture."

"Sounds like my dad," Mike says.

"Oh, really?" I ask, leaping at the opening. It strikes me right then that I am quite sick of ruminating on myself.

"They divorced when I was young," he says. "He moved out to California, so we got visits, maybe every year...then every other year...then every five years...then birthday cards when he remembered. You know, the usual 'Dad sucks' divorce story."

I nod, though I don't actually know this story very well. So we all have our baggage. Mine is just more convoluted.

"He's got a new family now anyway, new and improved. Young wife, young kids. We get Christmas cards."

"Lucky you," I say.

Mike laughs, a deep, strong laugh. "Lucky us is right." He clinks his bright-white coffee cup back in the saucer. Eddie is mopping up a spill next to him, the water beading on the dark wood.

Outside the window, Main Street is glowing red, green, and white. Lit-up candy canes, stars, and Christmas tree decorations line the street, casting soft shadows on the snow-banks. Sure, I'm Jewish, but I get it. I'd do the same thing if I made up 77 percent of the country: line the streets with menorahs, dreidels, and gelt all in blue and gold and pipe corny Chanukah songs in every storefront. "It's a holly jolly Chanukah, and in case you didn't hear..."

"Does it ever strike you," Mike says, "that you could be taking the wrong approach to this whole thing?"

"To what whole thing, my mom?"

"Yeah."

"What do you mean?" I ask, swallowing a bite of chocolate-chip muffin.

"Hypnosis for instance. Maybe it's all total bullshit."

I peel my heavy wool sweater off over my T-shirt, draping it over my chair. "The thought had occurred to me," I admit.

Mike taps his fingers on the table. Long fingers, like a basketball player. Jean Luc had long hands, too, veiny hands. I used to trace his veins right up to the crease in his elbow when I was learning to draw blood from patients. I told him he would make an excellent platelet donor. He told me that was quite a compliment.

"If I wanted to find out about my mother, for instance, I'd do some research," Mike says.

"Research. Like what?"

"I don't know. On the Internet. Hire a private eye, maybe, like they do on TV."

He's right of course, but then again, I'm not an idiot. I've done some research. I Googled her as soon as I was old enough to know what Google was. But she died before the Internet was truly alive and kicking. All I have is what my parents gave me: a copy of a newspaper article about the fire, her obituary, my birth certificate, and the dog-eared photo of us both. I've analyzed these images and words so often that they feel like memories. I do have some picture in my mind of who my mother was, riddled with holes maybe, but a picture.

But Mike has a point. I've never gone the next step because I never felt the need to. Or maybe I've just been subconsciously half-assed about the whole thing all along. As if all my efforts so far have been a way of being sure I could say I looked for the truth but couldn't find it. So maybe I'm not as ready to jump into my guilt-ridden nightmare as I profess. "Not a bad idea," I say.

We sit, staring at the fire in silence. Coffeehouse silence. With strains of samba and acoustic guitar playing Christmas songs. Next to me, a twentysomething wearing skinny black jeans and black high-tops (which, I am sure, were a downright pleasure in the snow) taps away at his computer, beside a stack of books including *How to Write a Best Seller*. Absently I trace the scars on my hands. I notice Mike looking, then not looking. So I hold them up, unashamed. "From the fire," I say.

"Really?" He grabs them to see, tracing them with his fingers. Like a doctor, not a lover. "How?"

"A piece of metal, something fell off the house during the fire, I guess."

"Hmm," he says, sitting back again. "They look like defensive wounds."

"What do you mean?"

He throws his hands up in a "stop" pantomime. "Trying to ward something off."

"Yeah, falling metal."

Eddie wanders up at that moment. "Want any more coffee?" he asks, barely making eye contact with me.

"Sure, love some. Thanks, Eddie."

As he pours, an ohm-sign tattoo peeks out from under his thermal sleeve. Mike signals that he'd like some, too.

"You're a regular, huh?" Mike asks as Eddie walks off, straightening up some chairs.

"Just keeping an eye on my brother," I say.

Mike looks up at the register. Scotty is flirting with a couple of girls. One of them is pretending to punch him. "Looks like he doesn't need any help," Mike says.

I sip at my coffee and he at his, the tinny sound of high hats from some inscrutable jazz album floating around us. In companionable silence, otherwise known as not knowing what the hell to say to each other. At work, we have a script. Here we are floundering, or maybe not. Maybe this is normal for a date. My brother would know what to do next, how to relate to someone without continually comparing him to an old flame. He would know how to move things seamlessly to the next level. Like Scotty with his video games, climbing effortlessly to level three, while all my wizards die one after the other.

A woman flashes by me through the window, running in navy spandex, her breath blowing out in bursts of smoke. I have a crazy urge to leap out the window and become her. Feet pounding the salt-covered asphalt in a comfortable rhythm, breath burning through my lungs. Escape the manufactured merriment and soft brown tones of the Coffee Spot and the floundering date with Mike.

"I have ADHD," I announce without any idea where it came from, except possibly my ADHD.

He looks at me as if I am an alien, then laughs, the same deep, full laugh as before. "I have high blood pressure," he says, "since we're sharing."

"Really?"

"Yeah, really."

"Why?"

"I don't know. They could never figure it out. Since senior year of high school I've been on medication. Lisinopril."

"Wow."

"Yeah, really. Fascinating, huh?" he says. "By the way, is ADHD actually a real thing? I always thought that was just another name for talking shit."

I take an oversized bite into my chocolate-chip muffin, something I must admit that the Coffee Spot executes exceedingly well. "Not exactly," I answer between chews. "There are lots of psych disorders where you talk shit. That's not a very discerning symptom."

"Yeah, okay," he concedes. "But it seems like this one is more or less an excuse for talking shit."

"Yeah, okay," I say. "I could go through the entire symptom list in the DSM V for ADHD, but I think that little ER brain of yours would get bored." Mike laughs, and I swirl the coffee around in my cup. "It's a dopamine thing," I say. "You wouldn't understand."

There is a shriek of laughter near the cash register, and Scotty has his arm around some large-breasted, big-haired, skinny-hipped woman sounding her mating call. He is immersed in Amusing Story #30-something. He has a catalog of amusing stories, a complex mating-call system of his own. Sometimes I think the whole thing is one unnecessarily elaborate charade. All this talking. If you want to sleep with someone, and you're just following your evolutionary calling, why chitchat about it? Do I really want to be sitting here having a conversation with Mike, when we could dispatch with the boring parts and go directly to bed?

Mike is looking at me with a grin, as if he is reading every thought in my head.

A phone text chirps, and I look down at my phone. Visit mother: 2 p.m.

I am forever leaving myself reminders, another "compensation measure" for my ADHD. Though, as Scotty once helpfully pointed out, "Not every idiotic thing you do is because of your fucking ADHD."

"You know," I say to Mike, "I actually have to get going."

"Oh yeah?" He sounds a little disappointed. "Anything exciting?"

"Extremely. I'm visiting my mom."

He stretches his arms out like a cat, yawning. "Want company?"

I pause, look at him. "Really?"

"Yeah," he says. "I've got nothing to do. Why not?"

"Really," I repeat. "Hanging out with my demented mother sounds like a good time?"

"Hey," he says, "it's a date. In for a penny, in for a pound."

"All right. You have no idea what you're getting yourself into," I say, giving him one last out.

"I'm ready," he says. "Let's go."

The nursing home lobby looks as if Father Christmas vomited all over the Victorian tearoom. Wreaths are haphazardly hung up, tinsel hangs in every corner, and ten different artificial Christmas trees are decorated with ornaments and fake presents underneath (fake presents, with their beat-up corners and brazen promises of nothing always depressed me somehow). There are elves planted all around, wearing garlands of red, green, and silver beads, as if it's Mardi Gras for little people.

"Wow," says Mike.

"'Wow' is right."

We make our way to Mom's room, where I notice a large construction paper sign reading "Celebrates Hanukah" in blue Magic Marker taped to the door. Subtle. I wonder if they will put blood on the door during Passover so no one will snatch her firstborn. When we peek in, my mom is staring out the window at an uncharacteristically sunny day. Dust particles dance in the stream of light, making the room appear a bit less depressing.

"Hello," I call, and she turns and gives me her ear-to-ear smile.

"Hello there, daughter," she says. I am hoping she actually knows my name. "And who's your friend?" She gestures to Mike.

"This is Mike," I say as he enters the room.

"Is this the Frenchman?" she asks, a mischievous glint in her eye.

I want to hide under her bed. "No, this is Mike," I repeat.

"Not the Frenchman?"

"Not the Frenchman."

Mike looks amused. "Mike," he says, shaking her hand. "Not French."

"Jewish?" she asks, ever hopeful.

"Sadly," he says, "not that either."

She shrugs dramatically, a "What's a mother to do?" shrug. "Oh well, that's okay," she says, sunny again. "Any friend of my daughter's... you know what they say." She has forgotten what they say. At this point, I truly wish I were under the bed. Bringing Mike here was beyond a bad idea, despite his claim that this is a perfectly legitimate way to spend his Saturday afternoon off. After that awkward introduction, we all sit in the room staring at one another.

"So, Mike," my mother says, her manners coming back to her, "what do you do?"

"I'm a doctor."

She nods enthusiastically. "What a coincidence! My daughter's a doctor."

"I know," he says with a smile, ready to please.

"She's a plastic surgeon," she says.

"Psychiatrist," I correct.

"Same difference," she says, waving me off in dismissal.

"Not at all, actually," I chime in, but she is focused on Mike. Whether she is flirting with him or making a good impression on my behalf, I am not sure. Mike is sitting back in the pale-pink love seat, comfortable as a clam.

"Hey, I think the Sabres are playing at three," he says, looking up at her clock.

"Oh, I love the Sabres!" my mom exclaims, which is a

complete lie. She struggles with the remote. My mother, never a TV watcher, has hardly ever turned on the set, a good-sized flat screen Scotty and I bought her out of guilt and in an effort to kill some of the bored silence during visits. Last time it took us thirty minutes to find the remote, which she had hidden in the bathroom because, she said, people were spying on her with it. That was one of her more paranoid demented moments. Mike stands up and leans over her to help with the remote, gets it to the right channel, then settles back in the love seat. The Sabres skate on amid strobe lights, pomp and circumstance, and an overdone national anthem from a local singer.

Mike is telling her the positive and negative attributes of each player as he skates onto the ice, and I stand up and start tidying. There's not much to tidy, mind you, but I am not a hockey fan, and Mike and my mom seem to have become bosom buddies. I stack the magazines on the tiny laminate nightstand, straighten the pictures on the windowsill, then wipe some dust off the binders of her books with my pointer finger, when I spy one of her high school yearbooks. Sophomore year. I pull it out and sit back down on the quilt.

The inside covers are filled with scribbles. "Never forget hot dog and 'root beer' night at Stacy G's!!!" Which is something she probably forgot two weeks later. Lots of smiley faces, hearts. A few pages in is a picture of two smiling girls with short hair on one side, permy hair on the other, which, heinous as it seems, must have been the style back then. My mom and a friend. The two are leaning toward each other, arm in arm, wearing togas. They have the relaxed posture of sisters, kids without any idea that life becomes harder, not easier. The blood-brother posture of best friends. And I know this, because I have never had one. I have had friends, but a best friend, never. I used to wonder how that would feel, to love someone so freely, so easily, like they were your own self. Someone you could tell secrets to on a sleepover, the hushed, safe whispers lulling you to sleep.

I recognize my mom in the picture, though not the friend. The picture is encircled by a heart in faded pink highlighter. "Never forget I love ya, babe. You will always be my best friend, Beth."

I trace my hand over the glossy smooth page, yellowing now with time, and wonder about this Beth. She bears no resemblance to the picture of my birth mother. This Beth is blond and blue-eyed, fresh as a daisy, with none of the dark-eyed mystery of my mother's face. And as far as my mom had always told me, she had met Beth at her job, a fellow social worker and dear friend. So obviously this must be a different one. There is, after all, more than one Beth on this planet.

"Oh!" Mike yells as the Sabres' puck hits the crossbar with a clang. My mom is staring at Mike in awe. She tosses her hair in a way that could be construed as coquettish. On the next shot the Sabres score, and a flash of white-T-shirted fans jump up in the stands. The sirens blare again, and the scoring player goes down on one knee and fist-pumps while the goalie hangs his head. My mother and Mike are high-fiving.

"This is a fun game, Zoe!"

"Yup," I answer, putting the yearbook back in the yawning space in the shelf.

"And I like your fella," my mom says, winking broadly at me. "But I still don't see why you call him 'the Frenchman.'"

"Yeah," Mike says, grinning at me. "She just insists on calling me that."

And they continue cheering, like peas in a pod.

Chapter Nineteen

Next week it's another Saturday, another day on Sam's stiff, brown couch. The pewter clock ticks through the silence of the afternoon.

"So," I say, after a moment.

Sam smiles at me encouragingly.

"I had a question about the hypnosis." The wind rattles against the windowpane. A tree stands out in the field, bone-white branches stuttering against the wind. "Why was my patient in the hypnosis last time?"

"You mean Sofia?"

"Yes."

Sam puts his elbows on his desk. The soft leather elbow patches squeak against the glossy surface. "That's the thing with hypnosis. It's what I warned you about. Sometimes the process doesn't uncover true memories. It's not uncommon to see people with a strong emotional link, or sometimes not even so strong, just part of your everyday life, pop up in these situations."

"Like day residue?"

"Yes," he says enthusiastically. "Exactly. What Freud calls 'day residue.' Just as you dream about the random things that happen during the day, even things with limited symbolic meaning, this may go on in hypnosis, too. So you may dream about studying for a board exam or playing a football game, just because it's what you're actually doing all day. And in this case, that is likely what happened in your hypnosis. You see this patient with a lot of emotional resonance for you, and she shows up in your hypnosis."

I nod, picking up the heavy iron puzzle on the table.

"It may also signal that you're not quite ready to go back to that night, the night of the fire. Your brain is good at self-defense. It usually won't go any further than it's ready to."

"Funny you should say that."

"What do you mean?" he asks.

"Because, actually"—I take a deep breath—"I was thinking maybe we should take a break. On the whole hypnosis thing."

"Oh." He nods, trying not to look too relieved. I am probably single-handedly destroying his psychiatry practice with my weekly mommy screaming. "I think it was valuable," I add, not sure if this is true or not.

"Right," he agrees, probably wondering the same. I feel as if this is a breakup of sorts. And we are telling each other: It's not you, it's me. "Any specific reason you want to stop right now? It did seem like it was bringing up some answers for you."

"I don't know. Like you said, maybe my brain was just trying to protect me. Maybe it's not such a good idea to go digging around in there." I play with the metal puzzle again. "We could always try again another time," I say, clinking two loops together. But I'm lying. I'd never go back there, to the sweltering pit of that laundry room, the bone-marrow-deep fear waiting in there. The wind whistles outside, and a shiver rushes through me. "So where do we go from here?"

"That's a good question," Sam says. "Maybe it's time to turn our focus on to what's happening with your mom."

"Which mom?"

"Your other mom. Not your biological mother."

"But why?" I ask. "Just completely give up on finding out about my real mom?" I sound peevish and whiny, even to myself.

"I'm not saying that exactly," Sam says. "But maybe we need to go in a different direction. As we already discussed, we think the reason you're so..." He pauses. I know he wants to say *obsessed*, but he decides that has too many implications for a psychiatrist-to-be. "Fixated on the idea of finding out more about your birth mother is that you feel like you're losing your real mother. So if we can get you to work through that issue in a healthier manner, maybe you can then come to grips with your relationship with your birth mother as well."

"Maybe," I answer as vaguely as I feel. I still feel finding out more about my birth mother is the key to everything, but I can't explain why, and I have to concede that I might be wrong. And, I will concede further, I might even be "fixated" on the subject, to put it nicely. "How's everything else going?" he asks. "How's Jean Luc?"

"Still in love with someone else, I assume."

"And your mom?"

"No change there either, I'm afraid."

Sam nods and, following the tick of the pewter clock, opens up his squeaky drawer and writes scripts for my scads of pills, with some extra Xanax for good measure.

I pocket my scripts and walk against the bitter wind to my car, past the bare white tree. The snow crunches under my boots, fine salt lines rimming the black leather. At once everything seems unaccountably sad to me, punctured. Jean Luc: failure. Hypnosis: failure.

My phone chirps a message.

what's up? It's Mike.

Not much, u?

any plans 2nite?

no, i am a loser

I get to my car. The door handle is freezing.

dinner at my place, loser?

I laugh. :) not feeling gr8 . . . maybe another time?

I don't feel like imposing my crappy mood on anyone else. This loser is having a glass of wine, a warm bath, then it's lights out.

u sure? I make a mean manicotti

I type in, another nite, I promise

ok, ttyl

ttyl

I sit on the cold vinyl seat, rubbing my hands together as the dusk darkens to night, while the whole evening looms ahead of me: the gray living room, the fake fireplace, the journal articles I should read but won't.

And I wonder why the hell I didn't just say yes.

Book Three: January

Chapter Twenty

Sofia is not her usual self.

Her casual, laissez-faire demeanor has evaporated. Sitting before me, gray, glum, and angry, she looks like a stranger. She is not drawing, she is not filing, she is just sitting, staring at the gray-blue wall in front of her.

"You look down today," I observe.

"Bad night," she says. Her voice is exhausted, as if she was up all night partying, though I know she wasn't.

"Couldn't sleep?"

"Yeah."

My brain catalogs medications for sleep. Ambien, Lunesta, Restoril. Xanax, too, but not the best if there's no anxiety, and I've never gotten the anxiety vibe from Sofia Vallano, except when her brother, Jack, came to visit. "Any particular reason?"

"Yeah." She doesn't offer more.

"Is it about Jack?" I ask.

"Kind of," she says. "Memories."

"They started coming back?"

"Yeah."

I wait, but Sofia doesn't say any more. She is oddly motionless. No flipping magazines, no examining her nails, no playing with her hair. Just this dead staring.

"Are the memories about that night?"

"No."

I don't want to play Twenty Questions, but I don't think she's goading me, more that she doesn't have the energy to explain. So we sit, her staring at the wall, me looking out the window. Gray sky, gray wall. No snow, no sleet, no rain, no wind today. Motionless, like Sofia.

I decide to change tacks. "Would you like something to help you sleep?"

"No. I don't need anything."

"Okay."

Sofia looks down at her bed, the bare mattress poking through one of the corners, worn white sheets rumpled up around it.

"Are you having any nightmares?"

"No," she says. "And yes." She slaps her hands together to catch a bug, then settles down to stare at the wall again. "Waking nightmares more like."

I nod. "Do you want to talk about it?" I ask, though it's obvious she doesn't.

She doesn't say anything for some time. "It's about my father," she answers finally, her voice toneless.

"All right." This is not the answer I expected. She's never

spoken of him before, except with Jack, talking about how he left them.

"My father was involved in that night."

"Oh," I say. This was not in Jack's account or any of the old notes. So if it's true, this is new information.

"He wasn't there, exactly," she says. "But he was involved."

"Can you tell me more about that?"

Sofia shakes her head. "Not now," she says, lying down on the bed, on her side. She cradles her head in her pillow. "I just want to go to sleep."

"Okay. I'll let you be for now. But tell one of the nurses if you need to talk. Or you need anything."

She nods, closing her eyes, asking for sleep.

"Yeah, I'm a cutter," the girl says as I'm examining her arms. She says it not as an admission, but as a challenge. Her arms are covered with soft, pink horizontal scars.

"What do you use?" I ask.

"Usually a razor," she says with a shrug. "Sometimes scissors if I can't get my hands on one."

I'm on call in the PER. She came in around seven, when I was just shoving the last of a turkey sub down my throat.

"You a cutter, too?" she asks.

"Uh, no," I say, caught off guard. We're not supposed to discuss our own state of psychiatric health. "Why do you ask?"

"I noticed your hands," she says. "I've never seen anyone cut on their hands."

"Oh," I say, putting my palms up reflexively. "No, that was from something else."

"I'm sorry."

"It's okay." I flip through her chart. "Do you want to talk about why you're cutting?"

"It's not even a big deal. My mom just freaked out about it." She motions her head over to the haggard, worried-looking woman in the waiting room. "I told her I wasn't trying to kill myself."

"Do you have any thoughts about that? Killing yourself."

She shakes her head no.

"So what are you trying to do?"

She shrugs. "Feel better, I guess."

I nod. "What's going on that you need to feel better about?"

She shrugs again. "Nothing special. Grades, friends, life."

She couldn't have put it better. Nothing special, just the everyday horror of high school life. It used to be a rarity, this cutting, but now I see it every day, kids cutting themselves to let the sadness seep out. As if it were that easy.

"Do you feel you need to stay overnight in the hospital?"

Unexpectedly, this question breaks down her well-constructed wall, and she starts crying. "Yes," she nods.

"You know"—I touch her arm—"you can tell me. You can tell me anything. Has anything happened?"

"No," she cries, a full-fledged sob now. "I don't even know why I'm so sad."

I hold her arm a second, my fine scars meshing with her new, pink, raised ones. "Don't worry. We'll get through this."

She nods, wipes her nose, and I hand her a tissue from the hospital-issued white box. The PER comes well stocked with tissue boxes. I leave the room to grab some order sheets and start writing up admission orders in the Fishbowl. I don't write for any medications yet, figuring the group will discuss this tomorrow. Most likely an SSRI with some antianxiety effect. I am signing the admission note when my cell phone rings. It's the psychiatric floor.

"Hello?"

"Hi, Dr. Goldman. You're on call, right?"

"That'd be me."

"Ms. Vallano told me you said she could talk to you? I told her we don't usually call the residents unless it's an emergency."

"No, that's okay. I'm here anyway. I'll shoot right up."

"Oh, great, thank you so much," the nurse says, relieved.

When I get there, Sofia is sitting on the edge of her bed. The sky is black outside the window, the outline of the maple tree barely visible.

"There's something I need to tell you," she says, launching right into it without even a hello.

"Okay."

She stares down at the tile floor, twisting a lock of black hair in her fingers. "It's hard to talk about."

"That's fine." I steal a forbidden glance up at her clock—it's nine. I fight back a yawn.

"It's about my father." Sofia shifts around on her bed. "He raped me."

Her eyes meet mine, then fall again. My exhaustion drops away instantly. "I've never told anyone before," she says, her voice soft and emotionless, flat.

"Do you know why not?" I ask.

She kicks her legs to and fro, like a toddler who wants out of the high chair. "I don't know. I guess I never wanted to believe it."

I nod. "And now?"

Sofia is twisting her hair again, choking the tip of her finger purple. "It's been on my mind for a while, since I saw Jack. But last night, I couldn't stop thinking about it. I had nightmares about it all night."

"Mmm-hmm."

She's silent.

"Why do you think the visit with Jack brought it on?"

"I'm not sure. But he looks just like my father. His hair, his freckles. I forgot how he looked, my dad. Completely blocked him out."

"Right."

"But then I forgot how my mom looks, too, so I don't know."

A food cart rumbles by the hallway behind me, sounding like a small earthquake.

"You were saying Jack reminds you of your father?"

"Yes," she says. "And these thoughts have been invading my head since Jack left. Things I thought I got over years ago." She lets out a tremulous breath. "Bad things."

"What kind of things?" I ask.

Sofia holds her arms as if a shiver ran through her. She twirls and untwirls her hair again, eyes still focused on the teal tiles. "The sound of his belt buckle."

I nod. "Okay?"

"It makes me want to throw up."

I run my fingers against the top of the vinyl chart. "I can understand that."

"But I can't get them out of my brain. All these images." She shakes her head as if trying to shake them out. "I thought I'd forgotten about them."

"Sometimes," I say, "an emotional event, like seeing Jack, for instance, can bring them up again."

Sofia swings her legs, creaking the springs in her bed. "When Jack was yelling at me, it's like I saw my father again. All those memories poured out, like the dam burst open or something."

"You don't have to talk about them," I say, giving her permission to stop.

"No, I think I need to talk about it or I'll go crazy." Sofia grabs the hospital blanket, grips it tightly. "My dad was always angry at me for something. Jack doesn't believe anything I say, but even he would admit that. He was just always mad. Yelling at me, grabbing my hair, slapping my face." Here her voice does gather some emotion, but she does not cry. "One time I had a bloody lip from him hitting me, and I was crying to my mom and she yelled at me. Yelled at me!" Sofia looks up at me, incredulous anger shining in her eyes.

"Don't talk back to him! You're just provoking him,

Sofia!" She says this in a whiny voice, imitating her mother. "Like it was *my* fault. My problem. She sat there drinking her vodka every night while he's holding me down, raping me in my bedroom, and telling me to stop being such a baby about it."

"Wow," I say. *Mmm-hmm* just doesn't seem to cut it. "What about your mom?"

"What about her?" she asks. Sofia's eyes have dark rings, as if they are black and blue.

"Did she know, do you think?"

Sofia laughs bitterly. "Of course she knew." She pulls her knees up to her chest, the bottoms of her white socks gray and dirty. "All the better for her. She didn't have to deal with the bastard anymore. Let her teenage daughter deal with him instead. Let *her* see how it feels to be raped." Her voice is pure venom.

"I can't imagine that, Sofia." I pause then, trying to arrange my words in the best way possible. "I could see how that could make a person extremely angry."

"Yes," she nods. "It did."

"Angry enough even, to kill."

There is no answer for a full minute. Sofia hugs her knees tighter like a life jacket, and I wait for her response.

"I could see it, too. It makes sense." Then she releases her knees and sits on her hands, as if she is afraid they might fly up and hit her. "But I still don't remember doing it."

I lean toward her. "I want you to know, though, Sofia, everyone would understand if you did remember. If you were so angry, so blinded by rage about what your father did, and your mother not doing anything, not protecting you, that you stabbed her to death."

She nods, eyes stuck on the floor.

"We would understand it," I repeat. "You were only a young girl."

"Right. But like I told you," she says, her voice harboring some irritation now, "I don't remember any of it." She sighs, as if she is telling a story she has already told a million times. "I remember getting high. I remember feeling unbelievably full of rage. I remember my brother being stabbed, seeing blood. That's all I remember. And believe me, that's more than enough."

I sit back in the chair again, folding my hands. Her speech sounds almost rehearsed. "Okay," I answer.

"Why? Do you think I'm lying about it? Do you think I actually remember killing her and I'm just not saying?" Her voice grows louder, accusing.

I don't answer her.

Sofia bounces on her hands, swinging her legs again. All motion. "You think I'll say whatever I need to to get out of here. Of course I want to get out of here. I'd be crazy not to. I want to live life while I can, while I'm young. Well, relatively young."

I nod, toying with the metal rings in her chart. Thirty-six is relatively young.

"I want to be released, Dr. Goldman. More than anything." Sofia's shoulders slump down. "But at the same time, I can only tell you what I can remember."

Chapter Twenty-One

It could be complete bullshit, you know," Jason says.

The next morning we are in the hallway, waiting for Dr. Grant to come out of a patient room.

"Pshaw!" Dr. A breaks in, looking up from his reading. I have never actually heard someone say the actual word *pshaw* before. "Who would lie about such a thing? No one in their right head."

"Yeah," says Jason. "That's the thing. I'm not sure we're looking at the poster child of mental health here."

"It would explain a lot," I say. "A possible fugue state. How she could have been pushed into killing her mother."

"But why didn't she kill her father then?" Jason asks.

"He was already gone. He wasn't an easy target. And she felt like her mother abandoned her to him, so she had a lot of anger."

He rolls his eyes. "I know this is heresy in our line of work. But what if she's just making shit up? I mean, really, she never told *anyone* all this before? Even when it could have helped her case? I don't buy it."

I tap my fingers on the table, thinking. "She said she hadn't thought about it for years until she saw her brother. His presence appears to have unleashed a torrent of memories."

"What about the sister, what does she say?"

"MIA."

"Still?"

"Yeah. We found Jack in, like, two seconds, but the sister appears to be lost in social-services-land somewhere."

Jason shrugs. "What did you say to the patient?"

"Not much. I gave her an out. Told her everyone would understand her killing her mother under such circumstances. I mean, some asshole rapes his fourteen-year-old daughter, there's bound to be consequences of some sort."

"Yeah," Jason agrees. "I just don't buy that it ends up in you killing your mother." He straightens out his bow tie, a purple that perfectly complements his lavender shirt. His bangs stand up stiff and glossy, as if on guard for his forehead.

"Nice tie," I say.

"Thanks. But do you think it makes me look gay?"

I titter, and Dr. A shoots us a look, then dives into his book again. He is memorizing the DSM V. I don't mean he is just reading it closely. He is actually committing it to memory. "It is quite annoying to keep having to look things up in the book" was his comment when I expressed some astonishment at the prospect.

169

While we're waiting, one of the patients pokes his head out of his room into the hallway. He is about sixteen, skinny and white, dressed in urban clothes with baggy jeans and his baseball cap sideways. "Hey, you got a clicky pen? Anyone got a clicky pen? Clicky pen?" He's jonesing for a clicky pen like he's dope-sick.

"Um, sure," says Jeff, the new medical student. He looks a lot like Kevin, the other medical student, and I keep mixing them up. He hands him a pen before the nurse can jump in.

"Oh, thanks, man!" the patient yells, escaping back into his room.

"Sure, no problem, man," Jeff/Kevin answers.

The nurse glares at him. "You didn't just do what I think you did, did you?"

"Um," he says, wondering where exactly he made his error. A medical student's life is full of these moments. And to be fair, her questions did have a lot of "dids."

"A clicky pen?" she asks.

"Uh, yeah. Well, I mean, he asked, so I didn't think it was a big deal or anything. I mean, was I...Was I not supposed to give him one?"

She points to the large handwritten sign drawn in blue Magic Marker on the door: No Clicky Pens, with pink highlighting around it and additional yellow highlighter arrows pointing to it like a huge traffic signal.

"Oh," he says, crestfallen. "Sorry. Do you, I mean, do you want me to go get it back from him?" Jeff/Kevin's face has turned so red that he looks like a tomato. Cartoon character embarrassed.

"Don't worry about it," I say, feeling sorry for the kid. "We'll get it later, when we visit him."

"Good luck with that one," the nurse snorts. And I can only guess what that means.

Dr. Grant emerges from the room next door. "Change the Valium to q six please," he says to the nurse over the divider. "The tremors are going down." He looks down the row of rooms. "So who's our next victim?"

"I'm, uh," struggles Jeff/Kevin. "We have Mr. Curtis Smith, sir."

"No need to call me sir."

"Yes, sir. Dr. Grant, sir. Dr. Grant, I mean. Just Dr. Grant."

Inwardly I sigh. I can tell Jason is inwardly sighing, too.

"Okay, fine. Tell us about Mr. Smith."

"Yes." He pulls out an index card. "Mr. Smith is a seventy-five-year-old white male with a history of hypertension, sleep apnea, and diabetes, who presents with an exacerbation of schizophrenia."

"Okay."

The clicky-pen man steps out of his room for a second, spies the nurse, and motors back into his room.

"Yeah, okay," says Jeff/Kevin, trying to stay on track, red splotches creeping up his neck like a vine. "He has been stable for some time in an assisted living facility, but recently he thought the TV was giving him a secret message that he was Jesus."

"Jesus?" Dr. Grant asks.

"Yes, Jesus," he confirms. Mr. Smith is a bit late on that one. In December, you tend to get a lot of folks coming in

171

here on the off chance that they might be Jesus. In January, not so much.

"Yes, all right. Any violence or aggression?"

"No," the medical student adds. "Just became very insistent with the staff and started writing messages all over his room about the Ten Commandments."

Wrong testament, I think but don't say.

"So." Dr. Grant looks over to Dr. A, who is overseeing the medical student on the case. "Dr. A, is this a typical presentation for schizophrenia?"

Dr. A nods vigorously. "Indeed, Dr. Grant. Delusions of grandeur such as believing you are God and ideas of reference such as the television having a conversation with you are quite typical and, in fact, in some ways characteristic of this disorder."

"Code Blue Emergency Team A. Code Blue Emergency Team A" pipes into the hallway. The operator's voice has a forced calm. Jeff/Kevin looks out toward the hall wistfully. I remember those days, running down the hallway, heart squishing in my chest, pulling out my Advanced Life Support card so I got nothing wrong. I have never been a cowboy. I did not enjoy barking orders, pushing IVs, leaning over my patient and rhythmically pushing my hands over a brittle sternum, face going blue before my eyes, and knowing, despite what they show in Hollywood, that the person was not going to live. I could never live Mike's life. Just as, I suppose, he could never live mine. Mike, who hasn't texted since I turned him down for dinner and gave me the curtest of nods when we passed each other in the ER last week. So someone else is in the picture, or he got tired of chasing the six-footer.

"All right," says Dr. Grant. "In full agreement. Shall we?" He points to the room, and we file in like geese following our mommy. Mr. Smith is pacing the room, muttering. He walks about two feet, his hospital slippers nearly coming off his cracked heels with every step, then raps with some violence two times on the window, then turns and repeats, like some endless hellish loop. His beard is scraggly, gray-black, and matted.

The medical student looks on with some degree of horror. Ophthalmology, I'm guessing. Jason is sprucing up his bangs.

"Hello, Mr. Smith?" Dr. A says. The patient keeps pacing in his worn track, not even looking up. He does wave him off with some annoyance, so at least we know he can hear us. "How are you doing today, Mr. Smith?" Dr. A asks, increasing his volume as if hearing loss were the issue here. "How are all of the things going for you?"

"What are his meds?" Dr. Grant asks.

"Abilify, ten. Humalog, Cardizem, and Inderal."

"Has he ever been on Haldol?"

Dr. A scans the chart. "Briefly, about five years ago. There was some concern regarding tardive dyskinesia."

"All right." Dr. Grant spins to me. "Would you put him back on it?"

I shrug. "I'd go up on his Abilify first."

"Jason, how about you?"

"I agree with Zoe."

"Dr. A?"

"Yes, I would also tend to agree on this treatment plan."

Dr. Grant looks at the medical student, who swallows, Adam's apple rising. "Me, too."

"Then we are agreed. Go up by five milligrams today, then go to a full twenty tomorrow." We leave the room, the patient ignoring us. Dr. Grant turns to me. "Any more news on Sofia?"

"Nothing more," I say. "She's still very definite on the sexual abuse from her father."

He gives a terse nod and marches down the hall. "Quite classic. Memory suppression due to trauma."

"Yes, but—"

"But what?" He turns back to me.

I hesitate. "I don't know. On the one hand, it makes sense for…everything really. But on the other hand…"

Dr. Grant stops short. "On the other hand?" he asks, staring at me. "There is no other hand, Dr. Goldman. If she says her father raped her, we have to assume that's what happened. Are you telling me you don't believe her?"

I swallow. "Not exactly."

Jason, who argued with me a minute ago that she might be "making shit up," is now steadfastly avoiding my gaze.

"Dr. Goldman, I know your patient has done some…unsavory things in her past. But she *is* your patient. For better or worse. And that means treating her as such."

I nod, chastened.

"And unless you can prove to me that she poses a direct threat to herself or anyone else, you need to start thinking

174

about a discharge plan. And you need to start thinking about it now."

Dr. Grant starts down the hall again and I walk fast to keep up with his angry stride, my face burning hot. So that answers that. According to Dr. Grant, Sofia Vallano is cured, right as rain, ready to go out and become a productive member of society. She'll never hurt anyone else, ever again.

And maybe he's right. But what if he's wrong?

Chapter Twenty-Two

That evening, Mom is waiting for us in her wheelchair by the large, rectangular French window in the lobby. The window frames a patch of dark sky, a few planets tentatively peeking out before the stars steal the show.

We're shaking clomps of snow off our boots on the black rubber entryway rug when she spots us and points, a smile filling up her face. "My kiddos!" she sings out.

Scotty smiles back, and we exchange our weekly hugs. We wheel Mom back to her room through reams of red hearts and lacy doilies running up and down the hall. With the rose-pink walls, it looks like Valentine's Day on steroids. Fat, half-naked angels are aiming their bows at us, though it's not even February yet.

"How's the Frenchman?" she asks as we cross the threshold to her room. Speaking of stupid and Cupid. Scotty smirks because he just can't help it.

"That's over, Mom," I say. I have told her at least ten times already.

"Oh," she says. "Okay, what about that other nice boy? The hockey fan."

"No, Mom. Nothing happening there."

Scotty double smirks. My mom takes her usual seat in her rocker, old lilac afghan hugging her shoulders. Scotty turns on the TV and puts his enormous, shiny, lime-green-sneakered feet up on the mahogany coffee table. Those sneakers probably cost him a week's pay. We are watching the news on CNN, though none of us are really watching, just some noise to drown out the beeping and moaning in the other rooms.

"So how's the Frenchman?" my mom asks again.

"What did you do this week?" I ask her, remembering the social worker's advice: "Try not to challenge, just redirect."

"I met a very nice man, actually," she says, her face lighting up.

"Really?" I say. Even Scotty turns to look at her.

"Tom Burns is his name. Tom Burns." She says the words like they are a delightful mantra. "'If I weren't a married woman, Tom Burns,' I told him. 'You'd be in some serious trouble.'"

"Yeah, but Mom, Dad's—"

She shoots me a frightened look, all glow fading away. "Dad's what?"

"Nothing," I say. It's just not worth it. "Just that Dad would like you to have friends."

"Yes." She nods thoughtfully. "I think so, too."

Graphs zip up onto the TV screen with a loud, over-dramatic announcer explaining them. Basically, red line for

Republican, blue line for Democratic, and ne'er the twain shall meet.

"Oh, I made something," Mom says, grabbing on the top of her dresser. She hands me a hot pink felt pillow. The white cotton stuffing is pouching out, with black Frankenstein stitching holding it together. It reads "I Love You" in glittery silver glue. "It's for you," she says.

"Wow," I say. "It's beautiful, Mom."

"Not for Tom Burns?" Scotty asks, teasing.

"No, I made him a purple one."

"Oh." I laugh. "So I know where I stand."

A commercial breaks into the show. A woman is looking forlornly at the residue on her just-washed dishes. I wish I had the time for such nonsense. The woman finally gets the right product and does a huge leap into the logo. Bored, I grab my mom's yearbook off her shelf again and start thumbing through the pages. I zero in on the picture of her and Beth, with the pink highlighter encircling it, then flip forward to the class pictures to find out this Beth's name, at least, and land on the group photo: a big mass of smiling faces with halos of windblown hair. It looks as if they took the picture in the fall sometime, outside on the football bleachers. Some of the boys look short and ten years old, others appear eighteen and muscular, ready for battle. Girls sit bracing against the wind, in various stages of maturity and social disarray. Some will go on to be doctors, lawyers, social workers. Others, too depressed to get out of bed in the morning, will be drunk by noon. Some could even end up on the couch in my office someday.

I scan the blurb of faces for names and I find my mom, curly side of her hair blowing into her face, and Beth right next to her. Scanning down to the names, I see Sarah Meyers, my mom, and next to her Beth Summers.

My breath catches. Beth Summers.

Beth Winters is my birth mother, Mom's other best friend. And her high school best friend is Beth Summers?

This seems perilously coincidental.

The rocker creaks away as the newest headline crawls along the bottom of the screen. My knees feel rubbery, and I slump back down on the corner of the bed, wrinkling her quilt. Maybe it is just a coincidence. They are different names after all, different people.

"Hey," Scotty calls to me, mouth full of pear from my mom's fruit bowl. "What's up with you?"

"Nothing," I say, my mind racing a million miles.

"You look kind of pale or something."

"Just tired."

"She works too hard, Scotty, don't you think so?" says my mom in a worried voice.

"She can't help it," answers Scotty, taking another chew. "It's like a disease."

Out of nowhere I think back to my college roommate, Natasha, who was majoring in psychology. She was the artsy type, with purple hair and black dresses, when everyone else was wearing jeans. We got in a debate over dinner one night over Jung (this passes for fun among us Ivy Leaguers), and I was arguing that what she called "Jungian synchronicity" was actually just a matter of coincidence.

"Ah," she said. "But that's where you are wrong. There is no such thing as coincidence."

Beth Winters. Beth Summers. What if Natasha was right?

I swallow. "Mom, do you know a Beth Summers?"

She stops rocking and stares straight at me, twirling the balled-up tassels of her blanket in her fingers. "Who told you about Beth Summers?" she demands in a whisper, almost a hiss.

Scott looks away from the TV and up at me. "What's going on, Zoe?"

"Nothing," I say, to tone down the tension in the room. "Beth Summers. She's in your yearbook. See?" I point to the open copy on my lap, and she lunges for it, falling onto her knees. The yearbook slaps onto the ground, my mom grabbing after it, her afghan tumbling off her.

"That's mine! Not yours!" she yells, gasping.

"Mom, it's okay," I say, fighting the quiver in my voice. "I'll put it back."

"No!" she screams, kneeling in front of the bed now, arms crossed over the book as if she is protecting her newborn from certain death. "Mine!"

"Mom, come on." Scotty jumps off the love seat and helps her up by the elbow. "It's okay. No one's trying to get your stuff. It's your yearbook. We get it." He guides her shakily back into her rocker, and she holds the yearbook on her lap with her hands guarding it, her knuckles a row of white knobs over the spine of the book. Her eyes are avoiding mine now.

Scotty gives me his best "What the fuck?" look and I answer with my best innocent eyebrow raise. But I know some way, somehow, I have to get my hands on that yearbook again.

Dr. Grant has asked me to arrange another conference with Sofia's brother, by phone if necessary, to discuss the incest allegations. He wants to wrap up all the loose ends before discharge. And despite being an overall believer in women not lying about being raped, I'm still not sure about Sofia. My intuition tells me that Jason could be right; she could be making it up. It would fit the narcissist-sociopath profile of her like a glove, a woman well schooled in the arts of manipulation and lying. But I have little to go on, except my intuition. And as Dr. Grant once sniped at me, "Just because you don't want to have tea with her, Dr. Goldman, it doesn't necessarily mean she's a psychopath."

Jack Vallano answers on the third ring, and I explain the situation to him.

He doesn't pause for a second. "She's lying!" he bellows. I have to hold the phone a couple inches from my ear.

"Okay," I say. "That's why I wanted to talk to you about it."

"I'm coming down there," he says.

"You can do that. But it's not a hurry or anything. Nothing's being decided today."

I can hear his fast breathing into the phone. Obviously

he is disturbed by this news. Jason sits to my right, scrolling through an *Up-to-Date* article on electroconvulsive therapy. Green stripes from the screen reflect on his forehead. Dr. A has his face buried in the DSM V, his left hand tying one-handed knots with prolene string. I didn't know it was even possible to tie one-handed surgical knots, let alone with the nondominant hand, let alone while memorizing a five-hundred-page text.

"I knew she would try something like this," Jack says.

"So, in your opinion, it didn't happen?"

"Didn't happen, couldn't happen. No way."

I can't help but think back to what Sofia said: "Of course he won't believe me. I'm the big, bad boogeyman."

"Listen," I say. The medical student across from me flips through index cards of his patients, perfecting his presentations. It looks as if he's dealing from a deck for a poker game. "I'm not trying to convince you of anything. I just wonder…" I take a deep breath.

There is a long pause on the phone. "Go on."

"Here's the thing: It would kind of make sense, if it were true. This is the kind of deep emotional trauma that can lead to a fugue state, even multiple personalities, in a child. Severe emotional stress leads the brain to break off from everyday life and go into another, safer world. It could even lead to murder."

"Right." Jack pauses to let this sink in. "I got to be honest with you, Doc. It sounds like a bunch of hooey to me."

"Maybe. You might be right. But it does sort of make the unfathomable more, well, I don't know, fathomable."

Jack sighs into the phone. "You know, Dr. Goldman, we all want to understand things. I get that. It's human nature. Even cavemen wanted to understand the world. But as much as we want to attach meaning to things, and nothing against your profession but that seems to be the main purpose of it, some things are *not* fathomable. Some things are just plain, unfathomable mysteries."

"Maybe so," I answer. I haven't had enough coffee for a philosophical discussion this early in the morning. "I think she might be telling the truth. But to be honest, I'm just not sure."

"And why do you think she is suddenly remembering this? Isn't that just a bit odd?"

"Actually, she says it was always there, in the back of her mind. She just didn't want to think about it. I don't think she fully believed it herself."

"So what's changed her tune now?"

I pause. "She says it was seeing you."

"Oh, right. And how did that work exactly?"

"I only know what she says. But she says you bear a striking resemblance to your father, and seeing your face brought it all back."

"How convenient."

"Maybe," I hedge again. "But again, not unheard of."

Dr. A has switched hands. His fingers arch in a blur. Jason is showing the medical student his patient's CAT scan. I can't help but glance over. Lots of atrophy, no big lesions. "Does he have boxcar ventricles?" the medical student asks. "Nope," answers Jason, tracing the caudate nucleus. "Just plain schizophrenia." The medical student looks disappointed.

"Do I get any kind of say in this whole matter?" Jack asks.

"Of course. That's why I'm calling you. Dr. Grant wanted me to set up a conference. Either via phone or you can come down again."

"Name the date," he says. "I'm coming."

Chapter Twenty-Three

I swirl the remains of the foamy milk heart around in my mug. Ragged and misshapen, it is a lousy metaphor for my own heart right now, à la Jean Luc, who has fallen off the radar. But then again, if he had called, I would have ignored him anyway.

Fake frost, the merry, sprayed-on stuff, coats the bottom of the storefront windows at the Coffee Spot. But the cheery Christmas messages—Let It Snow, Winter Wonderland, and Joy to the World—have been scrubbed out. Pretty soon, Be My Valentine and I Love You will be scratched in.

The matricide article I keep intending to read sits next to me in silent reprimand on the coffee table. Instead, my brain keeps circling around Beth Summers. I have searched for her on the Internet from my laptop but came up empty-handed. There are some matches, but they are all the wrong age or from the wrong country. And the closest ones look nothing like her picture from the yearbook. And I can't ask my mom without risking another outburst.

"You good?" Eddie asks, pushing in some chairs with a squeak.

"Yeah, thanks."

Eddie nods, heads off again. There's a certain bounce to his step, I notice. He looks good. He's even whistling. Scotty passes by him on his way over and splays out in the velour chair next to me.

"What's up with him?" I say, cocking my chin toward Eddie.

"Him? Oh, he's got a date."

"Oh." I raise my eyebrows theatrically. "A hot date?"

He shrugs. "She actually is pretty hot. He met her in yoga."

"Hot date with a hot chick from hot yoga." I laugh. "Calisthenics in a sauna—now that's my idea of a good time. Maybe she's got a matching ohm tattoo."

He rubs his hands together and jumps up from the chair. "Back to the grind. Pun intended."

"Hey, before you go. Remember Beth Winters?"

"You mean your birth mother, who is suddenly so fascinating to you?" Scotty motions practicing a golf swing, which is odd in the middle of winter, unless he's working on his Wii game.

"Right. Did you know then that Mom had a best friend in high school? Named Beth Summers?"

Scotty shrugs, dropping his pretend golf club. "From that yearbook?"

"Yeah."

"Okay. So what about it?"

"Doesn't that seem a bit odd to you? Beth Summers. Beth Winters."

"Seriously, what the fuck, Zoe?" he says, exasperated. "Who cares? What are you doing digging around in Mom's past anyway?"

"It wasn't intentional. I saw it in her yearbook when we were visiting."

"So fine. What about it?"

"I've been trying to get some info on Beth Summers. She's nowhere to be found on the Internet."

"And?"

"Well, I thought you might know better where to look." I point to my computer screen, giving him my most endearing smile.

Scotty huffs, bending down over my computer. Appealing to his superior computer skills always does the trick. "You're a pain in the ass, you know that?"

"I can't help it. I'm a psychiatrist."

"You're crazy is what you are," he mutters. He types her name into a couple of search sites, ones I haven't heard of. He is biting his lip unconsciously, scrolling in milliseconds through various Beth Summerses. But he gets no further than I do. "Why don't you just ask Mom?" He stands back up, knees cracking.

This gives me an idea. "You think she's still up?"

Scotty looks over at the clock, which has an odd, rectangular face with all the numbers melting like a Dali painting. The small hand nears a warped number eight. "Probably," he says. "I'd run over with you but I'm closing tonight."

I glance down at my matricide paper. Sofia Vallano will have to wait.

⌁

My mom is easy to spot in the audience; she is the youngest in the nursing home. Tonight's big show: a local middle school string orchestra. They are almost done butchering Mozart, the conductor waving his hands with great fervor, imagining himself perhaps a few miles down at the Buffalo Philharmonic. The children sit like statues, eyes focused on their rumpled scores, elbows jutting out of time with each other, scratching out incoherent notes. My mom sees me and waves me over, and I sit in the empty foldout chair next to hers, peering over at her program. Thanks be to the Almighty, there is only one song left—"The Pink Panther."

After many oohs and ahs, but mercifully no encore, the crowd of wheelchairs and walkers disperses, and we mosey back to her room.

"So," Mom says, settling into her rocker, afghan on her shoulders. "To what do I owe this pleasure?"

"Nothing, just wanted to see you."

"Oh," she says, eyes filling up with tears. "That is so sweet."

My mom was never a crier BD, but tears come unexpectedly now, as if she's making up for lost time. "Actually"—I sit down on my assigned corner of the bed, tossing my purse and brown leather satchel on the floor beside me—"can I ask you something?"

"Okay," she says, on the wary side. "About your birth mother again?"

"Not exactly."

"What is it then?"

"It's about Beth Summers."

Her face registers something. Her eyebrows furrow just an instant, her lips twitching downward, then the look pops off. "I don't remember a Beth Summers, honey."

"Really?" This surprises me, considering she nearly bit my head off over her name the other night. "It looks like she was a good friend back in high school," I remind her.

"High school?" she guffaws. "Honey, I had a ton of friends back in high school. You think I remember any dang-blasted one of them now?" Then she pauses. "Though the name does sound familiar. I knew a Beth Winters, I think."

"Yeah," I say. "That was my birth mother."

"Oh, right," she says. "I knew it sounded familiar." After a moment, she pats her knees. "I have to run to the potty," she says, standing up shakily from her rocker and heading toward the bathroom. She walks slowly without her walker. "Just be a minute."

As soon as the door clicks shut, I inch toward the book-case, slide out the three yearbooks (it seems junior year is missing), and stash them in my satchel. Mission accomplished. I feel guilty at how easily the deed was done. I think back to the day we packed up these yearbooks for her, along with a ton of other books she insisted on bringing, most of which ended up in a closet in our apartment. Scotty and I, moving boxes and bickering, Scotty was stinking of weed and denying it, and I was fresh off a plane from Yale and a teary farewell to Jean Luc. Not a happy scene.

Mom emerges from the bathroom and shuffles by inches over to her rocker, settling back down as if it's her throne. "How's the Frenchman?" she asks.

"Same old, same old," I say, which is easier than explaining that we've broken up for real this time, for the millionth time.

"How's Tom Burns?" I ask.

"Tom who?" she says, yawning, and I lean over and kiss her forehead.

"I've got to go. It's getting late."

"Okay, honey." She fights another yawn.

Driving home, I think of the look that flashed on my mom's face when I mentioned Beth Summers. Was that a relic of a memory, springing up before the holes of dementia sucked them back again? Or is it that she does remember, and she's lying to me?

⟵

"How's the Lexapro working?"

"Okay," Sofia answers, staring at the white ceiling tiles. Her face has a drawn look that tells me the Lexapro isn't working that well. Since she revealed her secret to me, her clinical disposition continues to worsen.

"Maybe this is the hump she needed to get over," claims Dr. Grant. I'm not so sure about that one. Her previously cocky, immutable demeanor now dissolves unpredictably into waves of tears, hours shut up in her room, refusing to go to group, lashing out at the nurses. It's the usual behavior in this place, unusual only in that it is Sofia Vallano, the former model patient, displaying it. It's as if she just figured out she's been committed to a mental institution for killing her mother.

"I drew a picture in art therapy." She snorts out the phrase "art therapy." I can't blame her. For her, other patients' artwork of rainbows and angry clowns does seem like some kind of bad joke.

"Can I see it?"

"Sure." She reaches over to the glossy white window ledge and produces it, then lies back down in her bed.

The picture, done with her charcoals, is frightening. That's the only way to put it. There is a teenage girl in one corner, black eyes, black hair, bony shoulders, her face the pale white of the paper. Above her, a leering face, the same wide face as Jack Vallano, but with sharper features, a beaked nose. This, I assume, is her father. His hands are huge, freakishly big for his frame, reaching out with menace. Her mother is another teeny figure in the corner, fetus-sized compared to the father. The mother is peering out of the page with a fearful look, her arms hugging herself even smaller. In another corner, I think I recognize a boy version of Jack Vallano. He is standing, arms too long and by his sides. His upright posture belies the fear buried in his eyes. In the last corner, a crudely drawn question mark. This is the first thing that draws your eyes.

"What's the question mark for?" The paper wobbles in my hand.

Sofia doesn't answer, and I wait a long minute as she stares, unmoving, at the ceiling tiles. "I guess I need a therapist to figure that one out." Her voice has just a hint of a sneer.

"Hmm," I say, not taking the bait and handing her picture back. She shoves it back on the ledge, where it rattles then settles down flat.

"Can we be done for today?" she asks.

I fight the urge to ask her if she's got big plans. "Sure." We are not accomplishing much anyway, except establishing that the Lexapro isn't working. "Maybe we should go up on the Lexapro?"

"Whatever," Sofia says, turning her back toward me, her body toward the gray-blue, pocked wall, girding herself for another morning of aimless sleep.

Over at the nurses' station, Jason is chatting with the nurses about the latest singing contest on TV. They're quite animated about their choices, though, to me, there are a million of those programs, all pretty much the same, none of which I've ever seen. I grab Sofia's chart when the scent of soft pine emerges next to me.

"Hello," says Mike with a smile. Not a warm smile, not a cold smile.

"Hello." I try to sound casual but end up sounding nervous.

He is scratching out a note as if he is in a race.

"What are you in for?"

"Oh," he answers, "bed seven." He motions that way with his head, still writing. "Taking out stitches from her wrist wounds."

"Oh right." Tanesha Johnson, Jason's patient. Tried to kill herself and did a decent job actually, for a woman. Went horizontal this time. Guess Mike beat Dr. A to taking out the stitches this time. "You're on surgery?"

He finishes the note and stacks it in the rack. "That I am."

"Thanks," I say. "If we get an appendix rupture, we'll call you."

Then he lets down his guard an inch and smiles, a bit warmer maybe. "See you around, Zoe." He loops his surgical pack over his arm and heads off to the stairs. And I know one thing for sure: I missed out on some mean manicotti.

Finally, after seeing all my patients, I have a chance to take a peek at the yearbooks. I sit ensconced in a library chair, the heater buzzing next to me. I start with sophomore year, but I've already thoroughly mined the contents of that volume and put it aside for senior year. A couple of medical students down the table laugh, catch the stares of the other library-goers, and pipe down.

Senior year. Within a few pages, there is a picture of my mom in a tight cable-knit sweater, her hair a softer brown wave now. The yearbook offers the usual senior year fare: togas, Spirit Days, pie-eating contests, handsome male teachers with a bevy of females students, and vice versa, football teams, hockey teams, debate teams, poetry clubs. The way we filled our lives when we were kids. But oddly enough, there is nothing more on Beth Summers. No class photo, no club pictures, no entreaties to "Never forget hot dog and 'root beer' night at Stacy G's!!!" It's as if she just fell off the map.

I flip through the book one more time. What the hell happened to Beth Summers? She probably just transferred out her junior year, the one yearbook my mother doesn't have, but that doesn't explain Mom's reaction when I first said her name. And it doesn't explain the too-close-for-comfort similarity to my birth mother's name. Curiouser and curiouser. I do a quick Google search for Beth Summers again, this time adding Glenview High School, and try the White Pages but come up empty there, too. Pulling out my phone, I notice the librarian giving me a cold stare, pointing to the No Cell Phone Use sign. I wander over to the library phone on the wall instead. The receiver is greasy and smells of aftershave.

"City and state, please?" the operator asks.

"Glenview, Illinois," I answer quietly, so as not to disturb the other patrons.

After some runaround, I speak to the principal of my mother's high school and explain the circumstances in ten words or less, including the case of the missing yearbook. I am told the following: Old yearbooks are stored in a warehouse in the middle of nowhere; she may or may not be able to round it up, and if so, she would then have to find someone willing to copy the whole thing and mail it to me, but if I want to come and personally visit the school, she would see what she could do.

Any half-sane person would have dropped it at this point but this I am surely not, so I set up an appointment for Monday. Which means a road trip and a bout of the flu planned for Monday as well.

I punch in Scotty's cell.

"Yo," he answers.

"Yo yourself."

"What's up? I'm busy."

"Are you off Monday?"

"Yeah, why?"

"Would you in any way be up for a road trip this weekend?"

"Where and why?"

"Where, Chicago. Why, on my never-ending quest for knowledge."

"And by that you mean all this bullshit with your mother?"

"Sort of. Beth Summers."

There is a pause. I stare at the corkboard by the phone. A glossy sheet announces flu shot times. "What the hell. Why not?"

"Really?"

"Yeah, really. Maybe take my mind off some things."

"Okay," I say, wondering what could possibly be weighing on the mind of my playboy, barista brother.

Someone calls outs out his name and he yells "One

minute," then returns the phone. "Okay, gotta go," he says, and the dial tone hums in my ear.

My cell phone chirps, to the ire of the librarian again, and I throw her a sorry look and pull it out.

Rounding: 1 p.m.

My rounding self-reminder. I stuff the yearbooks back in my bag and take a last look around the table for anything my ADHD brain forgot, ready to take on the world of Sofia Vallano and young girls with cutting scars.

Chapter Twenty-Four

So good to meet you." The principal shakes our hands warmly, and we take seats. Scotty and I spent an uneventful night in the hotel, other than his fairly eventful snoring. I called Dr. Grant with my raspiest sick voice first thing in the morning, and now we are in the principal's office, bright-eyed and bushy-tailed. The principal is a portly African American woman, very put together, wearing coral lipstick, sitting in a comfortable-looking office chair. I can't shake the feeling I'm about to get yelled at.

"I know you told me over the phone about your mother, and I am very sorry to hear about her troubles." We murmur our thanks. "Now, I did put a ticket into the warehouse, so hopefully we can get that by the end of the day. Though sometimes it does take longer."

Inwardly I gulp.

"Would you like a tour perhaps?"

Scotty looks at me, and I provide a solicitous smile. I can't

197

stop my eyes from fixating on her exquisite coral lipstick, which reminds me that I forgot to pack my pills. "I was really just hoping to get ahold of that yearbook."

The principal taps her long fingernails (exact same shade of coral) on her desk. It makes a pleasant thudding sound. "You know who used to keep all the old yearbooks..." she says, "is Mrs. Morgan." I nod with some hope, ready to hop on over to Mrs. Morgan's class. "But," she continues, "unfortunately Mrs. Morgan passed away last year." I nod again, hopes finely dashed. "Heart attack," she adds.

Scotty starts jiggling his leg, which is his "I'm bored" tell.

"Hey, I know someone who could help us. Bob Sulin, our librarian. When I need to find out just about anything that's who I ask." She lifts a long-nailed finger, motioning "Just a minute," and puts a call out to said librarian. Moments later, we are walking briskly (she is faster than her portliness would imply) down the hall, which looks exactly like any other school hall from time immemorial.

Dark, green-brown marbled cement under our feet and steel-gray lockers line the way, with posters of art projects, science photos, and inspirational messages such as Bullying hurts...don't do it. A bell clangs, and hundreds of kids spill into the hallways like ants, buzzing in a fever pitch. Sneakers and boots squeak down the hallway, girls laughing, lockers banging. I am transported back to high school for one vertiginous moment before we peel into the library and shut the door, quiet descending over the room.

Bob Sulin walks directly over to us, hand out, and the principal waves a good-bye and makes her escape. "Bob

Sulin, pleasure to meet you. What can I help you with today?"

I explain the situation, with Scotty leaning against a counter and tapping his foot, and Bob Sulin puts his chin in his hand like *The Thinker*. I have never actually seen anyone do this to think, except maybe as a PowerPoint icon, but Bob Sulin is doing it with brio. "We keep all the yearbooks in the warehouse at this point," he mutters into his fist. "I told them it was a bad idea, but they wanted to clear up the back room." After a full thirty seconds, his head pops up. "Okay!" he yells, making me jump an inch. "I got it. The answer, my friends, is microfiche." He smiles and gazes at us as if he is trying to convert us to Mormonism. "Have you ever heard of microfiche?" he asks earnestly.

"Uh, yes," I answer, and Scotty nods. I feel bad that I have heard about microfiche and have even utilized it before, because it seems to be a heartfelt cause for Bob Sulin, and one on which he'd like to expound a bit more.

"All righty then. Abso-tively fantastic," he says. Scotty tries to catch my eye, but I am assiduously ignoring him. Without my Adderall, riotous laughter would most definitely ensue. Bob Sulin leads us over to the microfiche machine in the corner and shows us the ins and outs, for over ten minutes, which doesn't sound like a long time, but believe me when going over the microfiche machine, it is. Bob Sulin has come up with the clever idea of sorting through the Chicago area newspapers for that time frame, on the off chance we could find out anything on Beth Summers. Meanwhile, he is going to double check the storage room in the basement, in case the missing yearbook hasn't been sent to the warehouse after all. The thought that I probably could have looked through microfiche at my local library does strike me, but I shove it down into the lowest mammalian part of my brain so I do not have an absolute breakdown at the microfiche machine about having driven twelve hours for a hopped-up lecture on the many attributes of microfiche.

We scroll.

It takes us some time, whipping through the gray, grainy images in the machine. I twist the knob until my hand is tired, while Scotty is relaxing in a chair, reading today's newspaper, his fingers flapping through each page. This is my craziness, after all.

"This is a lot of fun," Scotty says, folding up the sports section.

"Fuck off," I murmur, then realize I'm in a library, a high school library. And then out of nowhere, the name leaps onto the screen in front of me. Beth Summers. "I got something!" I yelp unintentionally. Scotty, for all his nonchalance, comes over to see. I read the article out loud from beginning to end: "Tragedy struck last night when seventeen-year-old Beth Summers was killed in a motor vehicle accident. The accident occurred on Hepworth and Main Street when the driver of the vehicle apparently fell asleep at the wheel and hit a utility pole. Estimated time of the accident was three a.m. There were no witnesses, but several neighbors came out after the accident occurred to investigate. Power was lost in several surrounding houses for nearly two hours. Miss Summers was pronounced dead at the scene. The driver suffered only minor injuries and was treated at Glenview Covenant Hospital. The driver's name is not currently being released, but she was reportedly a close friend of the victim."

There is a picture of a decimated car hugging a utility pole, a desolate night.

"Holy shit," says Scotty. I am speechless. Just then, we hear Bob Sulin clamber up the stairs, abso-tively beaming.

"Success!" He holds the yearbook up high like a trophy. "I remembered where I hid my stash." He cackles, then lays the yearbook open on a big wooden desk, a bit disappointed at our lack of excitement over his find. I shift over to leaf through the book while Bob Sulin leans next to us, the smell of his orange Tic Tacs wafting around us. The yearbook is un-remarkable on the whole. More class pictures, goofy candids, overearnest aphorisms in flowery italic print. Except for the last page.

This yearbook is dedicated to Beth Summers.
We will never forget you.

Underneath is a collage of photos of Beth Summers. The huge center photo is one of Beth and my mom, lying in a pile of leaves, throwing up handfuls and laughing. I smile just see-ing it—the joy is infectious.

"You can take it with you," Bob Sulin says. "If you promise to send it back."

"No, no," I say, my mouth bone-dry, feeling sick to my stomach. "Thank you. I think I got all I need."

The words from the microfiche article swim dizzy circles

in my head. "The driver's name is not currently being re-leased, but she was reportedly a close friend of the victim." The driver's name was not released, but I know her name: Sarah Goldman, née Meyers. My mom.

⌐

"Where are we?" Scotty asks.

"Not sure." I point to my navigator on the dashboard. "She told me to drive for the next sixty miles and turn right on Exit 54." "She" being my GPS, named "Karin" with an *i* and a mild Australian accent. That must be how they spell Karen in Australia.

"Hmmph." He unfolds the map. "If she told you to drive over a cliff, would you do it?"

"Probably." And I would. I trust her that much. Since I've been geographically challenged my entire life, my navigator has been a godsend. I have deep, questionably romantic feel-ings for my GPS with her Australian accent, her soft but confident voice, her gentle, chiding "Recalculating" when I make a wrong turn.

"Okay," he says, refolding the map with care. "We're in Morrison."

"Oh yes, that's right, I did see a sign for that." We ride through the flatlands in silence, the fields a monotony of tan and white, with patches of yellow grass poking up here and there through the snow, like stubble. A group of deer stands in the distance, their pelts the color of the trees.

The ride home is long. Scotty takes over as night descends, leaving me to stew about Beth squared.

"Do you think Mom remembers Beth Summers but just doesn't want to talk about it?"

"She sure flipped the fuck out when you took that yearbook," he says.

I shut my eyes, trying to sleep, but the rhythmic blare of the streetlights lighting up my retinas every four seconds doesn't allow it. I am moving the seat belt off of my collarbone when the question hits me. It is so obvious that I don't see how I have not asked it before.

Who is Beth Winters?

Assuming that Beth Winters is just a play on the name Beth Summers, and not actually a real person, then who is "Beth Winters," this person in the picture holding me? And is she even my mother at all?

Who is the person from all the articles? The images and words I know like the scars on my own hands. The woman in the social work agency picture, the obituary? The woman featured in the articles about the fire? Who is the Beth Winters on my birth certificate, and the name penned in blue on the back of the fuzzy-haired baby picture?

If there is no Beth Winters, then who is this woman?

"Scotty?"

"Yeah." He is moving out of the left lane.

"You know all the stuff I have on Beth Winters?"

"What do you mean?"

"The stuff Mom and Dad gave me. The picture, the copy of the newspaper?"

"Yeah, I guess." He taps his fingers on the steering wheel.

"Do you think they could have been faked?"

He groans. "What are you talking about now?"

"No, really. Hear me out a minute." I push the seat back to give me more legroom. "If Beth Summers was Mom's best friend, then maybe Beth Winters is a fiction, not my actual mother."

"Okay. That's a pretty big leap, but not impossible."

"Then how did she get in those pictures and all that stuff Mom and Dad gave me?"

Scotty doesn't say anything but crinkles his eyes. The wheels are spinning. A truck roars by us, spitting up gravel and ice. "You think they just fabricated them?"

"That's exactly what I think."

Scotty stares at me, not as if I've come up with a brilliant insight, but as if I am certifiable. "You know that sounds crazy, right?"

I shrug. "Crazy is what I do best." Though how I'm going to figure this out is not yet clear to me.

Scotty turns on the radio and twists around the knob through the static to find a station. Maybe he's trying to shut me out. We listen to aging rockers while my brain marinates on this newest bit of information. My focus has changed. I'm no longer "fixated" (as Sam would put it) on finding out more about Beth Winters. Maybe there *is* no Beth Winters. So the real question becomes who is this woman in the photo?

And who is my mother?

Chapter Twenty-Five

The next morning I have miraculously recovered from my flu and am getting ready to Skype with Jack Vallano.

I convinced him to Skype instead of making the drive from Chicago. But he didn't want to just talk over the phone because he still wanted to see me "face-to-face." He is on lunch at the post office in a back room that looks like a warehouse, stacks of boxes and tied envelopes everywhere. A friend helped him to set up the session on his computer. I am in the family therapy room again, the only room available for a private conversation right now. Jack is dressed in a dark blue postal uniform. He looks directly at me in the camera, one bright eye sparkling blue. His freckles stand out on the screen, which makes me wonder if mine do the same.

"I'm not used to this Skype thing," he says, playing with his screen. His face widens and distorts in the camera as he leans over to adjust something, then narrows again as he leans back.

"So we were going to talk about Sofia's claims," I say to start the conversation.

"She's lying," he says.

I tap my pen against her chart, thumping the page in a rhythm.

"Although I can't say for sure," he adds. "I've had some time to think about it since our conversation, and I should say that up front."

"Okay," I say.

"But I will say this: I met my father, and I just don't think he's that kind of guy."

I nod. But I'm not convinced. There aren't many child rapists out there with "I heart pedophilia" bumper stickers on their cars. "You say you met him?"

"More recently, I mean. Of course I have vague memories of him from when I was younger, but not much. He left when I was...I don't know, five, six maybe. But then I met him again as an adult."

"Mmm-hmm."

"Drinker. That was his vice."

Two security guards walk by my door, laughing, then it is silent again. "Was he abusive at all? Do you remember?"

Jack nods, as if it's an admission. "To some degree, sure, when he was drinking. Verbally, anyway. He'd get in your face and scream at you."

Which to me meant it wasn't a big stretch to turning physically abusive, too. Sexually abusive, hard to say. "Do you remember him leaving?" I ask.

"Kind of. I think basically my parents had one too many

shouting matches, we were going to get evicted, and my mom threw him out."

Sounds like a gem of a guy.

"I don't remember much about that time. But I remember the sad, gray feeling when he left. Like there was this pall that just descended on the house."

Which is exactly how Sofia described it, her mother falling into a severe depression after he left. Lying on a couch, drinking vodka, ignoring the phone, the doorbell, and everything else. Sofia pretty much picking up the slack and raising her brother. But maybe that's just what she remembers. Sofia the saint.

"I don't want to! I don't want to! I don't want to!"

Jack widens his eyes at the ruckus, which is loud enough to hear through the speaker, though he can't see anything. I recognize the voice as Trish, one of our more intractably psychotic patients. It routinely takes a few staff members to get her back to her room from lunch. I am so used to her bellowing by now that I don't even notice it. "It's like a loony bin in there, huh?" he says.

I smile in response. There is the thumping of feet and soothing words from burly male staff as a crowing Trish gets escorted down the hall.

"So your father wasn't there the night your mother was killed."

"No, he wasn't," Jack says, lifting his hand and cracking his knuckles. "That was a lucky break, huh?" he says, raising his eyebrows. His eye patch folds in, then out. "Not lucky for my mom, though."

"No. Not lucky for your mom. Or you either."

Jack attempts to crack his knuckles again without success. "He was an asshole, sure. But raping his own daughter?" He shakes his head, his face taking a pale greenish cast, though it could be the computer connection. "I just don't think so."

I tap my pen on the paper again. Wind rattles the window in my room, brushing snow against the glass. The room, with all its encouraging inspirational photos and mismatched furniture, feels empty, verging on deranged, with just me and my computer in it. "Sofia acted pretty sure about it," I say, trying not to sound accusatory.

Jack barks out a laugh. "Of course she does. She wants to get the hell out of there. What better excuse could she possibly have? She gets raped by her father, goes crazy, and then kills her mother half makes sense. But I ask you again, why would it come up now, after all these years?"

"Maybe she's just able to face it now."

Jack shakes his head. "It seems awfully convenient." He pauses, then exhales. "On the other hand, who the hell even knows?"

This seems as reasonable a statement as any. "I want to go back to something you said earlier," I say. "You mentioned that you met with your father when you were an adult. So did you lose touch with him after he left?"

"Lost touch," he echoes. "Yeah, you could say that. The man fell off the face of the earth. But about ten years ago, I reconnected with him." He puts his elbows on the table, the blue cotton stretched and worn, with the pink of his elbows showing through. "He tracked *me* down, actually. I had tried for a while to find him but I never could, and I guess my heart wasn't really in it anyway. So I gave up. But he ended up writing to me, telling me he was on his deathbed and wanted to make amends to everyone he had ever hurt."

I put my elbows on the table, too, my stiff white jacket scraping the surface.

"Twelve-stepper, you know. But he got there a little late—he was in liver failure."

"I'm sorry."

"Yeah, well. It was very sad." Jack pauses. "He told me he was never a good father or a good husband."

"Had he heard what happened to your mom?"

"No," he said. "He didn't know. He asked how my mom was doing, and I didn't have the heart to tell him the truth. I told him she died in a car accident, where I lost my eye." He looks away from the camera for a moment. "I don't know. Maybe I should have told him the truth. It just felt wrong to me. Like he didn't need to deal with that in his final days."

"That would have been a lot," I say, wondering what I would have done. It's beyond conception. "Did he ask about Sofia?"

"Yes. I told him she was in jail, that she killed someone. I figured that was close enough to the truth."

"What did he say to that?"

"That's a funny thing, you know?" Jack scratches the back of his head. "I never really thought about that until lately, when this whole thing was brought up. He said, 'There was always something not right about that girl.' I mean, he's on his deathbed, and if he had been"—he swallows—"abusing

Sandra Block

his daughter, you would think that would be a perfect time to admit to it. To make his final amends. But he didn't say that." He shakes his head again.

"Hard to know," I say. Yes, he might well have admitted this on his deathbed, but then again, maybe not. In the end, we all want to think well of ourselves, even pedophiles and rapists.

"I don't know. What do you think, Dr. Goldman?" Jack asks, staring directly into the camera, his blue eye looming out at me. "Do *you* think she's telling the truth?"

Chapter Twenty-Six

*T*he car is hot.

Sweat trickles down the back of my neck. The landscape whips by the window, and I turn to my mother in the driver's seat.

"Slow down," I say, but she is ignoring me. Or maybe she can't hear me. I reach over to shake her shoulder, and her head drifts down. Her eyes are closed, and she is nodding off.

"Mom! Mom!" I scream, shaking her with all my strength. She is leaning over the steering wheel now, the horn blaring, and I can't budge her. "Mom!" I am crying, but she is asleep or dead. She won't wake up.

The car is swerving; my stomach lurches. The guardrail expands in front of us and we are pitching. I hold on to her arm, not ready to die, and we are hurtling off a bridge, now falling slowly, dreamily. I am so high up that the ground below looks miniaturized, as if I'm on an airplane. Dark blue water crawls down below me, studded with whitecaps. We hang in the sky, a pearl-blue sky, and I think it would be so beautiful if we weren't falling.

In an instant, we are swooping down madly, a roller-coaster descent, and my mom awakens and turns to me.

"Mom," I say sadly, already mourning our death. But she does not look sad or afraid. She smiles, then her face changes into another face.

The face of Sofia Vallano.

"Sofia?" I say. I can't hear my voice over the engine and the wind rushing by. "Why? Why are you doing this?"

"Your father raped me," she says, with a chilling smile.

And we crash into the water.

Chapter Twenty-Seven

So what do you think the dream means?" Sam asks.

I am sitting in an oversized chair, boycotting the uncomfortable brown couch today, though the chair might actually be worse. I feel as if I'm sitting on a striped rock. "I'm not sure it means anything," I answer.

"Maybe," he says. "Maybe not."

This is exactly the annoying type of thing we psychiatrists say all the time. "I mean, I get the car."

"Okay."

"That's got to be about my mom falling asleep at the wheel and killing her best friend."

He nods. "Sounds right to me."

"So the question is, why am I her best friend, and why does she turn into Sofia Vallano?"

"Yes," Sam says. "Those are the questions."

This is what you call "reflective listening." I mastered this in my peer counseling group in college. It is so obvious to me at this point that hearing it practiced is just plain irritating. Or maybe I'm just in a shitty mood.

"Let's start with the friend part," he says. "What do you think that's about?"

I cross my legs, shifting in the chair. I have to talk to this guy about investing in some comfortable furniture. "I don't think my mother is trying to kill me."

"Okay," he says. "I don't think so either."

"And I don't really feel like I'm her best friend."

Sam leans back in the recliner. I notice he is no longer mirroring. "I don't think it has to be so literal."

"Okay," I say. I hate riddles, and my life is turning into one big riddle.

"What if," he says, "this is about betrayal?"

I look at my hands, tracing my scars. "Betrayal," I repeat.

"What do you think of that?"

I turn my head, catching my reflection in the nautical mirror. "She didn't mean to betray her friend."

"No, I don't think she did. That was just an accident."

"And Sofia betrayed her mother. Betrayed Jack."

"Certainly you could see it that way."

Then the lightbulb goes on. "She betrayed *me*," I say, at once feeling the full weight of it. "My mom betrayed me," I repeat, half to myself. "She's been lying to me about Beth Winters this whole time."

He doesn't say anything.

"The whole time," I say again, as this registers fully.

"Listen, we don't know if it's true," Sam stresses. "And if

she did, she may have thought she had a good reason to lie. But it doesn't change the fact that to you, it may feel like a betrayal."

I pick up a pillow that I had moved onto the floor when I sat in the chair. It is a needlepoint pillow of a cat. One of those folk-art designs. It does not remotely match the masculine decor of the room, let alone the striped chair. I examine it. Sam does not seem like a cat person either.

"It's a present from a patient," he says.

"Oh."

"How about we focus on the dream some more?"

"Okay." I put the pillow back down at my feet. "So why does she turn into Sofia?"

Sam twiddles his thumbs. "Why do you think?"

"Maybe it's just that day residue again."

"Maybe," he says, but I can tell he doesn't think so.

I lean over and pick up the pillow again, tracing the cat's overly long whiskers. "If it's about betrayal, then Sofia's committed the ultimate betrayal."

"Yes, I think you got it," he says.

I smile with satisfaction. "Freud was right. It's all about your mother, huh?"

Sam laughs then, a real laugh, as if maybe I'm growing on him a little.

Later that morning, I sneak the yearbooks back into my mom's room when she is in the cafeteria. As soon as she is wheeled into the room, I'm waiting for her.

"Zoe!"

"Hi, Mom." I give her a kiss and help her into her rocker.

"How are you?"

"Good," I answer, then take a deep breath. "Mom, I need to talk to you about something."

"Okay." She starts a comfortable rocking.

"I know about Beth Summers."

There is a pause. But she does not look stricken or even nervous. Just a touch confused. "Beth Summers?"

"Yes, Beth Summers. Your best friend from high school."

"Oh yes!" she says, as if the recognition just hit her. "Of course. Have you heard from her? I always wished I had kept in touch."

I stare at her a moment and decide she is not lying to me. Or if she is, she deserves an Oscar. "You don't remember? She died in a car accident." You killed her, I want to add, but I don't.

"Oh, that's right," she says, her face clouding over. "I did know that." She looks down at her lilac afghan and smooths it. "My memory's not what it once was," she says for clarification.

I bite down a laugh. Really now? I was wondering what we were doing in the nursing home!

"Patient in flight, room eight. Patient in flight, room eight," a female voice calmly announces over the intercom. There is a patter of footsteps past my mom's room as a man with a hospital pajama top and no bottoms streaks by and then a louder flurry of staff footsteps catching up to him. A high-pitched alarm stops as the escape hatch is closed.

"Come on now, Mr. Lampke. It'll be all right. Let's get back to your room and get some clothes on."

"Get away from me, you hear? I'll have you arrested, each and every one of you!"

"You know him?" I ask my mom.

She shakes her head. "Not really." She pauses and leans toward me in a whisper. "I think he's got dementia."

"Is that right?"

Mom nods and rocks some more in her chair. I notice the roots of her hair, bright silver. My mom looks old today. We sit in silence, staring out the window as snowflakes flutter around the lamppost like moths.

"I'm just wondering," I say, "doesn't it strike you? Beth Summers, Beth Winters. Kind of a weird coincidence, don't you think?"

Mom waits, then looks at her watch as if she has somewhere to go, and I realize I am holding my breath when she answers, "I don't know a Beth Winters. I know a Beth *Summers*. She was my best friend in high school. Beth Winters, I'm not so sure about that one."

"Beth Winters, my birth mother? You honestly don't remember her?" My voice is rising, my face getting flushed. "Mom, supposedly *she* was your best friend, from the social work agency. Beth Winters, the woman you've always told me was my mother."

She stares at me blankly.

"The name on the birth certificate: Beth Winters. The name scribbled on the back of my picture: Beth Winters. You're telling me you don't remember?" I take a deep breath to calm myself down. Getting angry isn't going to help, but I am angry, like it or not.

My mom continues to stare at me, bewildered. "Honey, I wish I knew what to say to you. I don't know why you're so interested in my high school friend, but I'll tell you what I can remember. It was forty years ago, honey. I don't remember her that well anymore." She pauses and looks up at the ceiling, as if searching for a memory. "I know," she says, her face lighting up, "she loved roller coasters, loved them!" She giggles like a high school girl. I imagine her elbow to elbow with Beth Summers, racing by the fair games and the spinning rides, riders squealing on high. "She once dragged me on Montezuma's Revenge seven times in a row. I remember because I got completely sick and threw up in the garbage can, and she was running onto the next roller coaster."

I have heard this before, yes, but I thought then she was talking about my birth mother. Beth Winters, not Beth Summers. "Do you remember anything, Mom, anything, about my birth mother?"

She flicks something off her sleeve that I don't think is even there. "It was a sad, sad story," she says.

"Yes?"

"Yes," she says, nodding. "There was a fire, I think."

"Right." I feel as if we are running upstairs in a spiral maze that has no end. No cheese for this rat to find.

"Did I tell you I met a very nice man?" she asks, changing the subject, or not. I'm not sure which subject she was on.

"Yes, you did mention that."

"I think"—she leans in—"he's got a crush on me. Not to toot my own horn," she says proudly, "but I'd lay money on it."

Later, at home, I am on my red corduroy couch, staring at the walls and listening to the grandfather clock ticking, trying to read about obsessive-compulsive disorder, when the thought hits me like a lightning bolt.

"Scotty!" I yell, putting down my hot chocolate. It is my third one anyway, and I am a little keyed up.

"What?" he yells back from his room, sounding huffy as usual.

I run over and rip open his door. He is in his boxers still, though it is past noon, typing away at his computer. Code or something, I don't know, I never got that. His room has that college dorm smell. "What the fuck, Zoe? Haven't you heard of knocking?"

"Have you heard of facial recognition?"

"Huh?" He doesn't look up from his screen. He is putting together a Web site, a hair salon maybe. Models with improbably shiny hair fill the screen.

"Facial recognition."

"What about it?"

"Can ordinary people do it?"

He taps his foot, waiting for something to load. "What are you trying to ask me, Zoe?" His hand flies on the mouse, moving text and pictures around the screen.

"If I wanted to find someone's identity, a picture let's say, could I use facial recognition to do it?"

Scotty shoots through a rapid series of mouse clicks and the font changes to an ornate italic, then the background to a creamy tan filled with seductive women in severely shaped haircuts that no one would actually get. I have to admit that it looks good. He shrugs, still moving text around. "It's doable. The FBI does it. Facebook does it."

"How about for me? Can I do it?"

"What do you need it for?" he asks, leaning into his computer screen. The blocks of colors reflect on his face.

I pause.

"And don't tell me it's this fucking Beth Winters thing again, because that shit is getting full-on annoying at this point."

I don't answer right away. "Okay, I won't tell you it's about Beth Winters."

He spins his chair away from the screen, looking at me. "What, you want to take her picture and do facial recognition on it?"

I raise my eyebrows. "I was thinking about it."

He shakes his head, clicking again. "That's beyond stupid."

"I know. But it's better than hypnosis."

"Well, that's for damn sure."

I wait for him to say more. Scotty runs his hand rapidly back and forth through his hair. "This Web site makes my scalp itch." He keeps working for another minute, and I stand, watching him decide. "I know there's some facial recognition shareware out there. I can probably work on it for you, but not today."

A grin fills up my face.

"Maybe next week. And no promises. It might not even work."

"Thank you," I say, leaning over to give him a hug.

He briefly relents. "You really are a pain in the ass, you know that?"

Chapter Twenty-Eight

It turns out that matricide is less common than you might think, if you thought about it much to begin with. Only a handful of cases per year. Infanticide has a much higher rate, though it's an undeniably easier affair. A couple of pounds of screaming newborn versus a hundred-plus-pounder who has raised you from birth. Most matricidal patients are schizophrenic (not the case for Sofia), whereas most patricidal patients have personality disorders and a long-standing relationship conflict with the victim (sounds like a better fit). Incest is a rarity, not the norm. And some old articles are still fixated on working the oedipal complex into the equation.

The library clock shows it's four. That means one more hour to wait around, which should be easy-peasy. I could take a chance and leave early, but that's just tempting fate for the dreaded 4:45 ER call. So I am spending a pleasant hour by the window in the hospital library, perusing the latest literature review on matricide in the *American Journal of Psychiatry* while the sun sets, turning the sky Creamsicle orange.

I figure if I can't solve my own life, I might as well work on the eternal riddle of Sofia Vallano. Putting down the article, I check my phone again for any new hits from the outside world. It is an ADHD tic, this senseless multitasking, and I know it, but knowing it and stopping it are two different beasts. I flip through another page in my article, and just as I'm about to check again, my phone pings happily with a new e-mail. I always picture the phone smiling, alive with promise: "Hey, I just got another one for you!" Usually this is a Nigerian prince asking me please, please to help him out, just this once, but I check anyway, because I'm nearing my next Adderall dose.

The e-mail is spam about making thirty thousand dollars working from home. I was hoping for something from an old friend from high school, Parker Bryant, who is working at the Syracuse newspaper right now. He was going to look into the paper's article about the fire. He is "on it," he said, in that officious way of his. Though he couldn't promise me anything this week. He's working on a big story about the mayor, so he says.

My pager beeps, a high-pitched, whining tone. I push the button and recognize the number with a sigh, internal and external. The ER.

It is 4:47, of course.

The patient in the ER is what you might call "floridly manic."

These are, in fact, the exact words I am writing in her chart. She is wearing a skimpy pink sundress, despite its being February in Buffalo, and reeling off, in rapid staccato, all the reasons she doesn't belong in the hospital, let alone the fine psychiatric ward where she will soon be heading. I am standing next to her because she refuses to sit.

"Normal?" she says. "What is normal really? I mean, I put that to you. Normal is a setting on a washing machine. Normal has no other meaning in my life. I am not normal, never have been normal, never wanted to be normal, never planned on being normal, never will be normal, and that's never going to change. Of course, lock up the woman for having some feelings." She pronounces this "feeeeelings."

"Give her a medication!" she continues. "God forbid she be allowed to *feel* something, *be* something, *ascribe* to something, other than the government's pseudobourgeois notion of emotion."

"Okay," I say calmly. Challenging these people is a bad idea and will result in further pressured speech for another good hour at the least. "I can understand what you're saying"—which is not 100 percent true—"but let me just ask you a few questions."

"Ask away," she says, waving her hand toward me with a flourish. "You're the examiner; I'm the examined. You do the touching. I am to be touched. I know our roles. I'm not igno-rant; I'm not childish; I'm not new to this land or ill versed in the ways of the world; I'm not—"

"All right," I break in. It is generally frowned upon to interrupt patients in psychiatry, but with manic folks, you sometimes have no other choice. "What are your medica-tions?"

"You mean the medications I'm prescribed, or the medi-cations I'm taking?"

"Both."

"The medications I'm prescribed would be Lamictal, 200 milligrams twice daily, Trileptal, 450 milligrams twice daily, with a side of Neurontin, 300 milligrams three times a day."

I am jotting madly.

"What I am taking is absolutely none of the above. Med-ications, I've discovered, are numbing agents, meant to anes-thetize your soul, and I for one have decided to fight back against the tyranny of big pharma, and big government, big hospitals, and all the rest of the bigs, and just lift myself out and feel life. Experience life, be life—"

"Yes, I can see that. Are you by chance taking any med-ications you weren't prescribed? Or anything over-the-counter?"

"No, I am a free vessel. I am open to life in its rawest form. I am striving to remove the barrier between me and the out-side world. Let the world attack me, I am ready for it. I am not afraid to feel the wind on my face, smell the grass, swim with the dolphins in the ocean of life—"

"That sounds good. Any allergies to medications?"

"Ferrets."

"Ferrets?"

"Yes. Ferrets. Not an allergy per se, but a genus I avoid if at all possible. I have discovered that ferrets are actually creatures of the devil. All creatures on the earth are divine, woven from God, to be treasured, loved, and respected, not eaten, mind you, because meat is murder. So, as I was saying." She breaks off and peers around rapidly, as if someone just ran in front of her, but I can attest that no one did. "Did you see something?"

"No." But I look just in case, because she is convincing.

Suddenly, she looks me straight in the eye. "You're rather tall, you know that?"

I pause to register this. Because while true, it is seemingly out of nowhere. But at least it means she is in touch with reality. "Um, yes. I did know that."

"Where was I? Ferrets! Ferrets! They are teaming with Satan."

Before I could hear the theory behind the demonic properties of ferrets, my text goes off. *Dum-dum-dum-dah.* Jean Luc. My heart goes squirmy.

Skype?

Can't now I type furiously.

Later?

Maybe. Got 2 go

I turn back to my patient, who has not paused for a breath. "Stare at me. Stare at me. Stare at the animal. Stare at the elephant in the circus. I am a trained elephant on a high wire..." She is pretending to walk a tightrope over the teal-blue tile, and I get an image of her walking on water. We are way past ferrets. I am picturing an elephant, trained or otherwise, on a high wire, and how that would not go very well in the end, and wondering what Jean Luc was texting about, and if my heart will ever learn to stop skipping at the mere glimpse of his number or whether it is destined to dangle, always, like an elephant on a tightrope.

"I think it's rather pretty, actually," the patient is saying. She is spinning, twirling the bottom of her dress. "My mother never wanted me to wear pink. Pink, pink, pink. '*Whores* wear pink, Claudia,'" she says, imitating her mother, her voice turning ugly. "Whore, whore, whore, whore!" she starts screaming.

I grab the curtain and find a nurse. "Can we get two milligrams Ativan, please?" I call out.

"IV or IM?" she asks.

"IM," I answer. "And pull five of Haldol, too, would you?"

"My pleasure," she answers, padding away.

"Nice place you've got here," Claudia says, circling around the ER cubicle as if she's just walked into a five-star hotel room.

"Not bad, huh?"

"My mom was a whore, my sister is a whore"—she counts on her fingers—"my first-grade teacher…the biggest whore."

My phone rings out the Fifth again, and I pull it out of my lab coat.

Forget Skype. Just call me pls.

My heart does the jig, but this time I ignore the text and tell my heart to go fuck itself.

My patient is now dozing blissfully in her five-star hospital room after two milligrams Ativan, and I am also near dozing blissfully in my eggplant settee at the Coffee Spot, Wagner droning on in the background. I hate their Wagner mix though I'm not sure why, could be a Jewish thing. I've bitched about it enough that Scotty usually changes it when I walk in.

Speaking of which, Scotty says he finally got the facial recognition software working so I'm waiting for him to finish his shift and show me. My DSM V book (which Dr. A has probably memorized by now) sits unattended on the table while I surf merrily on my iPad, indulging in my coffee with its disintegrating milk-foam rose, not one of Eddie's better designs. Eddie wanders by, wiping off a nearby table.

"So," I call over in a stage whisper, "how did the date go?"

He turns a dark crimson, a hesitant smile on his face. The coffee saucer clinks in his hand, trembling a second. "Good, actually." He glances down at the dark wooden floor, still smiling, then back up at me. "We're going on a second one."

"Good for you. You sly devil, you."

"I don't know about that," he says but looks delighted. "Hey, can I?" He points to my cup.

"No, I'm good."

He nods with half a wave and walks back to the kitchen. The bell tinkles pleasantly with a new customer arrival, a shot of cold air whisking through the doorway. I look over unintentionally and see a face I did not expect: Mike. And a woman. Wagner booms out of the background as if on cue.

I had braced myself to see him in the ER during the consult, but he wasn't there. I wasn't expecting him to infiltrate my favorite coffee joint. Though it is a free country, and they make good coffee. Grudgingly I would admit that he is allowed to patronize the place.

Mike glances at me, gives a cursory smile, and strides up to the counter to order. He leans into the woman, tall like he is (maybe he has a type?), and then orders. I flip open my DSM V, which is a good prop if nothing else, and put on my best heavily concentrating face. The woman laughs at something and punches him in the arm, and he laughs back. She has dark hair, long ringlets, a kind of Amazon beauty. It strikes me that she is a complete counterpoint to Melanie.

I focus my eyes on my book.

Depression:
A. Five (or more) of the following symptoms have been present during the same two-week period and represent a change from previous functioning; at least one of the symptoms is either (1) depressed mood or (2) loss of interest or pleasure.

The mnemonic for depression rings out in my head back from medical school:

SIG-E-CAPS. Sleep, interest, guilt, energy, concentration, appetite, psychomotor activity, suicidal ideation. And how does one Zoe Goldman fare this fine evening?

Sleep: pretty crappy, lots of nightmares, thanks for asking.

Interest: okay, if it's interesting.

Guilt: no problem there; it wasn't my fault.

Energy: the proverbial bunny.

Concentration: never been my strong suit.

Appetite: alarmingly good.

Psychomotor activity: jittery, but maybe that's the Adderall.

Suicidal ideation: thankfully, no, but Wagner isn't helping.

I hear Mike's big, bear laugh as he turns away from the counter. He and the woman are heading back my way, bright red Coffee Spot paper cups in hand. "See you later," Mike says to me, holding the tinkling door for his significant other as the cold air seeps through like a smack in the face.

"See you," I answer to his exiting back.

Scotty emerges from the back room, putting an arm through a sleeve of his puffy, black down coat and then pulling his winter hat down on his head, which flattens his hair like a monk cut. "You ready?"

Scotty places the picture of my brown-eyed mom and fuzzy-haired me on the scanner. "Now don't freak out if this doesn't work," Scotty says, which I suppose is his way of being supportive. "If the woman from your photo isn't on the Web, no facial recognition program will pick her up."

"Who's not on the Internet nowadays? She'd have to be from Mars."

"I agree, it's unlikely."

The scanner imports the picture with a buzzing noise, the white light flashing on and off. It does seem like science fiction, sending an unknown face out into the stratosphere and awaiting a match. Cue some heavy-handed orchestral music with lots of short notes, a hero wearing a shirt a few sizes too small and cracking the code with a password that's somebody's pet's name, and we could be in a Hollywood thriller.

It takes a while. Images shoot up on the computer screen in rapid succession, then are discarded back into the stratosphere. A hundred women with black hair and brown eyes file onto the screen one after another, faces eerily morphing together. I can't take my eyes off it. At last the dizzying parade slows to a crawl as the computer settles on three fuzzy faces. A red laser pointer traces every feature, crystallizing each one. Then the computer simulates the sound of a winning slot machine: the one-armed bandit creaking, three happy dings, and coins falling into the dish. Three Beth Winterses in a row.

Triple jackpot, we won.

"Who do we have here?" Scotty asks.

"Adelina Branco," I say, reading off the first one. "From Portugal." The face looks exact, her skin tone just a touch more olive. The hit is from a Web site for a bank in Portugal, with one smiling bank teller named Adelina Branco. Clicking on her bio, we get her high school and junior college history (where she maintained a 97 percent average) and also learn she likes handball and walks on the beach. Luckily, this narrative is given both in Portuguese and English, so we can easily rule out this suspect as my mother. Unless I'm secretly Portuguese.

"Not likely," I say.

"Okay. Let's move on to number two." He scrolls down on the screen and I crowd in to get a better look.

"Sylvia Nealon," I say. "She's from Cleveland. The other 'mistake on the lake.'"

"Yeah," Scotty mumbles, reading.

"Looks like the picture's from her Facebook page."

"Yeah, I'm pulling it up." Scotty gets into the Facebook site. His fish tank burbles, and three silver-streaked fish jet by in synchrony. "She doesn't share her whole page, just basic info."

I lean over his shoulder and read.

Relationships: single. Favorite book: Who has the goddamn time to read?

"A scholar," I say.

"Nobody reads, Zoe. She's just being honest."

"You read," I challenge him. "Just boring computer magazine crap."

Favorite movie: Il Italio.

"What's *Il Italio?*" I ask.

"No idea. Some movie. She probably thinks it's edgy."

"'Edgy' in air quotes."

"Right."

Occupation: medical biller. And there's a picture of her cat, a smoky fur ball of a thing, and a smiling Sylvia Nealon that looks a helluva lot like the photo, but kind of hard to tell with the shadows on her face.

"She's the right age," I say.

"Okay, so who's the last one?"

He scrolls back over to the facial recognition program. The third hit comes off yet another Facebook page: Mrs. Barbara Sanders. Fifty years old, living in Rochester, New York. She has two young boys, and her site is chock-full of pictures of them, children's artwork, "funny" things they said. She even Facebooked a straight-A report card. And her face bears an uncanny resemblance to my dog-eared photo.

Occupation: secretary.

"Ding, ding, ding!" I holler. "Folks, I think we have a winner. Good night, Beth Winters. Hello, Barbara Sanders. I want to thank you all for playing tonight."

Scotty is smiling, too, because his computer genius worked, and he is happy for me in spite of himself.

He starts closing up the program. "So what's the plan now?"

"Elementary, dear Watson. Go to Rochester. It's time to find my mommy."

Chapter Twenty-Nine

I am finally on my way to meet my mother, my real mother. At least I think so, though I have been wrong before on this account.

Jason agreed to cover me for a couple of hours so I took off early this afternoon to go to Rochester. The sun lights up the grime on my windshield, and my radio is playing mindless, hopeful pop songs, when Karin announces Pine Wood Road at the next left, which is Barbara Sanders's street, straight from her Facebook page. I crawl down the road, squinting at every mailbox for number eighty-four.

When I see it, my heart starts knocking against my sternum. I do some deep breathing, thinking I should have brought some Xanax, but I didn't want to be blotto for the meeting. Plus, I do have to drive home. I pull down the vanity mirror for a quick appearance check, which is never a good idea, take a final deep breath, and pull the car door open.

The house is smack-dab in the middle of suburbia, a pale taffy-pink color with stunted holly bushes attempting in vain to cover the foundation. The icy wind whips up, and I pull my black coat tighter around my neck. I push the cold, hard doorbell, sending a buzz through the house, and a little dog comes skittering down the linoleum. Through the window, I spy a well-coiffed shih tzu, dashing down the hall and barking like a possessed stuffed animal. He slams his miniature body against the window for all he is worth, to the point that I'm actually worried he could hurl himself through, when a muffled voice scolds, "That's enough, Tiffany. I know you're excited. Come on."

The woman opens the door halfway with a creak. She has gray, feathered hair, in a pseudomullet, and a faded yellow sweatshirt that reads "Jesus Loves You." My heart is now ramming into my throat.

"Hi," I say.

"Hi," she answers, not fully opening the door and looking at me as if I might be trying to sell her encyclopedias. My brain wonders for the briefest of seconds whether salespeople still sell encyclopedias before screaming at itself: *Focus!*

I pull out my picture, the one printed from Barbara Sanders's Facebook page, and then the dog-eared one of my mother. The resemblance is undeniable. "I'm looking for Barbara Sanders."

She grabs the picture. "Where did you get this?" she demands, her face losing color. "Who are you?"

"I'm Zoe Goldman. I tried to call but the number wasn't listed."

"Yeah?" she says.

"I found this picture on Facebook, and I just wanted to see if she lives here."

She stares at me, the light down on her top lip quivering. "What's going on here?" she asks. "What's all this about?" Her dog starts barking again. "Barbara has been dead three years now."

The wind whips up, sending freezing snow into my ears, and unaccountably, I start crying. "I'm looking for my mother," I say, realizing just how pathetic this must sound.

She stares at me again and shakes her head. Her shoulders relax. "I don't understand, honey, but come on in, it's freezing outside."

Fighting back tears, I follow her in.

❧

She pours me a "Jesus Loves You" mug of coffee, and though I am hopped up on three cups already and nearing palpitations, I don't refuse. She examines the picture of my mother, the one with the frizzed-out hair, holding the five-day-old me.

"You sure were a cute little thing," she says.

"Thanks, Mrs. Kopniak," I answer, nose still congested from my earlier emotional incontinence.

"You can call me Judy, honey," she says, drinking from her own bright orange "Jesus Loves You" mug. "How did you get Barbara's picture again?"

I explain the facial recognition software, the Facebook

page. She nods but does not really seem to be following. "Me and computers don't mix. My husband, Henry, he likes computers. He's always on that damn thing doing something or other."

I take a sip of coffee, which is bitter and burns the roof of my mouth. The kitchen is lemon yellow and small, but homey, decorated country style. Signs with fake needlepoint writing that read "God Blessed This Home" and "Home Sweet Home" abound, along with scads of references to JC and being saved.

"I'm sorry to hear about your daughter," I say.

"Thank you." Judy stares off in the distance. "I'm not over it, of course. I don't expect I ever will be. But that was God's will. Can't question that. She was too good for this world anyway. I always knew that."

It turns out that Barbara Sanders, her daughter, died of leukemia three years ago. She had two kids, Matt and Greg, the light of her life. But she is not the frizzy-haired woman in the picture, and she is not my mother. Judy admits it's an uncanny likeness, but definitely not her. And the Facebook page? Still up, now with Judy's address listed on it. Henry did that for any remembrances that people might send.

"Never had the heart to take it down," she says. "And the boys still post on it sometimes. I think it does them good, kind of a connection still."

"Hmmm," I say. "That must be hard." I can't help it, the psychiatrist in me is always ready pounce.

"It is," she agrees. "She was a good mom, a damn good mom. Loved those kids to death."

So she was a good mom, just not my mom. I play with the orange handle on the mug.

"I hope you find your mom, honey. But remember, your mom, the one who adopted you, is your mother, too. God gave you to her. And God always gets it right, even if we don't always understand."

"Well," I say, not sure what to say to that pronouncement. "Okay."

Judy bursts out with a laugh. "'Okay'?" she says, imitating me but not mocking me. "Someday you'll get it. Maybe when you're older." I can tell she feels as if she is talking to her own daughter. We finish our coffee leisurely, chatting about the weather and the ride home, watching the snow dance in swirls. Then we put the dishes in the scratched-up sink (where I spy "Jesus is my Main Man!" and "I'm Saved" mugs waiting). She leads me back to the front door with a subdued Tiffany at our feet, past a Precious Moments display in the teeny foyer.

"Thanks," I say, and we hug, not awkwardly. It's as if she's my long-lost grandma, not some stranger I just met. Tiffany doesn't even bark at me as I leave.

I drive the long hour back in silence. I don't have the heart to turn on the radio, the pop station now blasphemous somehow, until Karin's muted Australian tones finally lead me home.

Chapter Thirty

Have you been thinking of killing yourself?"

Sofia smirks at me. "Are you asking if I have suicidal ideation?"

"Yes, that's another way to put it."

We sit in the rec room, Sofia laying cards on a wooden table for a game of solitaire. Dr. Grant thought it might help her mood to get her out of her hospital room more, force her to interact with the other patients in situations other than just group therapy. Sofia draws a gaggle wherever she sits down, but she ignores the other patients. "Solitaire" says it all.

"I think about it all the time," she says. "It's a delicious thought."

I trace one of the scratches on the table. "How do you see that?"

"Suicide?" she asks, flipping over each card with a thwap. "It's the great escape."

"Escape from what?"

"From an empty life." Sofia may or may not be trying for irony. In any case, it's hard to argue with this. She has no visitors, no friends, no future. Her own brother despises her with good cause.

"You've made a life here," I offer.

She snorts. "Oh yeah. Art therapy. Group talk therapy. Recreational therapy. The fun never stops around here."

A laugh rings out at the next table over, as if to bely her point. My other patient, the teenage girl with the cutting scars, is sitting with a new patient, a heavy girl with an enormous butterfly tattoo starting at the back of her waistline and traveling up to her scapulas. It's unattractive to the point of tattoo artist malpractice; I can only imagine how it will look in twenty years. Both girls wear heavy, kohl-black eyeliner, cracking jokes to each other. In their hospital gowns, they are simpatico, fat and thin versions of the same girl: sad, artistic, misunderstood. I wonder if this is who Sofia Vallano used to be: sad, artistic, misunderstood. And matricidal.

"Were you happier in the old place?"

"What, you mean my former mental hospital?"

"Yes."

"Hmm." Sofia considers this. "Maybe." She layers her cards in a long row. The cards are tattered and marked from years of cigarette-stained fingers and coffee-cup rings. "I didn't think about things as much."

"But maybe it's good to think about things more. Face them."

Sofia smirks at me a second, then goes back to her cards.

"Good to face my father raping me every night? Good to face stabbing my brother? I'm not seeing how this is so wonderful."

I notice she didn't mention killing her mother. "Facing things isn't always easy, but it gets us somewhere."

"Yeah, well, I was fine with stagnant, thank you."

I decide to change tacks. "Did you have any friends there, at the old place?"

"Friends?" she repeats, as if this is a foreign concept. "Sort of, I guess. Mostly people who would come and go. No lifers like me. At least, no lifers you could actually carry on a conversation with."

"I could see how that would be."

"Not like you," she says.

"Like me?" I ask her, surprised.

"Yeah. Like you." She lays down another row. "I like you," she says, almost shyly.

"I like you, too, Sofia. And I want to help you."

She gathers her cards again and shuffles them with a loud rattle. "I don't know if you can."

"All I can do is try," I say.

She shuffles again, then taps the deck on the table. I see the patient who thought he was Jesus, milling about. He is asking the other patients for cigarettes, but no one gives him one. "Maybe if I had a goal," Sofia says.

"A goal?"

"You know, a purpose."

I can guess where this is going. "Such as being released?"

"Yes, that would be a good goal," Sofia says, flipping down a row of cards, not looking at me.

"Let's focus on getting you feeling better first," I say, avoiding the subject. "How's the Wellbutrin working?"

"It's crap," she says, smacking another card down.

"We just added it. It might take time."

"At the old hospital I had a goal at least."

"Okay. What was your goal there?"

Sofia's blue eyes narrow at me, then she returns to her game. "Maybe that's for me to know and you to find out."

And this from someone who supposedly likes me. She lays the bait, and for the millionth time, I don't bite. Though it's hard to know if these pissed-off moments represent Sofia the psychopath or Sofia the irritably depressed. To give her the benefit of the doubt, she does consider the thought of suicide "delicious."

I shut her chart. "I'll see you tomorrow, Sofia."

She doesn't answer, and I walk out of the break room with some relief, leaving her to the buzzing fluorescent light illuminating her cards. When I sit down in the room behind the nurses' station to check my e-mail on my phone, I see two voice mails waiting, both from Jean Luc. I put the phone up to my ear to hear the first message, my breathing speeding up.

"Please call me. It is important, Zoe." Loud breath, waiting. "Okay, talk to you soon."

Next message: "I know you are mad at me, Zoe. But I just need to talk to you. Please, Zoe, answer the phone." Here he waits a good thirty seconds, as if he doesn't get the concept that it's already gone to voice mail. "It's over with Melanie. C'est fini. Call me."

My heart goes into spasm. "C'est fini."

Whether he wants me back, though, or to lean on me in his time of need, I'm not sure. Blond, thin, wispy, beautiful Melanie. Jean Luc–beautiful. The kind of dreamy, mythical creature you might see walking down a red carpet, shyly smiling at her premiere, flashbulbs blinding her. And it's over.

Jason walks into the room and snags a nacho chip from the tray in the middle of the room. He crinkles his nose. "Stale."

"Yeah, that tray's been sitting there, like, all month."

He sits down beside me, flicks a thread off his knee. "I was hungry."

"I can see that. Hey, what are you doing in an hour or so?"

"I don't know, no plans. Why?"

"Want to go for a run?"

He lets out a loud sigh, patting his belly. "No, I don't *want* to go for a run, but the three pounds on the scale this morning tell me that's not such a bad idea."

"Delaware Park?"

"Sure. Where?"

"Zoo side," I say, smelling buffalo already. I walk to the elevators, passing the rec room and the silhouette of Sofia Vallano slumped over her cards.

"Why don't we live in California?" Jason asks, already short of breath in the first twenty-five yards. "No sane person chooses to live where it snows six months of the year.

There is no rational reason we are not currently in California."

"Did you apply for a residency in California?" I ask.

"Of course," he says, puffing. "Motherfuckers didn't want me."

"Okay. So that's the rational reason you're not currently living in California."

"You don't have to be so adamant about it."

"I'm not being adamant. I'm just being factual."

"Factual, my ass."

Which really invites no response, so we keep running. It is cold out, but a soft cold. The sun is setting, imbuing the air with a tawny, bronze light. It is my favorite time of day to run. My feet are hitting the street with a satisfactory pound, Jason's pace just off-step from mine. I fall into the rhythm of running, my brain smoothing scattered thoughts, my arms chugging effortlessly, and Jason's ragged breathing a soundtrack. Jason inserts his earbuds and turns on his MP3 for his own soundtrack, as he ineptly raps along to some hip-hop. I can hear the beats through the earphones.

My mind wanders pleasantly, released from its leash.

Rochester, no-go. So I have one more mommy to try from my facial-recognition hit. Sylvia Nealon from Cleveland. Doubtful, but worth a shot. One last-ditch effort to find my birth mother before I do as Sam says and let go of my obsession and work on things with my *real* not-real mom. I might ask Scotty if he wants to accompany me on the last stretch of the search, but maybe not.

The smell of buffalo dung is fading as the golden light

deepens into nighttime. Jason is keeping up, his breathing evening out now. I think again about Beth Winters. Maybe I will never know who she is, if she's my mother or not, and I will just have to accept that. But then again, maybe Sylvia Nealon can give me the answer.

My mind saunters over to Sofia Vallano again, slapping down her cards. Is she ready for release? Dr. Grant's plan: Get her depression under control, talk with Jack again, and "dismiss her from involuntary confinement to a mental institution." "With daily outpatient therapy in the hospital to start off," he said. "Of course we want to keep a close eye on her. And we also want her to be successful." In my heart of hearts, I think Dr. Grant is right. It's been twenty years. She deserves a shot. Even if I don't want to have her over for tea.

Next up on the thought parade: Dah-dah-dah-dum… Jean Luc! Who is no longer with the svelte Meh-lah-nee and may or may not want me back, just as I may or may not want him back. I have listened to his message at least a dozen times now, like an itch I can't stop scratching, but have shown inordinate impulse control and held off on calling him back. I picture the wine-scented cork, now long gone in a sanitation dump somewhere, paired with shame at my spectacular failure with Mike, who seems to have moved on swimmingly to a new Amazonian creature.

As we run on, feet banging the pavement, I hear the soft patter of hoofbeats and see a horse and buggy ahead, slowly clomping closer and closer to us. I've seen a few of these now in the park; it's a new thing for Buffalo. "Romance in

245

the Park" it's called. Freeze your ass off under a thin flannel blanket on a horse-and-buggy ride through the park, smelling horse dung instead of buffalo dung, *trés* romantic.

I am pondering the cruelty of putting blinders on these horses when a gunshot goes off somewhere. Maybe it was a car backfiring, but it sounded like a gun, and even more concerning is that the horse is spooked by the noise and is now bucking and zigzagging in our direction.

It all happens in a second.

The driver in his cheesy top hat, red-faced and yanking the reins with all his might, calls out "Whoa, Ginger!" The couple inside clings to the carriage bench for dear life, Jason rips out his earbuds, and my foot transforms into a ball of pain as the carriage wheel, quite unromantically, rolls over it.

My foot throbs with every pulse, as if someone is rhythmically dropping an anvil on it. I know this seems unlikely, but that is how it feels. I am trying not to moan and not to focus on it, which is like thinking of something else while someone punches you repeatedly in the head.

"Girl, you look like shit," says Jason, leaning on the bar of my gurney. We are in bed eighteen in the ER, not where I had planned on spending my Friday night.

"Thanks, Jason," I choke out. "I was running. I wasn't getting ready for a fucking pageant."

"I'm just saying. You should always wear something decent. You never know."

"You never know what?"

"Who you might meet! Your big Frenchman, Jean Luc. He could have been around the corner. Instead of that stupid horse."

Here I allow myself a loud groan. "Please don't say that name."

"Why? He was superhot," he says. "That boy was nothing to be ashamed of."

I know Jason is just trying to distract me from the pain, but he is just plain annoying at this point. Still, he did manage to call 911 and convince them that yes, I got run over by a horse and buggy and needed an ambulance, while the carriage driver put the horse-smelling, scratchy red blanket over me so I wouldn't go into shock. This is far better than Scotty, my usual running partner, would have done. He would have still been saying "What the fuck, Zoe? Seriously, a horse?"

Zing, zing, zing my foot is humming. I peek down at it, which is a mistake. A pot roast, purple with a hint of red, comes to mind. My foot has swollen to twice its usual size. I lean back again, light-headed.

"Ooh, girl, that looks nasty."

"Again, completely unnecessary, Jason."

Snatches of absentminded whistling echo closer and closer, then the curtain rips open, and of course, it is Mike peeking through. Here he whistles again, more of a "What the hell did you do to yourself?" kind of sound.

"Wow," he says, almost chuckling. "Zoe, that's impressive." He sticks his head back out the curtain. "Nicki, we're going to need ten milligrams morphine here."

Morphine. Thank God.

"So what the hell happened?" He looks Jason up and down to figure out the relationship. Jason is looking him up and down for a different reason.

"I was running," I say. "A horse and buggy rolled over me." Every word is excruciating.

"Of course. The old horse-and-buggy jogging injury." He flicks the X-ray up onto the light board. It is a half-inch lopsided. "See that?" he asks.

"No, Mike. I'm a psychiatrist. I tried to forget all the radiology I knew."

"Okay, then. That is a broken third, fourth, and fifth metatarsal."

"Holy shit," Jason says, looking at the film.

"What this means," Mike explains, "for the psychiatrists among us, is that you are going to get casted tonight, and you need to be off your leg for two weeks."

"Two weeks?"

"At least. Maybe more. No work for a month." He points to the syringe just handed to him. "How do you feel about the happy stuff?" he asks.

"Morphine?"

"Yup. Any allergies?" he asks, glancing at my chart.

"Nope. Bring it on."

Mike plunges the needle into the IV bag port with a grin. The morphine tingles over me like a wave, turning the anvil hammering into a soft hum. My brain is drifting, everything soft and gooey. Mike's face looms up in front of me. "You know, Zoe," he says, "if you wanted to see me again, there are easier ways."

I laugh, not a small titter, more of a rolling, elongated laugh. I have the odd feeling I will never stop laughing. Then my eyes start closing.

"Hey," I mumble, grabbing his arm. "Who?" I ask, forgetting for a second what I was asking, then grasping it right before I fade off. "Who was the woman?"

He looks confused for a moment. "What woman? From the coffeehouse?"

"Yeah." I am forcing my eyes to stay open, vision swimming double.

"Oh, that was my sister." His voice takes on a teasing twinge. "Why, were you jealous?"

Chapter Thirty-One

There is no comfortable place to put my cast on the couch, though I don't know why this should be a surprise. I give my toes, covered by an old navy-blue sock that has seen better days and smells like a locker room, a vicious scratch. I'm cutting down on the Vicodin, except at night, which has worked marvelously for my insomnia.

"You're not taking it with the Xanax, though, right?"

"Right," I answer. Well, maybe just a couple of times. Looking around the room, I sense that something is different, though I can't place it.

"So," Sam says, "about the incident in Rochester. Sounds like that was tough."

"Incident," as if it were a crime scene. "Yeah, it was disappointing. But I think I'll give it one more shot."

"Really?" he asks.

"I don't know. Cleveland's a quick drive, and I have some time off. It's worth a try. I'm not hoping for much. She's probably not going to end up being my mother."

He nods. "Maybe not."

"But if I don't see for myself, I'll never know."

"That's true."

"So if I go and it's not her—then it's not her. End of story, case closed. I can move on."

"Right," he says, nodding again, and we both wonder if this is true.

"It's the clock!" I yell out, and Sam turns to me, startled. "You changed the clock." The old pewter one is gone, replaced by a dark brown, wood-grained clock, also more nautical of course.

"Yeah, I don't know," he says, moving his head to look at it. "I thought the other one was ticking too loudly."

"Hmm," I say, nodding. So now who's got OCD? I scratch my knee. It's as if my knee and my toe are in a competition to see which can itch more.

"Tell me, what are you going to do if it's not your mother?"

"I don't know." I look out the side window at the parking lot. Piles of icy snow, frosted with dirt, stud the pavement. "I don't even know what's true anymore. I just don't understand why my mom lied to me."

"Why do you think?"

I work my fingers under the cast, dispatching another itch. "I honestly don't know. Except, maybe, in some misguided attempt to protect me."

Sam looks down at this desk. His face reflects off the gloss. "You know, I have kids, Zoe. And I would do anything to protect them. Anything. That's just how it is. It's a natural instinct."

"I'm sure that's true," I say, wondering at the fact that I had no idea that Sam had a family, and indeed no curiosity regarding the matter for nearly a year now. My therapist as an actual human being, what a concept. Sometimes my self-absorption knows no bounds.

"Maybe you'll never know the reason, but you might want to start thinking of it in a positive, rather than a negative, light at this point."

"What do you mean?"

"I mean, assume that there *was* a good reason for her lying to you. That she did have your best interests at heart, as she always has, and just try to leave it at that."

I nod. "Yeah, maybe." But I've never been much good at leaving it at that.

"So how's your patient doing?" Sam asks.

"Sofia?"

"Yes."

I shift my heavy leg, which is going numb, crumpling the leather.

"You can put that up on the table if you need to." He points to the cast.

"Oh, right. Thanks." I maneuver my leg onto the table with a minor crash, and he tries not to wince. He is probably going to disinfect that table from top to bottom as soon as I leave. "I haven't been to work all week, but I have checked in. Nothing much new, I think. Kind of in a holding pattern. She says she was molested; her brother says she wasn't."

Sam smooths his goatee. "In these types of cases, it is usually customary to believe the victim."

"Yes, I know," I say to his minipsychiatry lecture. "And as much as I hate to say it, I actually do believe her."

Sam twirls his pen in his fingers, a fake Montblanc. He has a few in the glossy brown pen box on his desk. "Why do you put it that way?" he asks.

"What way?"

"That you 'hate' to say you believe her? Odd thing to say about your patient, isn't it?"

My cast squeaks against the tabletop. "I guess."

He places the pen on his desk. "I'm sensing a conflict here. Are you?"

"What sort of conflict? An 'I'm angry at you because I'm looking for my mother and you killed yours' kind of conflict?"

A smile escapes from his lips. "Something like that."

I tap my good foot on the floor. "It's not that odd to be turned off by a matricidal maniac, is it?"

"Maybe not," Sam says, "for most people. But then again, she *is* your patient."

"Yeah, but it doesn't mean I have to like her," I return.

"No, I suppose not," he answers, looking down at his folded hands.

And I think we both know what he means by that one.

⤺

There are two messages blinking red on the answering machine when I get home, which uncharacteristically Scotty hasn't already erased. I push the button, then go to hang up my coat.

"Scotty, it's Shelley. Call me, please. We really just need to talk. You have my number." The voice is desperate. I feel sorry for Shelley. This isn't the first pleading "I've been wronged" phone message for Scotty, and no doubt it won't be the last.

The next message is unexpected. "Zoe, it's me. You won't answer your texts, and your message box said it was full, so I thought I would try you at home. Please call me." I don't get many pleading messages, though Jean Luc can hardly claim to have been wronged.

I ignore my heart, which is leaping and panting like a puppy, and plop down on the couch, clicking on our gas fireplace. My foot is throbbing like a toothache so I pop two pills and turn on the TV. I flip through some true-crime shows, which are usually my favorite, but today just seem depressing, and finally turn off the TV and crack open the DSM V, fighting the urge to doze.

Headlights flicker as cars drive by, shooting off snow in their wake. It is snowing in earnest now. They say every snowflake is a one and only, but each flake mounds ceaselessly on top of the other, linking crystals and giving up a unique pattern for the greater good of covering the ground. Which mostly means I will have to clean off the car if I want to go anywhere tonight.

The words swim as the pills soothe my foot and my brain. I put the DSM V on the floor and lay the soft mohair blanket (which Mom knitted BD) over my legs. The heater kicks in with a contented hiss, and I fall into a drugged, dreamless sleep.

When the doorbell pierces me awake, I panic for a confused minute, thinking it's morning and I'm late for work, but then glance outside at a darkening evening. On cue, the grandfather clock starts its stately chiming, one-two-three-four-five-six, seven pauses to take a breath, and then loud ticking resumes. The fireplace balloons in the reflection of the clock's brass pendulum.

The doorbell blares again, an annoying buzz I keep meaning to change before realizing I have no concept of how one would do this. Are there doorbell stores, for instance? By the time I think to Google it, my brain has already moved on to the next bright, shiny object.

Buuuuuuuzzzzz.

I am positive this blaring pedestrian at my doorstep is either some girl for Scotty or a Jehovah's Witness, which makes the noise all the more annoying, but I rouse myself and peel off my blanket, rubbing my arms in the dark apartment. My head feels groggy, my mouth furry, and finally my foot realizes it's awake and starts throbbing. "I'm coming," I call, or more accurately bray, out, gathering my crutches to get to the door. The door buzzes again on my way over, just to piss me off a little more. When I open the door, the snow blasts me right in the face.

My heart does the fox-trot.

Jean Luc is standing there shivering in a thin, light-blue spring jacket. "Zoe," he says, in his peculiar, lovely French way. A dark green compact car is parked in the driveway. I stare at him in shock, stock-still in the doorway. The snow lines his hair, and his lips are puffy with the cold, like rosebuds.

"*Je t'aime,*" he says.

He asks about my foot, and I explain the whole idiotic story, then there is an awkward silence. Jean Luc stands by the fireplace, rubbing warmth into his hands, while I sit on the couch.

"So what happened with Melanie?" I ask, getting right to the heart of the matter.

He exhales, as if he's just been through a trial. The flames from the fireplace throw shadows onto his face. "She went back to Robbie."

"Oh." I don't know what else to say. I could be angry, maybe I should be. But I'm not. I'm buoyantly, stupidly happy.

"It's for the best. She is too young"—he pauses—"too capricious." This is probably not quite the right translation of the French word he was thinking of. "And the truth is, I missed you."

I try to keep from smiling. "So it's totally over then?"

"Totally over," he says and walks over to me, the heat of the fireplace wafting off his clothes. He leans down over the couch to kiss me, his lips soft on mine. He lays his hand on my knee right above my cast. The patch of jeans lights up with warmth, and my heart thuds through my sweater, but I pull away, as if I'm pulling myself from a magnet.

"Jean Luc, I'm glad you're here. I really am. But I can't do this right now. I don't know." I shake my head, searching for words. "I don't even know how I'm supposed to feel."

His eyes stare into mine, deep and gray. He nods, as if he is mulling over a solution to a complex question. "I will just have to prove myself."

"I wouldn't put it that way," I balk. "It's not a test or anything. It's just...I need some time to figure this out."

"Yes. You are simply being logical."

"I guess," I say, though my heart is skipping illogically at the moment.

Jean Luc rubs his neck, which is lined with soft hair, like peach fuzz. "Let's go out," he says. "Are you okay to? With your leg?"

"Oh, that? Sure, no problem. You hungry for dinner?"

"Yes," he says. "Something from Buffalo, I will experiment." Then he crinkles up his nose. "Anything but sushi."

———

Beer and wings are meant for each other.

So much so that I'm on my second, maybe third beer. Maybe not the ideal plan with Vicodin in the mix, but what the hell, you only live once. The snow swoops and swirls outside, a pleasant contrast to the festive warmth in the restaurant. Rusted license plates line the walls in every shade and color.

"It wasn't a *total* failure," Jean Luc says, almost shouting to be heard above the music. "You remembered some things. I would say this is an achievement."

257

"I guess," I say, dabbing some chicken-wing grease off my chin.

He takes a long sip of beer. "Even if you stopped the hypnosis, you started the process. Maybe more memories will come on their own."

"Maybe," I say, with some cheer. This is a line of reasoning I hadn't considered.

The waitress wanders by. "Can I get you another, honey?"

"What the heck?" I say, handing her my glass, though my speech is already on the slurred side. Jean Luc signals for another, too.

"So," I continue, "Sam thinks my obsession with my birth mother has something to do with my mom's dementia."

He licks sauce off his lips. "Makes sense."

"You think?" I ask, chewing into another wing. "I don't think it's all that complex. I just want to know more about my birth mother. What's so wrong with that?"

"Nothing," Jean Luc answers. "We are all looking for our mothers, no?"

I laugh into my beer. Jean Luc makes everything seems so simple. "You would have made a good doctor," I tell him.

"Ah no," he says, with a mock-horrified face. "Talk, talk, talk to people all day long," he says. "I prefer to be left alone in my lab."

We both laugh. It is like his experiments, elegantly simple. The song pauses for a few seconds, then a new song starts up, a pounding drumbeat I can feel in my foot. "Do you think," he asks, wiping red grease from his hands on his napkin, "maybe I am *too* alone?"

I tap my palm to the music. "What do you mean?"

He shrugs. "Monica said I am too alone. Well, she said this in French, it translates a little differently. But basically, that I don't need anyone else but myself, and this is a problem."

Monica is his old girlfriend. They broke up a few months before he started dating me, after three long years with her in Paris and him at Yale. His debacle with Monica was an indictment against the concept of long-distance relationships, as far as Jean Luc was concerned. Which is why we broke up in the first place. Now it appears he's decided to repeat the experiment. "You're self-sufficient," I point out. "That's a good thing."

"It was more than that, though. She called me 'emotionally stupid.'"

"What?" I chew on a celery stalk from my basket. "Now that has to be a mistranslation."

"Yes, I suppose you are right. She said I have no 'emotional intelligence.' Not the same as stupid, I guess. What do you think of this—emotional intelligence?"

I have to pause on this one. Jean Luc once admitted to me that his laboratory sometimes felt more real to him than the outside world, "the one with trees, buildings, and people," he said. And the funny thing is that I understood him. After a lifetime of people waving their hands in front of my eyes, asking, "Hello? Anybody home?" and parents and teachers scolding, "Are you even listening to a word I'm saying?" Suffice it to say, I'm in my head a lot. But as a budding psychiatrist, I have emotional intelligence in spades. Jean

Luc is masterful at solving problems, but he is hopeless at understanding people. So maybe his ex has a point.

"I don't know," I say. "It's something you might want to work on."

At this, Jean Luc drops his head in his hands and bursts into laughter, his hair falling into his eyes. This is not at all the response I expected, but then, he is getting a bit pink-faced and drunk. "I'll be right back," he says, standing up to walk to the bathroom. I turn my head to follow him and notice my vision swimming, which makes me regret ordering my last drink.

A group of men at the next table shout out laughing, their faces flushed from heat, beer, and wings. The waitress brings by our new frosty beer mugs just as Jean Luc returns to the table, drying his hands on his jeans. There is a hole at his knee, pale skin peeking through. "I like these. What do you call them, 'wings'?" His bowl is a mess of chicken bones.

"You want to try one of mine?"

"Sure," he says, reaching over.

"They're hot, be careful."

Jean Luc takes a bite and in seconds starts coughing, his eyes filling with tears. "What is wrong with this?" he asks, grabbing for his beer.

"I warned you they were hot."

"That is not hot," he argues, sticking out his tongue and fanning it, which doesn't help. I know; I've tried. "This is more like unbearable."

"Unbearable is their Armageddon sauce. I had that on my wings once. Almost needed CPR."

"Zoe," he says, hoarsely, grabbing my hand. His eyes are still watering.

"Don't worry. I'll get medium next time. You just have to get used to it."

"No, no, it is not the sauce." He looks down at the table, then back up at me. "Listen, I should never have gotten involved with Melanie. She was all wrong for me, and it was a bad thing to do to Robbie. And to *you*, obviously," he adds, his emotional intelligence catching up with him. "You know me. I am not usually like that."

I nod, finishing off my last wing. "I don't disagree with you."

"I wanted to say I'm sorry. But I'm also not sorry, because it helped me see something very important. Something I hadn't seen clearly before, and perhaps I needed that variable to demonstrate it."

"Okay?" I say. I'm not sure what he's getting at, but I think he is comparing me to a chemistry experiment.

"It is this: I love you."

There is a pause, the music blaring around us, as I realize he never has said this in English before, though I always assumed he meant the same thing in French. Maybe he didn't, though.

"*Je t'aime*, too," I answer, and he gives me a bleary smile.

We walk back to the apartment, which is harder than it sounds on crutches in the snow. The snow is postcard perfect. The streetlights shine through the snow in a winsome blur, his hand steady on my elbow, until we finally get to the sidewalk that Scotty must have shoveled. The heavy oak door opens to the quiet apartment, and we head up to my bedroom

261

and sit on my bed. We stare at each other in the dark. The room is silent except for our breathing, and I grab the rough fabric of his shirt and kiss him hard, with something more than desire, something like desperation. As if I want to kiss every inch of skin on his body and mark him as mine.

Chapter Thirty-Two

The morning dawns gray and cloudy, with my head pounding and my stomach queasy. The bed is empty. "Jean Luc?"

"*C'est moi*," he answers, and seconds later he walks in with two steaming mugs of coffee. I forgot he was a morning person.

"One sugar and one creamer. Am I right?"

"You are right," I say. "And *trés* thoughtful." I take a long draught of coffee, which Jean Luc has made ultrastrong as usual, but which calms the thrumming in my temples now beating in time with my foot. "How did you sleep?" I ask, my voice husky from last night's beer and hot sauce.

"Not so good," he answers with a shrug. "Too much to drink. You?"

"Same," I answer.

He is sitting at my desk, drinking his coffee and reading through the *Sunday Times*. An image of him whispering into his cell phone in my desk chair from last night pops into my

263

mind. The visual is grainy, like a hallucinatory dream, mixed with a night of alcohol-laced anxiety dreams.

"Were you on the phone last night or something?" I ask.

"No." He shakes the newspaper straight. "Perhaps you dreamed it."

"Maybe."

"So what should we do today?" Jean Luc asks, flipping a page of the newspaper, the corner wilting over.

"I don't know. You're leaving tomorrow, right?"

"Yes, in the morning, to avoid the traffic." He moves the paper so I see half of his face.

"Okay." I mentally peruse things to do in Buffalo when a crazy idea strikes. "How about a trip to Cleveland?"

Jean Luc raises an eyebrow. "Cleveland? I don't know," he hedges. "It seems like a long drive for the rock-and-roll things."

"No." I laugh. "To see my birth mother. Well, I don't know if she's my birth mother. My maybe–birth mother."

His eyebrows furrow with unease. "How does this follow again?"

"You remember the facial recognition I was telling you about?"

"Right," he says slowly, dipping back into the conversation from last night's debauchery.

"It's the last one from the program. Sylvia Nealon."

Jean Luc's jaw clenches, and he flips another page.

"Or what the hell," I say. "We don't have to. It's a stupid idea. We could go to Niagara Falls if you want."

He lowers the paper, staring out the window. "No, let's do it. Let's go to Cleveland."

"You sure?"

"Yes, Zoe. If I can help you, then I should help you. Let's go find your mother."

His face contorts with dismay. "She doesn't know we are coming?" Jean Luc has always been an open book. A psychiatrist's dream.

"Sort of," I lie. "Well, I left quite a few messages, but she never exactly answered."

"Oh," he answers doubtfully, as Karin reminds him to turn left in three-quarters of a mile.

I wipe the powdered sugar off my lips from our Tim Hortons doughnut run. Jean Luc takes dainty bites of a croissant and leaves the other half in the bag. His car is pristine, unlike mine, which looks like a mixture of my office and a locker, and somewhere a homeless person might live. I had wanted to pack some goodies and magazines but he said, "Why would we do this? There are stores on the way, no? If we are hungry?" Completely missing the point of a road trip, even a three-hour one.

We listen to NPR while I rearrange my cast in a million uncomfortable ways and try to ignore the burbling in my stomach, which may be a consequence of my hangover or a response to the impending reunion with my maybe–birth mother. When I see the sign for Cleveland, I want to puke. We pass by stately brick homes with stately brown trees, then by scaled-down suburban new builds for scaled-down American dreams, and finally to rows of cramped, beat-up houses with dirt-streaked vinyl siding, for those who have just about given up on the American dream.

Karin states that we have arrived, and the nerves squeeze in my chest. Jean Luc pulls to a stop on the opposite side of the street, and we both stare at the house as if we're on a stakeout. I stretch my legs and take a deep breath.

"Do you want me to come in with you?" Jean Luc asks, though I can tell the thought makes him nervous.

"No, she probably won't even be home. You stay. I'll be right back." I hobble out the door and across the slushy street. Another doorstop, another mother. I stare at the door a moment, at the peeling, pale lavender paint. The stoop is covered with fungus-ridden Astroturf, like all the other stoops in the row. Breathing in deeply, I am about to ring the bell when the door swings open and a woman steps out.

At first glance, I know this is my mother. I know it in my bones. She is the picture, aged twenty years, standing before me. Her frizzy hair is a head full of black curls now, veined with wiry grays. The sun is bright, shining behind her, framing her head like a halo. I stand there staring slack-jawed at my mother, who obviously did not die in a fire or otherwise, and incidentally does not recognize me.

"Hello?" she says. It is not a nice hello. It is an annoyed, "What are you doing on my doorstep staring at me?" hello.

"I'm Zoe Goldman."

"Okay. I'm Sylvia Nealon. Can I help you with something?" She has a thick New York accent.

"Um. I did leave a few messages, but I never heard back so..."

"Oh," she says, looking at me anew. "*You're* the one leaving those freaky messages on the machine?"

"Yes, well, I saw your picture on the Internet, and you look just like my mother, and I'm looking for my mother, and I thought maybe you were her." I could not sound more imbecilic. I thrust the picture out toward her, the one of me and my frizzy-haired mom, almost toppling off my crutches to do so.

"How did you get this picture?" she asks, suspicious now.

I'm too shocked to answer.

"I repeat: How did you get this picture?"

"From my adoptive parents," I say as calmly as possible to calm her down, too. The picture sways in the breeze as she grips it. "It's the only picture I have of my birth mother before she died. She was killed in a fire, at least that's what I was told, and so that's me, right there, five days old. The baby. That's from—"

"Wait," she says, cutting me off. "Break here. Hold on a second. That is my picture, and that is a baby, but that is not you, baby doll. I don't know who you are, or what you are trying to pull over on me here, but that is my daughter, Robyn."

Here we gaze at each other in silence, miles of bewildered confusion between us. As if the earth tilted off its axis, and we are in parallel worlds.

"My parents gave me the picture," I repeat, like a robot.

Sylvia turns over the photo. "And who in the hell wrote on the back?"

I swallow. "My adoptive mom."

267

"And who's your adoptive mom?"

"My mom is Sarah Goldman, used to be Meyers. And my dad died. But his name was Terry Goldman."

She pauses. "Terry Goldman? From GIK Finance?"

That was the name of Dad's consulting group, for Goldman, Irwin, and Kennedy. "Yes, yes, that's right."

"He was my boss," Sylvia says.

"I don't...I don't understand."

"Join the club, honey. I spent two years as a secretary at that office when I lived in Syracuse. Terry was my boss. I had the baby around that time, and he must have got ahold of the picture somehow."

"Oh," I say, confused. So my father *stole* her picture and pretended she was my mother? Why in God's name would he do that?

"I quit soon after anyway."

"How did you end up in Cleveland then?"

"It's been twenty years, honey," she says. "I relocated for my husband. Who went and took off with his secretary. Asshole," she mutters, leaning her arm on the spindly, black iron railing. "Not that it's any of your business."

"No, I suppose not," I say in a daze.

"Your father wasn't so bad, though. He was a nice-enough guy. I'm sorry to hear that he died."

I nod slowly, as if there is gauze around my head. "Car accident," I mumble.

A sports car with red spoilers speeds by us on the street, as if it's on the autobahn and not a broken-down, outer-ring suburb of Cleveland. I get a glimpse in Sylvia's doorway of white walls, shiny black furniture. It smells like cigarettes. "I still don't understand how you thought I was your mother, though," she says.

I adjust my crutches, taking some weight off my armpits. "I don't know either. It's just what I was told."

"That's pretty screwed up," she says.

And for the first time in the visit, I fully agree with her. "Can I keep the picture?" I ask as an afterthought.

Sylvia pauses, considering, and hands it to me. "Why not?" she says. "I have enough pictures of Robyn. This one reminds me of the asshole anyway." She steps back in the door, and as I pivot on my crutches on the Astroturf to leave, she calls out, "Hey, good luck finding your mother."

"Thanks," I say and turn to hobble off her step, grateful, at least, that it wasn't her. When I get in the car, Jean Luc is saying good-bye quickly in French and powering off his phone.

"How did it go?" he asks.

⌐

Jean Luc is in my bedroom finishing up a few e-mails before dinner when I hear his footsteps shuffle down the stairs. I'm thumbing through *Archives of General Psychiatry*, where I have just learned that in a questionnaire study of a hundred patients with insomnia, 92 percent claim to be tired during the day. Staggering. I wonder how much government funding the researchers absconded with for that study.

"Zoe, we need to talk," Jean Luc says, dropping his packed-up duffel bag on the floor. The thud hits me like a sucker punch.

"What about?" My psychiatry journal flaps shut on my lap.

He shoves his hands in his jeans pockets, jangling his car keys. His light-blue spring coat is half-zipped. "This isn't working."

I stare at him, stunned. "What do you mean?"

Jean Luc pauses, looking down at his brown leather shoes, which have dark stains from the snow. "I'm sorry, Zoe. I don't know what to say. Today just felt..." He searches for the word in English. "Not right. You could feel it, too, couldn't you? Like we just could not connect to each other?"

"Today wasn't the most spectacular, I'll admit," I say. "But I mean, consider the circumstances."

"Yes, maybe." He sounds resigned.

I sigh. "I should never have dragged you there, Jean Luc. It's my fault. Next time we'll go to Niagara Falls. How about this, let's do steak tonight, okay? No sushi."

He looks at me in a sad silence.

"Why, were you planning on leaving right now?"

"I think it would be best."

I stare into the blue gas flames, trying to piece together what exactly happened here, where things fell apart. The ride home was quiet, but not uncomfortably so, and I wasn't exactly in a chatty mood. Just now I figured we were relaxing before dinner. And...

"Who was on the phone, Jean Luc?"

270

He doesn't answer, bending down to straighten out the twisted luggage tag.

"In the car, after I saw Sylvia Nealon. Who was that?"

"Oh, no one," he says, color flooding into his cheeks. Again, the proverbial open book.

"Let me guess," I say. "Three syllables, starts with an M."

He looks up at me. "It is not what you think."

"Yeah, right," I say. "It's exactly what I think. She calls, and you come running."

"I was leaving tomorrow anyway," he argues.

"Obviously you can't stand to be here another second."

Jean Luc doesn't say any more, just stands in the middle of the room, his shadow a beastly profile on the wall.

"It was her on the phone last night," I say. "Wasn't it?"

Jean Luc doesn't say anything but at least has the decency to look guilty.

"So what was last night then at the restaurant? What was the 'Now I see how much I love you' all about?"

Still he is silent.

"Was that part of the experiment? You introduced a variable and got the wrong result?" I slap the journal onto the coffee table, standing up from the couch with some difficulty. "I bet I wasn't even the variable at all...I was probably the fucking control group!"

He swallows. "Zoe, I'm not sure I understand the protocol—"

"You know what? Don't call me. Don't text. Don't ask me to Skype. When she dumps you for Mr. Washington again, I don't want to hear about it. It is over. Not maybe it's over,

Sandra Block

maybe it's not. Maybe I love you, maybe I don't. It's over. *C'est fini*. I was doing just fine before you decided to swoop in and fuck up my life."

Jean Luc stares at me, and the grandfather clock gongs out five long tones. "I am sorry, Zoe," he says, waiting for an answer, but I have none to give. He loops the duffel over his shoulder, zips his jacket, and walks out the door. I hear the trunk slam shut, the engine start, and then he is gone.

Chapter Thirty-Three

W as she wearing purple?" Jason asks.

He is inquiring about my manic patient, Claudia, who is improving. This morning at least she didn't way the word "whore" once, and I could get a word in "edgily" as Dr. A would say. And she is back to accepting medications into the holy temple of her body. As usual, we are waiting in the resident room for Dr. Grant to start Professor Rounds. A week after my disastrous Jean Luc/not-birth-mother reunion, I am back in the saddle at work.

"No," I say, thinking back. "A pink sundress. Why?"

"I have a theory. All manic women wear purple."

I raise my eyebrows. "Wow, that's reductionist."

Dr. A looks up from the DSM V that he is halfway through memorizing. "Zoe! That is an excellent use of the word 'reductionist.'"

"Thank you."

"You people are beyond help," Jason mutters, pulling out his phone to check e-mail.

"You're wearing purple," I point out, noticing his lavender shirt and matching tie. "So does that mean *you're* manic?"

"No, that means I'm gay."

Dr. A shakes his head at us as if we are children, and just then Dr. Grant sticks his head in the doorway unexpectedly. "Dr. Goldman, can I see you for a moment?"

"Sure," I say, standing up clumsily on my leg.

"Let's go in my office," he says. Dr. A and Jason watch us, thinking for sure I'm about to get fired. I am wondering what on earth I could have said to the manic patient. His office is cramped with piles of books stacked on the floor, as if a hoarder might live here. We sit across from each other with his desk, which is buried under academic articles, between us. He has a poorly drawn cartoon framed above his desk with a lightbulb saying "Q: How many psychiatrists does it take to change a lightbulb? A: One, but it has to really want to change." Despite myself, I chuckle.

"Zoe," he says. I realize he has never called me by my first name. "I wanted to talk to you about your patient."

"Claudia?" I swallow. "I think we're getting somewhere, but we still have a few weeks for the meds to really kick in and—"

"No, no, not that one. Sofia Vallano."

"Oh, okay. What is it?"

"Well," he says, pulling some large drawings from the side of his desk. "It appears she may have developed a sort of unhealthy attraction to you."

"Oh?"

Dr. Grant pushes some charcoal pictures my way, and I lean over to look. There are about ten pictures in all.

In one, I am smiling, my stethoscope hanging lopsided on my neck, mid-speech, seriously engaged in therapy. Another shows me standing tall, framed by the doorway, even catching the sheen of my name tag. Sofia has nailed every detail: my minimally uneven incisor, my eyes looking round and fishlike when I get excited, the slant of my lab coat against my chest, pockets stuffed with papers.

One in particular strikes me. I am sitting, thoughtful, by the window. My face is pale against the night sky, the moon a white ball in the corner of the page. The shadow of the tree branches can just be seen reflecting off the wall beside me. This must have been from the one time I went to see her at night, when she told me about her father.

"Interesting," I say, leafing through them. Maybe I have made more of an impression on her than I thought. "They are intense. But innocent, I would think. What did she say about them?"

Dr. Grant rubs his hands together. "She said she connected with you."

Her words come back to me. "I like you, Dr. Goldman." But was that *like* like?

"It's funny. I feel like we haven't really connected at all."

He clears his throat and inches his chair closer to the desk. "I do have to ask, in these circumstances…" There is a pause. I know what he is going to ask, and it is horrifying. "Is there any type of"—he barks out a cough—"romantic relationship, possibly, between you?"

"No," I say. Once, firmly, that's all. No explanation needed.

"Okay." He looks relieved. Then he quickly adds, "If there

were, we could talk about it. It's not an uncommon part of the transference/countertransference process. Even if it's emotions that haven't been acted on yet. That's the best time to catch it."

"No, Dr. Grant. I appreciate your concern, but I don't have any strong emotional attachment to Sofia Vallano." Other than the fact that she's invaded my hypnosis sessions and my nightmares.

He bites his lip, thinking. "You know, the pictures might actually be a positive sign then. A signal that she is trying to connect with people again."

"Maybe," I say, though I'm not so sure.

"In any case, I'm transferring her to Jason on Monday, just to be on the safe side." He puts his hands on the desk as if he's about to stand up.

"Actually, there is something about Sofia that I wanted to discuss."

He drops his hands back on his lap. "All right."

"I just"—I say, struggling with how to put this best and decide to keep it simple—"I just don't like her."

Dr. Grant smiles, then stops, trying to be serious for my sake. "Empathy, Zoe, is something we can work on. It doesn't come naturally with every patient, especially one like this. There are exercises we can do, steps we can take. Sometimes, honestly, you just have to fake it."

"So here's the scoop, Zoe." It's my high school friend Parker, the Syracuse reporter extraordinaire. No one else would actually call it a "scoop."

"Yes," I say, reaching for the back of my patient printout to write down notes. I push Sofia Vallano's chart to the side, and it sticks to some invisible stain on the Formica table at the nurses' station.

"Here's the short version: I can find no evidence of a fire."

"Really?" Dizziness washes over me. "Are you sure?"

I hear banter in the background, laughter. No typewriters, though, because this isn't the movies. "I only got a couple of minutes here, but I'll tell you what I found. I went back through all the potential years, from a few years before your birth to five years later."

"And there were no Syracuse fires in all that time?"

"I'm not saying that," he clarifies, a bit testy. "There were a dozen restaurants with suspicious fires, arson of a suspected heroin den, several house fires, but definitely nothing at the address you gave me. It was a new build, you're right there. But the land had been a wilderness preserve for a rare tree species, fought over for years before a new pro-business mayor came on board and the rules changed. That was the big news on that address, if you can call that news."

"And nearby, no fires?"

"A young mother dies in a fire? We would have found it, Zoe. Nothing that fits your description. Sorry."

I pause. "What about the article on it?"

"Oh yeah," Parker says. "That's another thing. We

couldn't find that file in the archives at all. Same with the obituary."

A nurse comes into the room, grabs an IV bag, and leaves again. "What do you mean? Was it lost maybe? Do your archives go back that far?"

"Yes, they do," he says. "We have issues saved from that year, but that article wasn't in there. Neither was the obituary. In fact, they don't even look like actual articles from our paper."

"I don't understand."

"It's weird. The header is from our paper; that's for sure. But the margins are off, and they have a different font than we were using back then."

"So you're saying the articles aren't real?"

"That's what I'm saying. I think somebody cobbled them together, forged them. Maybe someone gave your parents fake copies or something? I don't know."

Or maybe my parents gave *me* fake copies.

I hear Parker's name yelled out in the background. "Hey, I really got to go. Call me later if you need to."

"Yeah, thanks," I say, staring at what I have written on the back of my patient list.

No fire
Suspicious fire restaurants
Heroin den arson
New build, new mayor
Fake article?????

It looks like a bizarre haiku. My life feels like a bizarre haiku.

I open Sofia's chart again when a familiar form walks by with his usual confident stride: Mike. He leans over the counter across from me, pointing at my cast. "I distinctly remember stating, 'No work for one month.'"

"It's *been* a month," I argue.

"It's been two weeks."

"Oh well, you know. A month, two weeks..."

"You were bored?"

"To death."

Mike swings around into the nurses' station, looks through the chart rack, grabs a chart, and sits next to me, perusing it. "How's the leg doing, anyway?"

"Okay." I start my note while he flips through pages of his chart. The fluttering of the pages echo in the silence. "You know, Mike?"

"Yes, Zoe."

"I'm sorry if I was a jerk before. I was just...in the process of getting over someone."

"Would this be the Frenchman your mom was so fond of?"

"One and the same."

Mike keeps flipping through his chart. "And where might the Frenchman be now?"

"Back in DC," I say. "With his new girlfriend."

Now he looks up from the chart. "Apology accepted."

"So, in that vein, I was thinking we could maybe try the dinner thing again."

Mike slaps shut the chart and grins at me. "Why, Dr. Zoe Goldman, are you asking me out on a date?"

Sandra Block

"What are you doing next Saturday?"

"Hmmm, let me think." He looks up at the ceiling. "Nothing. Did I let an appropriate number of seconds go by before admitting that?"

I smile. "I think you're in the clear."

"So what are we doing?" he asks.

"Dinner, my house, seven sharp."

"*You're* making dinner?" he says, not hiding his disbelief.

"What, you think I can't cook?"

Mike stands. "I guess we'll just have to see," he says with a grin and walks down the hall, whistling.

BOOK FOUR: FEBRUARY

Chapter Thirty-Four

My mom is putting together a puzzle. I think it is a kitty. She never used to like puzzles ("What a goddamn enormous waste of time") or kitties in the past, but that was all BD. We have some time to visit before my "hot date with Mike," as Scotty called it. Scotty actually likes Mike, whom he deems "a million times better than Frog-Boy." Sun streams through the curtains of the window, striping the varnished table. My mom maneuvers another piece while Scotty works on a corner. I toy with a couple pieces myself.

"How did you break your leg?" My mom looks up at me from the puzzle, tapping one of the pieces on the table. This is the third time she has asked me this visit, and I am not counting the previous visits.

"I was running." I leave out the horse part this time; that was just too confusing. And admittedly, even for a person without dementia, the scene was confusing.

"Why were you running?"

"Exercise. Mom, you know I run."

"So you weren't running away from anyone?"

"No. Why would I be running away from anyone? I was just running, you know."

"Okay. You were running, I get it."

Scotty already has a good chunk of the corner done. I keep getting mismatches for my one piece. I have never been good at puzzles. The cafeteria doors open, and a strong meaty smell wafts through the air.

"Meatloaf, my favorite," my mom says, sounding like her BD sarcastic self.

I finally find a match and search through the pile for another. Scotty has assembled the mouse kitty toy. My mom is working on a cloud. I think I'm making a whisker. "So, Mom," I say, unsure how to proceed.

Scotty shoots me a warning glance, which I ignore.

"About the fire."

"Yes, dear," she answers, sliding around her cluster of pieces.

"*Was* there actually a fire?" I ask.

She doesn't answer for a bit, searching for another piece, though it occurs to me she might be stalling. "Of course there was a fire."

Scotty is silent. He is irked at my "obsessive" insistence on finding my real mother, but since the facial recognition fiasco, he himself admits the pieces aren't adding up.

"It's just...I researched it, Mom, and there was no fire at the address you gave me."

"Maybe you got the address wrong."

"No," I counter. "I didn't."

"Then maybe I got the address wrong. Zoe, it was over twenty years ago. I told you I've been having memory problems," she says, her volume escalating.

"Okay." I slap the picture of my supposed mother down onto the table. The frizzy-haired mother, who in truth used to be my father's secretary and who left me devastated, with sore armpits, on her disintegrating Astroturf porch. And by the way, the adorable, puffy-eyed, five-day-old is named Robyn, not Zoe. "Who is this?" I ask.

Mom drops her puzzle pieces, the cloud falling apart. Scotty pushes away the cat toy he was creating. The room is emptying, walkers inching toward the dining room, aides coming and rolling patients away. "What are you asking me, Zoe? What do you want me to tell you?"

"The truth," I say, staring right into her eyes. "That's all I've ever wanted."

Mom chews on her bottom lip. Tears spring up in her eyes. One pools over and a tear falls onto the tip of her nose. She wipes it away, as if she's surprised to find it there. "Zoe, I'm sorry. I love you, honey. I love you more than anything. I don't know what else to tell you. *I'm* your mother, honey. *I'm* your mother." Then she starts really crying.

Scotty flashes me a look of pure disgust, which is exactly how I feel about myself right now. I scoop up the photo without a word and put my arm around my broken, breaking-down mother. She is my real mom, she's right. Maybe there was no fire. Maybe there was no Beth Winters. Just a reborn version of the best friend she killed. But *here* is my real mom, right in front of me, and I am making her cry. And maybe she had her reasons for lying. And maybe she doesn't even remember the reasons anymore. Sam is right: You would do anything for your kids. Anything. Maybe it's time to take his advice and assume the best.

"I'm sorry, Mom," I say, rubbing her bony shoulders, noticing how thin she has grown. "I love you, too. I don't care about the fire. I don't care about any of it."

She nods, her hiccups calming. We continue working on the puzzle in silence. Scotty has nearly half of it done, and my mom has reassembled her whole cloud, cotton floating through a blue puzzle sky. I was wrong about the whisker; I'm not sure what I'm making. She looks up at me, then at my cast, her face registering surprise. "How did you break your leg?"

A sweetish smell floats up from the crinkly plastic as I unwrap the flowers.

The sunset is a cold pink, mixed with creamy orange, the same color as the flowers. I am almost done tidying the apartment, dusting side tables, piling books and magazines, vacuuming in high-traffic areas. I'm not the cleanest person alive, as Scotty would attest, but I'm making an effort. I spritz some air freshener in every corner for good measure, then admire the bouquet on the dining room table. Flowers do spruce up the place.

Scotty is over at Random Girl #38's house tonight, and

Mike is coming at seven. Mike was right: I don't make a mean manicotti, or a mean anything, except maybe a mean tuna-fish sandwich, and I'm guessing that's not what he had in mind for our romantic dinner. Scotty (an excellent cook, actually) taught me how to make my own marinara, which isn't bad, so I'm going for simple: angel hair pasta with marinara. It's not going as well as planned, however. Chopping the tomatoes, I am making a watery mess. Scotty always made this part seem effortless (though maybe he wasn't using a bread knife) while I was very helpful at pouring the wine, or even going as far as to lay out some cheese and crackers on a plate. The sky has darkened to blue-black out of the square of the kitchen window, the outline of two planets shining through like dot-to-dots. My cell phone rings. It is the number for the hospital, the psych floor.

"Hello?"

"Hello, is this Dr. Goldman?" a female voice asks.

"This is."

"Yes, all right. We know you're not on call, but we're having a bit of an issue over here."

"Okay?"

"Your patient Sofia Vallano—do you remember her?"

"Yes, I remember her." To say the least.

"She says she refuses to take any of her meds unless she sees you."

"Did you call the on-call doc?"

"Dr. A is here. She won't listen to him."

"So one night without meds won't kill her. I can see her in the morning."

"She said she would hurt herself."

I give my leg a ferocious scratch. It tends to act up when I'm annoyed. "Did she specify?"

"No, she didn't."

"Can you make her a one-on-one?"

"Listen," the nurse says, not unkindly, but tired of the conversation. "I already ran through all this with Dr. Grant. I asked if it would be okay to miss one night of medication. I asked if we could put her one-on-one tonight."

"And what did he say? Did he tell you she's not even going to be my patient after this weekend?"

"Yes, he did. He said as of tonight she still is your patient, and he would like you to come in and work with her."

I clench my teeth, wanting to throw a tomato at him. If this is one of Dr. Grant's tricks for teaching empathy, it's not effective. I am feeling lots of things, but empathy is not one of them. I look at the grandfather clock and figure I should be okay if I delay the date by an hour. Worst-case scenario, I could call in pizza, my usual dinner fare. "Fine. I'll be there."

I send out a text to Mike. Something stupid came up with patient. Make it 8?

His answer pings right back. NP. Watching bad reality TV. No hurry.

Then a :) comes on my phone screen, and I send one right back. And as I march out into the frigid night air to face my manipulative, narcissistic, sociopathic, matricidal patient, I am smiling like an emoticon.

Chapter Thirty-Five

The snow wafts up in ghostly drifts.

It is a steep trek up the ER parking ramp, something I never noticed before breaking my foot. The wind pushes me back, my crutches slipping in the newly fallen snow. The flag in the distance bangs against the pole, a rhythmic tong, tong, tong, like a bell. Long wisps of clouds race against the sky.

I pass Dr. A on the way to Sofia's room.

"I am tremendously sorry," he says.

"That's okay. Thanks for trying."

He shakes his head with some consternation. "I think it was inappropriate to call on you. One night without meds is not the biggest deal in the century. And I also doubt her claim to hurt herself. I suggested a one-on-one aide for her."

"As did I," I say, shrugging. "I'm here, no big deal. You might as well go home."

"Unfortunately, this is not within the cards tonight. Consult on eight north." He adjusts his metal clipboard. Dr. A always has a clipboard.

"Let me guess," I say. "Delirium."

"Most probably so," he answers with a smile and heads to the elevators.

So there is nowhere left to go except Sofia's room. And I don't have a ton of time to work with, considering I drove through a blizzard and hiked up Mount Kilimanjaro to get here.

"So," I say, entering the room. I sit down, leaning my crutches against the wall, and dispensing with chitchat. "What's up?"

Sofia is sitting on the edge of the bed, legs dangling, rubbing her feet together. Her pajama cuffs are dirty. "I want to talk to you about the pictures," she says, just meeting my eyes.

"Okay. Go ahead."

She crosses her arms, and I see goose bumps running up and down them. The room is cold and gray. The one dim overhead light buzzes and flickers at random times, about to burn out. Through her window is a blackening sky, icy white moon. Like the moon in her picture.

"It's not what you think."

"Okay. Tell me about it." I reach over and prop up my crutches, which were threatening to slide down the wall.

"It's not about being in love with you," Sofia says stridently, almost angrily.

"Okay." I pause. "I didn't think it was, if that makes you feel any better."

She picks up the pink nail file lying on her blanket and starts mindlessly filing. "Dr. Grant made it sound so bad. But it wasn't bad," she insists, "I just...I just have a connection to you."

"A connection is good," I agree.

Scrape, scrape, scrape.

"So what is this business about not taking your medications then?" I ask.

Sofia keeps filing. "I didn't know how else to get through to you," she says, which is honest at least.

"Okay," I say, thinking, It couldn't have waited until Monday, until after my date? "So you got me here. Anything else going on?" I scoot my chair farther in toward her, which is an awkward effort with my cast. She inches closer toward me on her bed. It is unclear who is mirroring whom.

"I just needed to talk to you."

"Okay. Tell me." I fight the urge to look at my watch. The caged clock above her bed is calling out to me like a siren.

Sofia stops filing, and the light flickers again. "Do you really not know?" she asks, with a hint of desperation.

"I don't think so."

"You don't know me at all?"

"I don't understand what you mean, Sofia."

"You don't know me," she repeats.

"I know you," I say.

"No, you don't." Sofia lets out a bitter laugh. "You don't know shit."

I swallow, unsure how the conversation took this turn, but I need to get out of this room in twenty minutes for a date, whether she takes her damn meds tonight or not. I am way past being concerned about empathy. I shift in the chair to adjust my leg. "Tell me, Sofia. Tell me what I don't know. I can't help you if you won't tell me."

"I'm not looking for your help."

"No?" I ask. "Then I'm at a bit of a loss here. What are you looking for? I'm not angry about the pictures, if that's what this is about."

Sofia turns to look out the window, filing her nails again. The grating sound fills the room. Squeaky sharp, like fingernails on a chalkboard. "Did you recognize the moon? In the one picture?"

"Yes, actually. I was thinking that when I walked into the room tonight. You captured the moon quite nicely."

"I'm not talking artistic technique here," she says. "Did you *recognize* it?"

"What do you mean?"

"Did you recognize the moon," she says slowly, "from that night?"

"From which night?"

"From which night?" she repeats in a mocking tone. "I thought you, of all people, would remember the moon on that night, Tanya. Tanya Vallano."

My mouth goes dry as dust. "What did you just call me?"

"I'm afraid you may have developed an unhealthy attachment to your doctor here, which is completely normal, very understandable, I might add," Sofia says, doing a bad, nasal Dr. Grant imitation. "Please." She draws out the word with the disgust. "As if I'd want to fuck my own sister."

My whole body trembles, and I feel weightless, light, floating. My body has disconnected from my brain.

"What?" She laughs. "You think you're invisible? You think I wouldn't find you eventually? I may not have gone to Yale, but I'm not stupid, Tanya. Or wait a second, I'm sorry, not-Tanya. I'm supposed to call you 'Dr. Goldman.'"

Words falls out of her mouth, a waterfall of words. I watch her lips moving. I cannot process them. My brain will not hear them.

"You really didn't recognize me," Sofia says with disbelief. "I thought you were just playing me, and playing me damn well. I'll admit, I was actually impressed. And then, when you didn't break the facade for Jack, your big hero of a brother, I started to wonder. Maybe you weren't trying to play me. Maybe, just maybe, you really didn't remember me."

I am seeing the eye patch, Jack's face, aging backward into a young boy, wiry, scared. The boy from her picture, hurling his body over mine and screaming, "No, Sofia, stop!" I can hear him shrieking and see him hunched over, holding his hand over his eye. Blood streaming between his fingers.

"Sofia," I say, remembering.

She smiles, the warmest smile I have seen yet. "Now you remember me."

↩

The scene gels together in slow motion, jagged pieces coming together like a mirror breaking backward.

My mommy is screaming, the sound of fabric tearing, over and over, and her screaming every time. It looks as if Sofia is punching her with a knife. (The big, shiny knife in the drawer my mom told me never to touch. "Sharp," she said, explaining. "Don't touch.") Spots of violet bloom on my mom's dress, spreading together. She falls against a mirror on the wall. Pieces crashing, breaking.

"Run," Mommy whispers to me. I see my reflection broken up and grotesque in the pieces of mirror on the floor. "Hide." Her voice is hoarse, fading. Her blue, blue eyes clouding over, losing focus. I remember my mother's face.

I run, I hide. I hardly understand what this means, but I always do what Mommy tells me to do. My feet scurry up the stairs, well-worn, green-carpeted stairs, my socks slipping down off my heels. I don't know where to go, but a deep force steers me away from Sofia's room. Sofia is nice and not-nice. Sometimes she fills me with happy warmth, deep-blue eyes I trust. Sometimes she turns cold, not-nice, and I don't want to be near her. Her room down the hall is blaring dark orchestral music. I smell a spicy, warm, cedary aroma floating from her room. Pencil sticks with wisps of smoke curling up on top, a column of ash. Thinner than my mom's cigarettes. ("Incense, don't touch," Sofia told me once when I reached out to play with these long, maroon, hard sticks. "Hot, do you understand? Hot.")

I run into the laundry room, turn off the lights, shut the door as quietly as I can. The dryer is humming, a rhythmic sound. I crouch down beside it, leaning my whole body against it. It is warm, soothing. Moonlight streams through the window, spattering on the tile floor. The tree branches move on the floor, like witch *fingers. I hear footsteps and see a shadow slice through the light shining under the door.*

"Tanya?" I hear a sweet voice calling. Is it my mom? Or is it Sofia? I remember my mom's eyes, glazing over. It is Sofia. Run, Mom told me, hide.

"Tanya?" I hear again, but I do not answer. It is not-nice Sofia. She sometimes tries to trick me.

But the door flies open, bright light blinding me. I am shivering, teeth chattering, wetting myself, and afraid I will be in trouble for having an accident. Sofia grabs my wrist hard and yanks me into the hall. The music is hurting my ears, the smell, sickly sweet. I fall to my knees, stiff carpet brushing them, throw my hands up to protect myself and through the slats of my fingers see the silver knife edge glint in the overhead light. I stand up on wobbly legs to push her away, but the knife descends in lightning strokes, my fingers burning now, dripping onto my nightgown. I stare at my hands, are these my hands? Blood, slick, springing up from my hands. Blood, red as finger paint.

In the corner of my vision, I see Jack (best friend, always-nice Jack) talking on the phone. He is yelling into the phone. He is saying our address. I know our address. I memorized it in day care. Then Sofia turns from me and leaps at him, plunging forward with the knife again. He is screaming, holding his face, when she turns back to me, and he jumps on me, covering me with his heavy body. "It's okay," he whispers, blood pouring out of his face.

And then there are sirens, blasting, blaring sirens, drowning out the music from Sofia's room. And someone, an adult, is dragging Jack off me, and I am clinging to him and screaming "Mommy!" and my hands are burning. I see Sofia standing, ghost-pale, skinny elbows, staring in a daze without her knife, and someone (a fireman? How did a fireman get in here?) is wrapping a large white bandage around Jack's head, as if he is a mummy from Halloween. (He was actually a mummy last year, and I was Raggedy Ann.) Somehow we are downstairs now, and someone put a black sheet over Mom's head. I want to take it off, but they carry me away, and someone hands me my beloved Po-Po and we go in a car with a bed, and Jack is lying next to me, and voices are trying to talk softly to us, but there are so many voices.

And I just want my mommy.

"Mommy," I whisper.

"You're pathetic," Sofia says. "Your mommy isn't here, re-member? I killed her."

"But," I say, trying to focus on her face, "why?"

She laughs then, almost a cackle, not-nice Sofia. "You really want to know why?"

I nod, not trusting my voice to speak. I feel my knees trembling, even in my cast.

Sofia rises off the bed, slow and deliberate, so her face is inches away from me, eyes boring right into mine. "Because," she says, and I can feel her breath on my face, "I wanted to."

The scene tumbles back to the present as her hand reaches out and plunges the nail file in my neck. I cannot turn my head away quickly enough, as if I'm stuck in molasses in a nightmare. Jets of blood shoot out in pulses even as I feel the dull blade ripping my skin. I am clawing at Sofia with one hand, flinging the file out of my neck with the other, thinking in an oddly clinical manner: jugular or carotid? If it's carotid, I'm already dead. If it's jugular, I might have a chance.

I clutch at Sofia, desperately trying to gain a grip on something. I am clawing with all my might, a nose, an eye. I feel blood under my fingers and keep squeezing. I hear yelling. I don't know if it is Sofia or me. My mind is floating, my arm is going numb, tingly, but I keep squeezing. I cannot let go; I will not let go. There is the patter of feet running into the room, and I see brown, sensible leather shoes bounding toward me. I wonder what kind of shoes those are, then realize the absurdity of the question as possibly my last observation in life, and I feel myself floating.

I am not floating above my body. I am on a clear, deep, blue lake. Blue water sings around me. Jewel-blue skies high above me. The boat is small with a fresh coat of red paint. "Zoe" is written in black script on the corner. I am rowing, in perfect rhythm, my arm, my oar, the water, the sun, the sky, all one, all together. My brain is quiet, resting, at peace. I can hear my name, far, far in the distance, like an echo over a mountain.

"Zoe...Zoe...Zoe..."

But the call turns into a whisper, and then it stops.

Chapter Thirty-Six

I fade in and out.

I can't keep my eyes open. Beeping noises. Rough hands searching my arms for veins. Voices, sometimes loud, sometimes hushed, unintelligible. The face of my birth mother hovers over me, face blurred but concerned, her blue-blue eyes. Then I see my mom, BD, her face smiling, her warm hand holding mine, calling my name. I think I am alive, but I am not sure. I fight to keep my eyes open, but I usually lose. I don't know how long this goes on, could be hours, could be days.

Then one day, I open my eyes. I recognize the teal-blue tile, the gray walls with black scuff marks from inaccurate bed-drivers, and the thin, navy-blue blanket laying on me. First, I realize I am at the county hospital. Then I realize I am alive. Exhausted, worn down, but alive. My eyes move over to the window, and Scotty is asleep, lying in the chair, his head arched back with his Adam's apple sticking out.

"Scotty," I call out, but my voice is a hoarse whisper. "Scotty," I try again, and he bounces up from his chair. He runs over to the bed, hair disheveled, eyes bloodshot.

"You look like crap," I whisper, expecting a hearty *What the fuck, Zoe?* in return, but instead he reaches over, clutches my hospital gown, and starts crying. His face is buried in my chest, wetting my shoulder, head shaking. I am patting his head. "I was so afraid," he says, his breath ragged, sobbing.

"It's okay," I say back, patting his back now, though my arm is tired.

He cries into my chest for another long ten seconds, then takes a deep breath and gives my shoulder a squeeze, which is a little painful. He stumbles back into his chair, giving his eyes a vigorous rub. They are red and swollen.

A nurse bustles into the room, heading over to change the IV bag when she looks down. "You're awake!" she says. "I was wondering when you were going to join us."

"Could I have something to drink?" I ask, noticing my throat is bone-dry and sore. "Wait," I say to the nurse, the thought dawning on me, "was I intubated?"

"You sure were," she answers. "A drink I have to ask the doctor about. But these should do for now." She empties some ice chips into a Styrofoam cup. I scoop the icy pebbles up with my fingers, letting them melt on my tongue. I have seen ice chips adorning patients' bed stands for years. They become part of the furniture. But I have never actually tasted them. And let me tell you, they are delicious.

Scotty procures me another cup, and I keep chomping until my tongue is numb. He lumbers down in the chair next to me, yawning and crossing his long legs. He looks dog tired. "Do you mind if I put the TV on?" he asks.

"Sure," I say, yawning. He clicks through channels, each one thrumming a different ad, until he settles on—big surprise—hockey.

"I think I might rest a little more," I say, apologizing as if I have a guest over but can't quite stay awake. The odd thought shoots in my head that maybe someone drugged the ice chips.

"Go ahead," he says, patting my leg, his ring knocking against the cast.

"Hey," I call out before I can forget, "how is Sofia?"

The answers dribble in over the next two days, as I rejoin the land of the living.

Sofia severed my jugular, not my carotid, and Dr. A came to my rescue. He told the nurse he felt guilty when he heard I was still dealing with Sofia so he stopped back on the floor to see if he could help. Security was called when Dr. A heard screaming in the room: Sofia, it turns out, from me clawing her face off. Dr. A knelt down to find me pale and dying on the teal-blue tile and, in an instant, whipped out some prolene and a hemostat and stitched me right up on the hospital floor. It shames me to think that if the roles were reversed, I would have been ill equipped to save the day. I might have inquired, "So how do you feel about dying at the hands of your murderous sister? Should we try to reach some closure on this?" while leaning out of the way to avoid the spurting blood. But Dr. A is not afraid of blood, and of course he had his surgical bag on him "in case it ever comes in overhanded."

I am ready to leave the hospital already and have been telling anyone who comes near me about this desire, but my body is not quite on board with the plan. I walked three feet in physical therapy yesterday, and my good leg felt like jelly, with bones aching that I can't even name.

"Who are these from?" I gesture to the huge yellow-and-red bouquet on the side table. The sweet floral smell mixes with the stale smell of my hospital sheets.

"I don't know," Scotty says, flipping through a *Macworld* magazine.

I tear open the envelope with my finger, pulling out the little square card with boxy blue writing.

There are better ways to avoid me.

Mike

I laugh, which makes my chest ache.

"Oh, Jean Luc sent some, too." Scotty glances around. "They're here somewhere."

My heart does not cha-cha, fox-trot, or engage in any other dance. "You called him?"

"Yeah. We weren't sure at first, you know." He smooths out a page, then takes a picture of the ad with his phone camera. Because God forbid he write the information down manually.

I scratch at the tape on my hand, the IV tugging at my skin. "Does Mom know?"

Scotty looks up from his magazine. "I didn't tell her. I didn't want to say anything until I knew...either way," he says awkwardly.

"Yeah, I probably would have done the same."

There is a loud knock on the door and a burly man comes in, wearing a tie and jacket. His belly hangs over his belt as if he is pregnant, the buttons stretching over his "baby" and threatening to pop. "Zoe," he says, shaking my hand. His hand is huge, like a bear paw.

"Hi," I say, wondering if I am supposed to know him.

"Hey," says Scotty, who obviously does.

"Do you remember me?" he asks me.

"I'm sorry, no..."

"Detective Adams," he says. His voice is low and gravelly, but friendly. "Don't worry about it—you've been pretty out of it."

"I met you?"

"Said a couple of slurred words, more like," he says.

I attempt to sit up in the bed, which is a mistake. Pain shoots through the incision in my neck. The detective winces. "Quite a gash you got there," he says. And he's right, I saw myself in the bathroom mirror. The light was forgiving, but even so, I look like Frankenstein. Now the victim will have no problem describing me to the criminal sketch artist after I rob the liquor store. *She was tall, over six feet, nondescript features, but a very large, nasty scar on her neck.* "I have a couple of questions for you," he says. "If you don't mind."

"Sure," I say. "But can you tell me something?"

"I'll try," he says, which is different from yes.

"How is Sofia doing?"

He nods. "She's okay," he says but doesn't go any further. "Can you tell me what happened, from the beginning?" He grabs a spare chair next to Scotty and pulls it up beside my bed. He barely fits in it.

I tell him everything I remember, including the story of that night when I was four, and Sofia telling me she was my sister. Scotty's eyes are glued on me throughout the story. He has heard bits and pieces from me so far. The detective is scribbling in a notebook, the way they do on TV. I am surprised they don't have iPads by now.

He smooths his tie, a cheap maroon number. "How do you think she found you?"

"Honestly, I have no idea." I shift my casted leg, which is prickly and falling asleep. Every time I move, the bed tries to move with me with a mechanical moan. It is maddening, keeping me up all night. I will never forget to write sleepers for my patients ever again. "Do you know anything about how she found me?" I ask.

Detective Adams doesn't answer right away. "We have looked into it."

"And?"

"And it seems she has been following you for many years, since she was in the previous institution in Syracuse. She apparently had access to a library computer in the hospital, from someone in security."

Yeah, I'm sure Sofia was quite popular with the folks in security. "So she found out I was a doctor?"

"Actually, she's been following you for quite some time. We found Web-site hits all the way through college and medical school."

I shiver, as if someone walked on my grave. "And it's just a coincidence that she got transferred from Syracuse?" Of all the gin joints.

"Sort of," Detective Adams answers. "It wasn't a secret they were thinking of shutting down the hospital. It was all over the news in Syracuse for some time. They tried to save it, but when push came to shove, it was a for-profit hospital, and it wasn't making enough money. So they closed it."

"So you're saying she had time to plan."

"In a manner, yes. Sofia knew from a nurse she befriended that only the most stable patients were going to be transferred to Buffalo. The rest were going to Albany. So she had to shift gears and be on her very best behavior. She wasn't always such an angel. But she managed to convince everyone she had changed. She saw her golden opportunity, and she took it."

I am suddenly exhausted. My head is pounding along with the stitches on my neck. The metal clock above the whiteboard reads three o'clock. A quick calculation tells me it's about time to score another pain pill. "So can you tell me where Sofia is?"

"She's here, on another floor in the hospital."

"What?" I say, sitting up again, my bed moaning.

"Don't worry. There are two policemen with her. She's handcuffed to the bed. And no more nail files. That's a security breach that, believe me," he says, "will never happen again." He shakes his head and mutters, "Giving a psych patient a nail file..."

⟵

The room is blazing.

My body grows warm against the dryer, the whirring sound vibrating through me. My fingers smooth the hem of my favorite powder-blue, frilly nightgown.

The room is dark but lit up by the moonlight, spattered in checkers on the floor. I touch the cold tile to feel the moonlight, but it slips away under my hand. The sweet smell of cedar fills the air.

Jack is asleep, but I don't want to wake him up. Mommy said to run, hide. What if Sofia finds him, too? Punches him with her knife? I huddle by the warm dryer, squeezing my eyes closed. Maybe, if I can't see them, they can't see me.

Footsteps thud by me. "Tanya? Where are you?"

I curl into a ball. Don't answer her. Mommy said to hide.

"I won't hurt you. Come out, Tanya. We can play makeup."

Makeup is my very favorite game, where Sofia puts lipstick on me, blush and eye shadow. Her hands touching my face, smoothing the soft brush across my eyelids with a wonderful tickle. Sofia smiling at me with her pretty teeth. "You look like a princess!"

But that is nice Sofia. And this is the other one, the witch who comes out and tries to trick me sometimes. Told me it was apple juice and gave me a bitter, blue, scratchy drink and closed her bedroom door and laughed when I threw up and Mommy had to help me. Not-nice Sofia, who stuck her leg out and tripped Jack. Pretended to soothe him and even touched the blood as it beaded up in needlepoints on his knee, but then I saw her dip her blood-smeared finger in her mouth when she thought no one was looking.

"Come on, Tanya. Hide-and-seek is over. Time to come out. We can play tea party."

Then the door flies open, light filling the room, blinding me. A huge figure towers over me, like a monster. Sofia, her blue eyes blazing. I cower in a ball, warm wet seeping into my undies and my powder-blue nightgown.

Then her face looms up in front of me.

"Someday," she says, with her Mona Lisa smile. "Someday I'll get you."

Chapter Thirty-Seven

This is all we got," the woman says, handing me a dark-green file folder. She is an overweight woman with big, gold hoop earrings and a shirt revealing impressive cleavage that's hard not to stare at, even as a heterosexual female. It makes me think back to a Get Your First Job seminar at college, where the PowerPoint bullet point admonished us to "play up your attributes!" Though it is doubtful this is what they had in mind.

"Thank you," I say, signing a form and leaving her a credit card and driver's license for the privilege of taking the folder to a cubby five feet away. But I have waited over an hour in this overheated room that smells of new carpet, discussing my admittedly complex situation with the above-mentioned amply cleavaged woman, along with a manager and supervisor, before establishing that I should be allowed access to the folder. The clerk and manager were still refusing with polite bureaucratic rudeness when the supervisor actually remembered the case, got a human look in her eye, and made the decision to let me see it. At that point, I would have given my firstborn to have a glance at that thing.

I scoot out a gray plastic chair under the gray Formica table. Along with the gray walls and the new gray carpet, it seems the interior designer of the Syracuse City Court had hopes this room would just disappear. I take a deep breath and open the file.

A picture of my mom jumps out on the top of the pile, from the crime scene. She is a beautiful woman, more beautiful than I would have remembered, wearing a light pink dress with a mauve orchid design, now stained mostly red with blood. There is a lot of blood on the robin's-egg-blue wall, seeped into the oriental carpet. Her eyes are Sofia Vallano–blue and clouded over.

Underneath is a picture of Sofia, from the crime scene as well. Age fourteen, looking both scared and matricidal, pale, skinny, her hair dyed black, and black nail polish dotting her fingers. And then there is a picture of Jack, impossibly young, with his sandy red hair, freckles on his face dark as dirt, his eye already swollen shut. There is even a photo taken of me, little Tanya, my face red from crying. I could be straight out of central casting for Little Orphan Annie with my pudgy, freckled, round face and smeared cheeks.

Also included in the file is my real original birth certificate (not the reissue that I have from my parents after the name change), a picture of my mother, alive, from her passport photo. She wears a mysterious smile that reminds me of Sofia.

There are just those few items from the night of the murder. The supervisor explained that most of the information and evidence surrounding the crime is in a separate unit in Albany. So it will be a separate trip and a separate fight, a separate gray room with a separate gatekeeper, to get a glimpse of that file.

Most of the papers in the forest-green folder start with my post-Tanya life. I piece together the story from the faded copies.

My adoptive mother was a social worker at New Horizons, an agency that worked with Sofia Vallano on her drug addiction and truancy issues, though my mom was not the direct worker on the case. After the murder, a search for suitable family members to care for Jack and me was carried out, and it was established that my biological father, James Vallano, a homeless alcoholic, was not fit for this role. There were also no available grandparents, as James Vallano's mother was dead and father in prison and both of Annette Vallano's parents were deceased. Jack was sent into foster care, and my parents petitioned to be my foster parents. An application was made for formal adoption as soon as legally allowed, followed by a speedy name change. Then we moved to Buffalo, and the trail goes cold.

I flip through the file one more time to establish that I've seen it all, which I have, and I hand back the folder and am returned my ID and credit card.

"Can I make a copy of the paperwork?" I ask.

The supervisor overhears from her computer and answers without looking up. "You need a 104-app for that. Tayisha, go get her a 104-app, please." Tayisha complies, but I can tell she's none too pleased at being bossed around by her, well, boss, and her days at the Syracuse City Court are numbered. I take the application, which is a good twenty pages and more complicated than my college calculus final.

"Okay, then, thank you," I say, putting on my heavy wool coat and gathering my crutches. Time to leave the gray room. "Good-bye."

"Good-bye," they answer in unison, neither looking up from her computer screen.

I find my car easily in the nearly empty parking lot. The Steri-Strips on my neck are itchy, peeling, and nearly off at this point. I drive the snowy, boring highway home with Karin for company, filled with sadness and relief.

It is over. No fire. No Beth Winters. No Beth Summers. Just Annette Vallano, James Vallano, and my brother and sister, Jack and Sofia. A do-good social worker turned mom: my real mother. And a new life for Zoe Goldman. The riddle is solved; there's nothing left to see here, folks.

Time to put my obsession away.

Chapter Thirty-Eight

 D o you feel better now that you know the whole story?"
Sam asks.

I am back on Sam's couch. Gone is the uncomfortable,
stiff, brown one, however, and a cushiony blue couch is in its
place. "I feel worse, actually."

Sam nods. "Watch what you wish for."

"Something like that. Can't argue with the truth,
though," I say, stretching out my legs on the new couch. "The
truth will set you free."

"So they say," he says, brown eyes smiling. "Be patient
with yourself, Zoe. It will take time."

Right. Time to get over the fact that your patient was actually your sister, who killed your mother, and that your other
mother has been lying to you for your entire life and is now
slowly dying of dementia. Yes, I would say it will take time to
process all of this.

"When are you planning on going back to work?"

"Monday," I say.

Sam's eyebrows arch up. "Are you concerned that may be too soon?" If I'm not, obviously he is.

"Not really." The truth is, I can't handle another minute cooped up at home plodding though this dreary month. I've read every psychiatry journal I can get my hands on, taken up cross-stitching, and my unrelenting presence is driving Scotty up the wall.

"I was afraid you might feel too raw to get back into it so soon."

"Maybe," I say. But really, I think nothing is as therapeutic as helping people who are more screwed up than I am. "I think I'll be okay. They've done all the investigation about the case that they need. They had me talk with the chairman to make sure I wasn't too bat-shit crazy to start seeing patients again."

"And they decided?"

"No crazier than any other psychiatrist."

Sam smiles politely, but I don't think he finds it funny. The sun glints off the glass on the diplomas above his desk. His new clock ticks loudly. I think it is actually louder than the pewter one. "You know, Zoe, you shouldn't try to hurry this. You're dealing with a lot. A lot to assimilate."

"I know," I say. I don't know how I'm supposed to feel. Angry maybe, or afraid. But I don't. All I feel, quite simply, is sad. Sad for everyone, for Sofia, Jack, my birth mother, even Tanya.

"There are support groups you might want to look into."

"Support groups?"

"Yeah."

"For people in my situation?" I can't imagine that is remotely possible. It would be a pretty lonely support group. Lots of coffee and stale cookies for everyone.

"Not precisely. For those who have been affected by a murder."

"Oh." Now that one seems overly vague. I find myself nitpicky these days, but I figure I'm allowed a degree of low-grade depression, all things considered.

"Any PTSD symptoms going on?"

"Probably. I jumped a foot in the air when Scotty grabbed my shoulder the other day."

"He probably shouldn't approach you from behind."

"Yeah, I think he's learned that." I lift my leg onto Sam's coffee table. I am sporting a new metal Aircast, which has been a delightful change for my leg. My foot, pale and atrophic as it may be, can finally breathe. It is a walking cast, too, so my crutches have been happily relegated to the garage. But the damn thing still aches.

"And how's your mom doing?"

"Not great. Still declining."

"Hmm," Sam says. "Did you end up telling her about Sofia?"

"No. I didn't think it would help anything. Like you said, she was just trying to do the best she could. A made-up story about a fake mom and a fake fire was probably better, in her mind, than the real thing."

"She gave you a new life."

"Yes, she did. In Buffalo, where no one would even know

the story." A car revs out of the driveway, muffler on the fritz. The snow clumps in damp, melting gray patches on the pavement.

"Imagine how your life would have been different if you had known the truth."

"Yeah," I say. "That's true. Probably not in a good way either."

"Hard to know."

I nod, but I can't imagine too many positives there, starting off your life as damaged goods, ready-made excuses for failure in hand, and a chip on your shoulder as big as Montana. Would I have gone to Yale? Would I have become a doctor? Probably not. But then again, Sam is right: It's hard to know these things.

Sam leans back in his office chair, then glances at the clock, and pulls out his script pad. "Adderall dosing okay?"

"Yeah," I say, though my thoughts have been zipping around like atoms lately, if atoms indeed zip around. "Or should be, anyway, once I'm back to work."

"Xanax?"

"Don't think I need that right now."

"No?" he says, surprised.

Knowing that both my parents were alcoholics, Sofia into PCP, and Jack heroin, I think it's time to cool it with the Xanax. Might just be hereditary. "Not for now," I say. "We'll see how it goes."

"Okay," Sam says. "See you next week. Call me if you need to. I'd like to keep an eye on things pretty closely right now."

Translation: I want to make sure you're not too bat-shit crazy to be seeing patients again.

⟵

I attempt to sneak late into Professor Rounds, having picked my first day back to oversleep. But it's hard to be inconspicuous when you are over six feet tall, limping, a ghastly wound on your neck, and with all assembled aware that your psychotic patient, who was actually your sister, tried to kill you.

The conversation in the room, needless to say, comes to a halt.

"Ah, Dr. Goldman," says Dr. Grant. "Nice of you to join us." He points to the chair next to him. "Have a seat."

I sit next to Dr. A, who clasps my arm with a smile. Jason sticks his tongue out at me, and I wave to the gaggle of new medical students. So it's pretty much business as usual. I pull in my chair, knocking my metal cast against the leg of the table, which sends a jolt of pain down to my toes and gives the old desk another scratch to add to the collection.

This is not the first time I've seen my colleagues since my hospitalization. They came to visit me once during that hazy recovery time, and in one awkward moment, I sobbed a heartfelt (and possibly narcotic-induced) thank-you to Dr. A, who accepted this graciously in an "All in a day's work" kind of way, with Dr. Grant scratching his head and Jason observing, "Wow, I feel like we're in a soap opera."

Dr. Grant's phone rings, and he walks out of the room

talking. I take the moment to hug Dr. A, which he accepts with bemused embarrassment. "My hero," I say lightly, but I mean it through and through.

"Pretty nasty scar there," Jason says. "Looks like Dr. A's got to bone up on his stitching skills." I expect Dr. A to whip out his notebook and add "bone up" to his look-up-later list, but he does not. "Did you hear?" Jason says. "Dr. A's going to be leaving us next month."

"Really?" I ask with some shock. "Why? Where are you going?"

"Not far. A spot opened up in the neurovascular fellowship, and our Dr. A got it," Jason answers proudly.

"Yes," says Dr. A. "One of the fellows, unfortunately, developed an alcoholism problem." He purses his lips, in recognition of this unfortunate circumstance. "So I applied for the position, and happily I was accepted." Dr. A clasps his hands together, as if to rein in his delight. I wonder if stitching up someone's jugular in twenty seconds flat had anything to do with it.

"That's great, Dr. A," I say, sad that our triumvirate will be breaking up, but happy that he will be where he belongs. "But what about the DSM V? Did you ever finish memorizing it?"

"Only half," he admits.

"And what about all of your idioms?" I tease him.

"This is no longer a concern." His face opens in a smile. "There are no idioms in anatomy."

Dr. Grant returns to the room. "Okay, are we ready?" The medical students pull out their pens, like a synchronized swim team. Dr. Grant starts: "Forty-five-year-old woman with diabetes, hypertension, and a new onset of visual hallucinations. As per her son, she has been complaining of seeing dinosaurs in the backyard."

A surge of contentment runs through me. Dinosaurs in the backyard.

My beloved, chosen field: psychiatry.

Chapter Thirty-Nine

We huddle by the grave at Syracuse Forest Cemetery. The sky is gun-metal gray, churning out sleet. My coat is wet and heavy with it, my black leather boots soggy. Jack smokes a cigarette and the smell is heavy, but I wouldn't deny him this meager comfort right now.

My mother has a large gray tombstone, the same gray as the sky: "Annette Vallano. Much Loved, Much Missed."

Jack blows out a mouthful of smoke. "Sometimes I think about Sofia, and I wonder if sometimes God makes a mistake." He crushes his cigarette butt with his boot and then picks it up and holds it. Jack Vallano will not litter his mother's grave.

I find a small, smooth stone and put it on the top of the rough gravestone. "You know," I say, "I feel like I owe you thanks. Thanks I never even knew to give you."

"No, no," he says quickly. Bits of sleet land on his eye patch, then melt into the fabric. "That's not necessary. You

318

were my little sister. I just did my best to protect you. I wish I could have done more."

I pull my hat tighter, the sleet hitting my ears.

He eyes me a second. "Dad was tall, too, you know. Super-tall, like six-feet-six. Every one of them giants on his side."

"Oh," I say. So that explains that. "Freckles?"

"Them, too," Jack says with a smile. He wipes away some sleet that snuck under his eye patch. "This whole thing is pretty fucked-up, huh?"

"Yeah. That about sums it up."

Jack stomps his feet, trying to get rid of the cold. "You ready to go? I think we've paid our respects."

"Sure," I say, happy to leave, and we start the trek back to our cars, the grass prickly under my boot. My metal cast is icy cold.

"Hey, you want to have a quick lunch? I know an old-fashioned diner not far from here, makes a good burger."

"Okay," I say, though I'm not hungry. But I would like to talk more with Jack, my new brother. Really talk, outside of the ragtag family conference room, outside of the gray of the graveyard and the sleet lining the stones. Maybe he can finally tell me about my mother. After a short ride, with me following his silver car down the highway, ignoring Karin and her chiding, we reach the diner.

The restaurant is warm, the aroma of hamburger grease filling the air. We peel off our coats, rubbing our hands. The glum atmosphere of the grave site seems to lift away as well, crowded out by the shiny black-and-white-checkered floors, pink-and-orange neon signs, and jangly music. *I love you, Peggy Sue, with a love so rare and true . . .*

Sandra Block

Soon we are digging into burgers and fries. I take a long sip of pop, the ice cubes clinking in my glass. "So what can you tell me about our mother?"

Jack lathers his fries with ketchup. "Unfortunately, I don't remember much. A lot of things around that time I just don't remember. Suppressed the memories. Or so I read," he says with a grin.

An imagined picture of Jack's apartment pops up in my mind. Small, dark but cozy, with a heterogeneous mix of books on every shelf. "All I can remember," I say, "is going to a fair with her, winning a blue bear named Po-Po," I say.

"Oh yeah," he says, his face lighting up. "Dad won you that bear, actually, from the fair. A dart game I think it was. Man, that was a long time ago," he says between chews. "He left a few months later, right after we started school."

I will myself to remember something of my father, but I can't. I don't even remember him leaving. "That must have been hard," I say, hating how much I sound like a psychiatrist.

"It was." Jack stares out into the parking lot. "It's funny. I remember that time frame in colors, if that makes any sense. More than actual memories, colors. Red and yellows right before Dad left. I had a bowling birthday party, and they let me keep a pin, and all the kids signed it. And one night I fell asleep on Dad's shoulder at a drive-in movie." His voice fades. "Then it's gray and black. Dad leaves. Mom is pale, crying all the time, lying around on the couch. Sofia wearing all black. 'Goth' they call it now. Black hair, black fingernails. And then it was just me and you, kid."

320

"What do you mean?"

"I practically raised you, Zoe. I was a little kid myself, but I could see even then that no one was stepping up to the plate."

I pop a french fry in my mouth. "It's funny. The way Sofia tells it, *she* was the one who took over parenting after our father left."

He nods thoughtfully. "Well, I don't remember it that way. Doesn't mean it didn't happen, I guess."

A man from the booth across from us wanders over to the old jukebox, lights running and flashing down the sides. He fishes in his back pocket for some money.

"So our mom basically checked out after Dad left?"

"Yeah, pretty much. But I remember her being kind. Teaching me to ride a bike, giving me Superman Band-Aids, you know, good stuff like that. But there were dark times, too, even before Dad left." Jack raps his knuckles on the pale pink Formica table. "When I went to see Dad, you know what I remembered?"

"What?"

"First, let me tell you there were wine bottles everywhere, I mean, everywhere in that apartment. It stank to high heaven, and there were red circular stains all over, on the nice wooden floors, even on the furniture. Damn near ruined that apartment. Probably the cheapest stuff he could find."

"Yeah."

"And then it hit me all of the sudden, a memory from my childhood: vodka bottles, not wine bottles. Rows and rows of vodka bottles, little blue circles on the glass, all lined up like

321

toy balls. But those were Mom's bottles, not Dad's. I remember them clinking around when Mom took out the garbage." He pushes a french fry around the plate, not eating it. "She had her problems, Zoe. She wasn't a saint. Hell, nobody is. I still think about that shit every single day. If I didn't work the program, I'd be shooting up tomorrow." We sit there in silence, Jack slurping the remains of his milk shake. When the waitress drops off the bill, he grabs it despite my reaching for it. "You'll pick it up next time."

"Okay," I say, though I'm not sure there will be a next time. There is no book of manners for this situation. What do we do now, start exchanging Christmas cards? I grab my coat, which smells like french fries, while Jack lays out some cash. "Do you think it was true, what Sofia said? About our father?"

Jack sighs, shaking his head. "Honestly, I don't think he ever laid a hand on her."

"It's weird she would say that, though, out of nowhere."

"Probably just angling a way to get out of the hospital."

"Yeah maybe. But I've wondered about that. If that was really what she wanted, why would she try to kill me then? If her ultimate goal was to get out, that doesn't seem like a very good way to go about it."

"No, it's not," Jack admits. "Maybe she changed her priorities on that one. Who knows? One thing about Sofia: She lies a lot. Always been that way, even as a kid. I think she just can't help it."

Sofia's a liar; this is perhaps the kindest defense he can give her. It's hard to know, though, what Jack remembers, and what he thinks he remembers. Jack has his version, Sofia hers. And then there's mine: a blank slate dotted with broken memories. Maybe Sofia was right about our father. Maybe that's why our mother was so broken. Maybe she kicked him out after Sofia told her that he was raping her. And then our mother didn't have any life left in her to fight.

As we scoot out of the booth, the waitress wipes up the table behind us, the smell of Windex mixing with the grease. Outside, the day is still gray, the sleet dying down now.

Maybe the truth is this: There is no truth. I don't know what happened to Sofia, my mother, my father, or even Jack. And the harder truth is, I never will.

Jack climbs into his little silver car, heading back to Chicago, and I climb into mine, heading to Buffalo. I wonder if I'll ever see him again. A chirping text interrupts my thoughts.

Hey gimpy, how r u? It's Mike.

Good, u? I manage to type, without crashing the car.

Feel like coffee?

On this gray, sleety day, nothing sounds better. Spot?

where else? what time?

I glance at the clock on the dashboard. 4?

C u there.

My heart does the smallest pirouette.

"Hey, look at that!" Mike says as he walks into the Coffee Spot, pointing to my new metal cast.

"Not bad, huh?" I say.

He goes to the counter to order. A bluesy guitar sounds in the background. I sip the heart-shaped foam, and Mike comes back with a coffee in hand and sits down. "So what's new?"

"Not much," I answer. "How about you?"

This makes us titter, then full-out laugh, his rolling, bear laughter drawing stares.

"So how come you didn't come to visit me in the hospital?" I poke his arm.

He looks puzzled. "Really?"

"Yeah, really. I mean it's not a big deal or anything."

"No, I *did* visit you. Multiple times."

"You did?"

"Yes, I did."

"Did I say anything interesting?"

He takes a sip of coffee. "Actually, you weren't making a ton of sense."

"Ah, yes. I had a few of those conversations."

Mike stirs some creamer into his coffee. "I have a question for you, though."

"Sure, what is it?"

"How did the patient find out about you? I mean, how did she even know you were in Buffalo?" he asks.

"It's pretty scary, actually." I adjust my metal cast. "It was just a total coincidence. UMHC had a subscription to the *Buffalo News*, and one day she happened to see a picture of me in there."

"What were you in the news for?"

"Oh, it was just in the local section. *Mary Poppins*, back in fourth grade."

Mike lifts his eyebrows. "You were Mary Poppins?"

"Not exactly. I was a suffragette." I still remember the picture vividly. It was on our refrigerator forever, newspaper edges turning brown. Standing tall with rouged cheeks, singing loudly and off-key with my Give Women the Vote sign. (My first and last foray into the theater; turns out there's not a huge demand for exceedingly tall women who can't act.)

"And she recognized you?"

"Not only did she recognize me, she got my new name from the caption."

"Really?" Mike takes another sip of coffee. "They gave your name?"

I shrug. "I guess they weren't as careful back then. I mean, it wasn't exactly the *New York Times*."

"I guess." He shakes his head. "That is bizarre, though."

"It is."

We pause then, listening to the blues guitar, orders called out, snatches of other conversations. I adjust my brace again, and Mike surveys the room. Eddie is drawing hearts with arrows running through them on the frosted glass and his shirt rises up as he leans, revealing a new, dark-blue tattoo on his back, some Celtic-looking design. Scotty is manning the register. The silence builds to just past comfortable.

"I like you, Mike," I say out of nowhere, maybe because my Adderall is about an hour from peak or maybe just because I mean it.

He tilts his head and looks at me, as if he's looking at a painting in a museum. "I like you, too, Zoe Goldman," he answers.

I pick up my coffee cup, the heart dizzily spinning. "Maybe we can give dinner one more try. I promise not to get stabbed in the neck this time."

Mike smiles, a broad smile. His gray sweater hugs his shoulders just right. I realize it's the same sweater he wore to our first coffee foray. "Okay. What are you doing this Saturday?" he asks.

"Why, what are you cooking?"

"I make a mean manicotti," he says, his eyes twinkling.

Chapter Forty

Hello!" my mom calls out, seeing us in the hallway. She stands up from her rocker and pulls me in for a hug. My mother, BD, was not so demonstrative and would have shied from these open displays of affection. But maybe it's time to stop comparing my mom to herself, AD, BD. She is who she is right now. Maybe she'll be different tomorrow. But then, so will we all.

Scotty gets a hug, too, then yawns, stretching his arms up to almost touch the ceiling. "I'm going to grab some coffee from the lobby. You want anything?"

"No, thank you," Mom says.

"Sure," I say. "I'll take a coffee."

After he leaves, the room is quiet a moment. The sun shines bright through the window, a light snow dusting the ground. I pull my leg higher on the bed; my brace keeps slipping off the quilt.

"How did you hurt your leg?" she asks.

"Running," I answer quickly. "Mom?"

"Yes, honey," she answers, leaning toward me in her rocker. Her face is peaceful and open today, not the worried, bewildered visage I have seen lately.

"I know I've been a little difficult about trying to find out about my biological mother."

"Oh, honey, that's natural. That doesn't upset me. I wish I could tell you more. But I don't remember so much about Beth these days. And the fire."

"I know, I know. And that's okay. What I wanted to tell you is, it doesn't matter. The only thing that matters is that *you're* my mother." I reach over and touch her knee. "And I love you."

I think of my other mother, my other poor, dead mother with her vodka bottles, her alcoholic husband, and her daughter dressed in black, tattooed with death. I feel sorry for her. But I never knew her enough to love her. And if I had to choose, I would choose my mom, my real mom, BD or AD. I would choose Zoe, not Tanya.

"I love you, too, honey," she says.

We hear the squeak of Scotty's shoes returning.

"They were closed," he explains.

"Oh well," I say.

"There was quite a scene out there," he adds.

"Oh yeah?" my mom says.

"Yeah, this guy out there kept yelling about gorillas in the dining room," Scotty says, lifting his tangerine-orange sneakers onto the coffee table. "He seemed pretty convinced about it. Finally some staff had to come and calm him down."

"Oh," my mom says. "That's old Dr. Horner. That man is always going on about the gorillas."

I chuckle at how matter-of-fact my mom is about this. My mother, who in an unguarded moment told me they put cameras in the bathroom to spy on her. It's hard to judge, really, who's crazy and who isn't. Sofia, who killed our mother because she wanted to; Jack, who still thinks about heroin every day; Jean Luc, who can understand any chemical equation but not love. And me, who needs Adderall to keep my thoughts from flying. Gorillas in the dining room, dinosaurs in the backyard. That's the least of it.

The truth is, we are all a little crazy.

Reading Group Guide

Dear Reader,

Walking up the stairs one night, I saw the reflection of the moon on the tile of my laundry room floor. This seems an innocuous-enough image, mundane even. But somehow the way the light was bent and scattered, it looked almost like blood spatter. (Yes, as a rabid mystery reader, I find my imagination tends toward the gory at times.) A line came into my mind: "Moonlight spattered on the floor."

What was this then? A poem? An image to file away? Over the next few days, the vision wouldn't leave me alone. Instead, it grew. There was a girl hiding there, in a room lit only by the moonlight. What was she doing? From whom was she hiding?

By inches, the girl started to fill in. She was injured by whatever she saw, changed. She was flawed and insecure, brilliant and a little nutty all at the same time. Therefore she had to be a psychiatrist. Thus Dr. Zoe Goldman was born.

Now all good protagonists need a quest. And as her boyfriend Jean Luc says, "We are all looking for our mothers, no?" Of course, there is Freudian play in this, but taken to another level. Zoe is not only subconsciously but literally looking for her mother: her "real" or birth mother. And at the same time, she is also searching for her adoptive mother, who is disappearing behind the veil of early onset Alzheimer's disease.

The mother quest turns out to be quite a challenge. Many would-be mothers pop up in the book, including the mother of the imposter Beth and the woman in the picture, Zoe's fading adoptive mother, and the ghost of Sofia's mother.

In another nod to Freud, the very answer to Zoe's search is locked deep within her own subconscious memory, tantalizing but unreachable. She stabs at it through hypnosis and dream analysis but to no avail. And all the while, the answer is staring her right in the face—but Zoe's conscious mind refuses to see it. Puzzles are laid out through the book (see if you can find them all) that her conscious mind struggles to solve, but they are grasped only by her subconscious.

Ultimately, however, *Little Black Lies* is more than just a Freudian nightmare. It is about family, the constant mutation, strain, and repair of the bonds that connect us. Zoe does find her mother in the end, both mothers. She fills in the missing piece, the hole punctured in herself on that moonlit night, with the discovery of her own empathy. Zoe gains empathy for her patients, as well as her family, for her mothers, her brothers, herself—and yes, even Sofia.

I hope the story will stay with you long after you've read the last page.

All my best,

SANDRA BLOCK

DISCUSSION QUESTIONS

1. Could you relate to Zoe? Did you get a sense of how exhausting it is sometimes to be in her head? Do you ever feel like that yourself?

2. Do you have any friends or relatives with ADHD? Do you feel reading this book helped you understand them better?

3. Zoe often seems uncomfortable in her own skin. Why do you think this is? Her height? Her ADHD? Her age? Do you recall feeling that way in your life?

4. What do you think of Zoe's relationship with her brother Scotty? Do you like Scotty? Can you see how living with Zoe all these years may have been difficult for him at times?

5. Do you relate to Zoe's desire to connect with her birth mother? Why do you think she felt the need to do this after all these years?

6. Do you think her adoptive mother remembered the truth

at this point? Do you think she was still lying? Why didn't she tell Zoe the truth in the first place?

7. Do you blame Zoe's adoptive mother for keeping the truth from her? What would you have done in her situation?

8. During her residency, Zoe and her resident friends (Jason and Dr. A, for instance) are in constant contact with a stream of patients. Did their attitudes surprise you at all? Did this behind-the-scenes look at Zoe's residency interest you?

9. Zoe has her share of romantic troubles. Could you understand her attraction to Jean Luc? Do you think he was right for her?

10. How are Mike and Jean Luc different? Which one do you think Zoe should end up with?

11. Did you guess, before Sofia's revelation, the answer to Zoe's quest for her mother? Looking back, can you find the clues that lead us there?

12. Many puzzles are scattered throughout the book. Can you identify some of them? Why do you think this is? What does the puzzle represent here?

13. Why do you think Sofia killed her mother? Is it because she "wanted to"? Was she just "God's mistake," as her brother, Jack, wonders? Do you think she was sexually abused by her father?

14. Do you think Zoe will maintain a relationship with Jack? Would you?

15. Forgiveness is one of the themes in the book. Who should be forgiven? Should Zoe forgive Sofia? Should she

forgive her adoptive mother for lying? Should she forgive her birth father for leaving them? Does Zoe herself deserve forgiveness? If so, what for?

16. Another theme throughout the book is the idea of a continuum of "craziness." Who gets to define *crazy*? Do you agree that everyone is a "little crazy"?

17. The book relies heavily on Freudian theories of the conscious and subconscious, probably part of Zoe's training. Do you subscribe to these theories? Are you aware of decisions or actions in your own life that have seemed more due to your subconscious than to your conscious mind?

THANK YOU:

Rachel Ekstrom, who called one day and said, "I liked your book, actually *loved* your book" (I still have the phone message saved!) and offered to take me on. To this motorboating adventure and many more...

Alex Logan, who didn't just tell me the book could be better but showed me how.

My agent-sibs (you know who you are!), for giving me all that twitter lovin'.

Maxine Rodburg, who treated me like a writer when I was really just an annoying college freshman.

Allison, Becca, Kath, Maye, Nell, Bissell, Leela, Melissa, and all the others (yes, Facebook friends, that's you!), who cheered me on.

All my coworkers at the best sleep center in town (Buffalo

Thank you:

Medical Group, of course), who had to hear about every twist and turn on the publishing road.

Nanette Burstein, for taking the time to read it. Ed Park, for all your help. Bill Smith, for giving me advice on this go-round, and Emily Smith, for reading my first awful attempt all those years ago...

Margie Long, who read the manuscript and told me she had "quite enough" of the villainous Sofia.

My brother, who always has my back (and who doesn't swear nearly as often as Scotty).

My mom, who loved my book as only a mother could. (And yes, my agent *had* read more than one book when she offered to represent me...)

My dad, who is still doing my homework.

Owen, who practiced his reading over my shoulder.

Charlotte, who told her teachers on a school trip that I was a writer, which made me realize that I actually was.

Charlotte and Owen, who brighten my world every day.

And finally my husband, Patrick, who gave me his tough love in red writing in the margins, who gave me Saturdays to write, and who loved me even when I was at my most writerly unlovable. You will always be my favorite heavyweight.

About the Author

Sandra Block graduated from college at Harvard, then returned to her native land of Buffalo, New York, for medical training and never left. She is a practicing neurologist and proud Sabres fan and lives at home with her family and Delilah, her impetuous yellow lab. She has been published in both medical and poetry journals. *Little Black Lies* is her first novel.